Tactics of Mistake

"is very early in the cycle that the author is writing about the Dorsai, that planet of people who are bred, live and die as the toughest, most expert mercenary soldiers mankind has ever seen. In fact, this is the book in which we learn how the Dorsai pattern was formed and the Dorsai race started on its straight and narrow course of purposeful evolution. . . .

"In their day, Isaac Asimov's future of the Foundations and Robert Heinlein's of the 'Future History' seemed impressively complex and real. Quietly, Gordon Dickson has been building a future of his own that is far more logical, more humanly real, and with a stronger philosophical foundation than either of those classics. . . ."

—P. Schuyler Miller, *Analog*

"The situations are so complicated and imaginative and there is so much action that it kept me continuously interested."

—James Blish

"Dickson has no problem bringing new thought and freshness to the story line . . . reading provides new insights. *Tactics* is a thoroughly good adventure story with some depth. . . ."

...ster Del Rey, *If*

Trouble rather the tiger in his lair than the sage amongst his books. For to you Kingdoms and their armies are things mighty and enduring, but to him they are but toys of the moment, to be overturned by the flicking of a finger. . . .

LESSONS: *Anonymous*

TACTICS
OF
MISTAKE

GORDON R. DICKSON

DAW BOOKS, INC.
DONALD A. WOLLHEIM, PUBLISHER

1301 Avenue of the Americas
New York, N.Y.   10019

Published by
THE NEW AMERICAN LIBRARY
OF CANADA LIMITED

PRINTED IN CANADA
COVER PRINTED IN U.S.A.

1

The young lieutenant-colonel was drunk, apparently, and determined to rush upon disaster.

He came limping into the spaceship's dining lounge the first night out from Denver on the flight to Kultis, a row of bright service ribbons on the jacket of his green dress uniform, and looked about. He was a tall, lean officer, youthful to hold the rank he wore in the Expeditionary Forces of Earth's Western Alliance; and at first glance his open-featured face looked cheerful to the point of harmlessness.

He gazed around the room for a few seconds, while the steward tried unsuccessfully to steer him off to a booth nearby, set for a single diner. Then, ignoring the steward, he turned and headed directly for the table of Dow deCastries.

The white-faced, waspish little man called Pater Ten, who was always at deCastries' elbow, slipped away from his chair as the officer approached, and went toward the steward, still staring blank-faced with dismay after the lieutenant-colonel. As Pater Ten approached, the steward frowned and bent forward to talk. The two of them spoke for a moment in low voices, glancing back at the lieutenant-colonel, and then went quickly out of the lounge together.

The lieutenant-colonel reached the table, pulled up an empty float seat from the adjoining table without waiting for an invitation and seated himself across from the tawny-haired, beautiful young girl at deCastries' left.

"Privilege of first night out, they tell me," he said pleasantly to all of them at the table. "We sit where we like at dinner and meet our fellow passengers. How do you do?"

For a second no one spoke. DeCastries only smiled,

the thin edge of a smile that barely curved the lips in his handsome face, framed by the touches of gray in the black hair at his temples. For five years, now, Secretary of Outworlds Affairs for Earth's Coalition of Eastern Nations, he was known for success with women; and his dark eyes had concentrated on the tawny-haired girl ever since he had invited her—with her mercenary soldier father and the Exotic Outbond who made up the third in their party—to join his table, earlier. There was no obvious threat in that smile of his; but reflexively at the sight of it, the girl frowned slightly and put a hand on the arm of her father, who had leaned forward to speak.

"Colonel . . ." The mercenary wore the pocket patch of an officer from the Dorsai World, under contract to the Bakhallan Exotics, and he was a full colonel. His darkly tanned face with its stiffly waxed mustache might have looked ridiculous if it had not been as expressionlessly hard as the butt-plate of a cone rifle. He broke off, feeling the hand on his sleeve, and turned to look at his daughter; but her attention was all on the interloper.

"Colonel," she said to him in her turn—and her young voice sounded annoyed and concerned at once, after the flat, clipped tones of her father, "don't you think you ought to lie down for a while?"

"No," said the lieutenant-colonel, looking at her. She caught her breath, finding herself seized, suddenly like a bird on the hand of a giant, by the strange and powerful attention of his gray eyes—entirely at odds with the harmless appearance he had given on entering the room. Those eyes held her momentarily helpless, so that without warning she was conscious of being at the exact focus of his vision, naked under the spotlight of his judgment. ". . . I don't," she heard him say.

She sat back, shrugging her tanned shoulders above her green dinner gown, and managed to pull her gaze from its direct link with his. Out of the corner of her eye she saw him look about the table, from the blue-robed Exotic at its far end, back past her father and herself to the dark, faintly smiling deCastries.

"I know you, of course, Mr. Secretary," he went on to deCastries. "In fact, I picked this particular flight to Kultis just so I could meet you. I'm Cletus Grahame—head of the Tactics Department at the Western Alliance Military Academy until last month. Then I put in for transfer to Kultis—to Bakhalla, on Kultis."

He looked over at the Exotic. "The purser tells me

you're Mondar, Outbound from Kultis to the Enclave in St. Louis," he said. "Bakhalla's your home town, then."

"The capital of Bakhalla Colony," said the Exotic, "not just a town, nowdays, Colonel. You know, I'm sure we're all pleased to meet you, Cletus. But do you think it's good judgment for an officer in the armed forces of the Alliance to try to mix with Coalition people?"

"Why not—on shipboard?" said Cletus Grahame, smiling unconcernedly at him. "You're mixing with the secretary, and it's the Coalition who's supplying Neuland with arms and material. Besides, as I say, it's the first night out."

Mondar shook his head. "Bakhalla and the Coalition aren't at war," he said. "The fact the Coalition's given some aid to Neuland Colony is beside the point."

"The Alliance and the Coalition aren't at war," said Cletus, "and the fact that they're backing different sides in the brush war between you and Neuland's beside the point."

"It's hardly beside the point—" began Mondar. But then he was interrupted.

There was a sudden hush in the buzz of conversation about the lounge. While they had been talking, the steward and Pater Ten had returned, behind an impressively large, uniformed man wearing the stripes of a spaceliner's first officer, who now reached the table and dropped a big hand heavily on Cletus' shoulder.

"Colonel," said the shipman, loudly, "this is a Swiss ship of neutral registry. We carry Alliance and Coalition people, both, but we don't like political incidents on shipboard. This table belongs to the Coalition Secretary of Outworlds Affairs, Dow deCastries. Your place is back there across the room . . ."

But from the first word, Cletus paid him no attention. Instead, he looked back to the girl—at her alone—and smiled and raised his eyebrows as if leaving it up to her. He made no move to rise from the table.

The girl glared back at him but still he did not move. For a long second her glare held; then it wavered and broke. She turned to deCastries.

"Dow . . ." she said, interrupting the ship's officer, who had begun to repeat his words.

DeCastries' thin smile widened slightly. He, too, raised his eyebrows, but with a different expression than Cletus. He let her gaze appealingly at him for a long second before he turned to the shipman.

"It's all right," he said, his deep, musical voice stilling

7

the voice of the other, instantly. "The colonel's just making use of his first-night privileges to sit where he wants."

The shipman's face reddened. His hand dropped slowly from Cletus' shoulder. Suddenly his size made him seem no longer large and impressive, but clumsy and conspicuous.

"Yes, Mr. Secretary," he said stiffly, "I see. Sorry to have bothered you all . . ."

He darted a glance of pure hatred at Pater Ten, which affected the little man no more than the shadow of a rain cloud affects the glowing radiance of a white-hot iron ingot; and, carefully avoiding the eyes of the other passengers, he turned and walked from the lounge. The steward had already evaporated, at deCastries' first words. Pater Ten slid into the seat he had vacated earlier, scowling at Cletus.

"About the Exotic Enclave at St. Louis," Cletus said to Mondar—he did not seem to be disturbed by what had just happened—"they've been very good about lending me library materials for research."

"Oh?" Mondar's face was politely interested. "You're a writer, Colonel?"

"A scholar," said Cletus. His gray eyes fastened now on the Exotic. "I'm writing volume four right now, of a twenty-volume work I started three years ago—on tactics and strategical considerations. But never mind that now. May I meet the rest of the people here?"

Mondar nodded. "I'm Mondar, as you say."

"Colonel Eachan Khan," he said, turning to the Dorsai at his right, "may I introduce Lieutenant-Colonel Cletus Grahame of the Alliance forces?"

"Honored, Colonel," said Eachan Khan, in a clipped, old-fashioned British accent.

"Honored to meet you, sir," said Cletus.

"And Colonel Khan's daughter, Melissa Khan," went on Mondar.

"Hello." Cletus smiled again at her.

"How do you do?" she said, coldly.

"Our host, Secretary Dow deCastries, you've already recognized," Mondar said. "Mr. Secretary—Colonel Cletus Grahame."

"I'm afraid it's a little late to invite you to dinner, Colonel," said deCastries deeply. "The rest of us have eaten." He beckoned the steward. "We can offer you some wine."

"And, finally, the gentleman on the secretary's right," said Mondar. "Mr. Pater Ten. Mr. Ten's got an eidetic

8

memory, Colonel. You'll find he's got an encyclopedic fund of knowledge on just about everything."

"Pleased to meet you, Mr. Ten," said Cletus. "Maybe I ought to arrange to borrow you, instead of library materials, for my next research."

"Don't bother!" said Pater Ten, unexpectedly. He had a creaky, high-pitched, but surprisingly carrying, voice. "I looked at your first three volumes—wild theories, backed up by warmed-over military history. They must've been going to kick you out of the Academy if you hadn't requested a transfer first. Anyway, you're out. Now, who'll read you? You'll never finish a fourth book."

"I told you," said Mondar in the conversational pause that followed this small verbal explosion. Cletus was gazing at the small man with a faint smile not unlike that of deCastries, earlier. "Mr. Ten has an encyclopedic fund of knowledge."

"I see what you mean," said Cletus. "But knowledge and conclusions are two different things. That's why I'll be finishing all sixteen of the other volumes in spite of Mr. Ten's doubts. In fact that's why I'm headed for Kultis, now, to make sure I get them written."

"That's right—haul victory out of defeat there," creaked Pater Ten. "Win the war at Bakhalla in six weeks and become an Alliance hero."

"Yes, not such a bad idea," said Cletus, as the lounge steward deftly slid a clean wineglass in front of him and filled it from the bottle of canary-yellow liquid on the table. "Only it isn't either the Alliance or the Coalition that's going to win in the long run."

"That's a strong statement, Colonel," said deCastries. "Also, a little close to treason, isn't it? That part about the Alliance, spoken by an Alliance officer?"

"You think so?" Cletus said, and smiled. "Is someone here thinking of reporting me?"

"Possibly." There was abruptly a note of something chilling in deCastries' deep voice. "Meanwhile, it's interesting to hear you talk. What makes you think it won't be either the Alliance or the Coalition that'll end up having the strongest voice among the colonies on Kultis?"

"The laws of historical development," said Cletus, "are working to that end."

"Laws," said Melissa Khan, angrily. The tension she had been feeling beneath the calm talk had become too much to bear. "Why does everybody think"—she glanced a moment, almost bitterly at her father—"that there's some impractical set of principles or theories or codes that

9

everybody ought to live by? It's practical people who make things happen! You have to be practical, nowdays, or you might as well be dead."

"Melissa," said deCastries, smiling at her, "honors the practical man. I'm afraid I have to agree with her. Practical experience works."

"As opposed to theories, Colonel," flung in Pater Ten, gibingly, "as opposed to bookish theories. Wait'll you get out among practical field officers in the Neuland–Bakhalla jungle in a practical fire-fight, and discover what war's really like! Wait'll you hear your first energy weapon sending its sizzle overhead, and you'll find out—"

"He's wearing the Alliance Medal of Honor, Mr. Ten."

The sudden, flat, clipped tones of Eachan Khan chopped across the small man's tirade like an ax. In the new silence Eachan pointed a steady, brown forefinger at the red, white and gold bar at the far right of the row of ribbons decorating Cletus' jacket.

2

The silence continued a moment at the table.

"Colonel," said Eachan, "what's the trouble with your leg?"

Cletus grinned wryly. "It's part prosthetic about the knee, now," he said. "Perfectly comfortable, but you can notice it when I walk." He looked back at Pater Ten. "Actually, Mr. Ten's pretty close to being right about my practical military experience. I only had three months of active duty after being commissioned, during the last Alliance–Coalition brush war on Earth seven years ago."

"But you ended up those three months with the Medal of Honor," said Melissa. The expression with which she had watched him before had now changed completely. She swung about to Pater Ten. "I suppose that's one of the few things you don't know anything about, though?"

Pater Ten stared hatingly back at her.

"Do you, Pater?" murmured deCastries.

"There was a Lieutenant Grahame decorated seven years ago by the Alliance," spat out Pater Ten. "His division had made an attack drop and landing on a Pacific island held by our garrisons. The division was routed and cut up, but Lieutenant Grahame managed to put together a guerrilla force that was successful in bottling our people up in their strong fortified areas until Alliance reinforcements came a month later. He ran into a traveling mine the day before he would have been relieved. They stuck him in their Academy because he couldn't qualify physically for field duty after that."

There was another, but shorter, moment of silence at the table.

"So," said deCastries, in an oddly thoughtful tone, turning in his fingers the half-filled wineglass on the tablecloth before him, "it seems the scholar was a hero, Colonel."

"No, Lord no," said Cletus. "The lieutenant was a rash soldier, that's all. If I'd understood things then as well as I do now, I'd never have run into that mine."

"But here you are—headed back to where the fighting is!" said Melissa.

"That's true," said Cletus, "but as I said, I'm a wiser man now. I don't want any more medals."

"What *do* you want, Cletus?" asked Mondar, from the end of the table. The Outbond had been watching Cletus with an un-Exotic-like intensity for some few minutes now.

"He wants to write sixteen more volumes," sneered Pater Ten.

"As a matter of fact, Mr. Ten's right," said Cletus quietly to Mondar. "What I really want to do is finish my work on tactics. Only I've found out first I'm going to have to create the conditions they'll apply to."

"Win the war on Neuland in sixty days!" said Pater Ten. "Just as I said."

"Less time than that, I think," said Cletus, and he gazed calmly about at the sudden changes of expression on the faces of all but Mondar and Pater Ten.

"You must believe in yourself as a military expert, Colonel," said deCastries. Like Mondar's, his gaze upon Cletus had grown interested.

"But I'm not an expert," said Cletus. "I'm a scholar. There's a difference. An expert's a man who knows a great deal about his subject. A scholar's someone who knows all there is that's available to be known about it."

"It's still only theories," said Melissa. She looked at him puzzledly.

"Yes," he said to her, "but the effective theorist's got an advantage over the practician."

She shook her head, but said nothing—sinking back against the cushion of her seat, gazing at him with her lower lip caught between her teeth.

"I'm afraid I'd have to agree with Melissa again," said deCastries. For a moment his gaze was hooded, as if he looked inward rather than outward at them all. "I've seen too many men with nothing but theory get trampled on when they ventured out into the real world."

"Men are real," said Cletus. "So are weapons. . . . But strategies? Political consequences? They're no more real than theories. And a sound theorist, used to dealing with unreal things, is a better manipulator of them than the man used to dealing only with the real tools that are actually only end products. . . . Do you know anything about fencing?"

DeCastries shook his head.

"I do," said Eachan.

"Then maybe you'll recognize the tactic in fencing I use as an example for some I call the *tactics of mistake*. It's in the volume I'm writing now." Cletus turned to him. "The fencing tactic is to launch a series of attacks, each inviting ripostes, so that there's a pattern of engages and disengages of your blade with your opponent's. Your purpose, however, isn't to strike home with any of these preliminary attacks, but to carry your opponent's blade a little more out of line with each disengage so gradually he doesn't notice you're doing it. Then, following the final engage, when his blade has been drawn completely out of line, you thrust home against an essentially unguarded man."

"Take a damn good fencer," said Eachan, flatly.

"There's that, of course," said Cletus.

"Yes," said deCastries, slowly, and waited for Cletus to look back at him. "Also, it seems a tactic pretty well restricted to the fencing floor, where everything's done according to set rules."

"Oh, but it can be applied to almost any situation," said Cletus. There were coffee cups, as yet unfilled, spaced about the table. He reached out and captured three of these and lined them up, upside down between himself and deCastries. Then he reached into a bowl of sugar cubes standing on the table and brought his fist back to drop a cube onto the tablecloth by the central cup.

He covered the sugar cube with the central cup and moved all the cups about, interchanging their positions rapidly. Then he stopped.

"You've heard of the old shell game," he said to de-

Castries. "Which one of those cups would you say the sugar cube's under?"

DeCastries looked at the cups but made no attempt to reach out to them. "None of them," he said.

"Just for purposes of illustration—will you pick one, anyway?" asked Cletus.

DeCastries smiled. "Why not?" he said.

He reached out and lifted the middle cup. His smile vanished for a second and then returned again. In plain view sat a sugar cube, white against white on the tablecloth.

"At least," said deCastries, "you're an honest shell-game operator."

Cletus took up the middle cup, which deCastries had set down, and covered the sugar cube. Once again he rapidly switched around the positions of the overturned cups.

"Try it again?" he asked deCastries.

"If you want." This time deCastries chose to lift the cup at the right end of the row as it faced him. Another sugar cube was exposed.

"Once more?" said Cletus. Again he covered the cube and mixed the cups. DeCastries picked up the cup now in the center and put it down with some force when he saw the sugar cube he had exposed.

"What's this?" he said. His smile was definitely gone now. "What's the point of all this?"

"It seems you can't lose, Mr. Secretary, when I control the game," said Cletus.

DeCastries looked penetratingly at him for a second, then covered the cube and sat back, glancing at Pater Ten.

"You move the cups this time, Pater," he said.

Smiling maliciously at Cletus, Pater Ten rose and switched the cups about—but so slowly that everyone at the table easily kept track of the cup deCastries had last handled. That particular cup ended up once more in the middle. DeCastries looked at Cletus and reached for the cup to the right of the one that plainly contained the cube. His hand hesitated, hovered over it for a moment, and then drew back. His smile returned.

"Of course," he said, looking at Cletus, "I don't know how you do it, but I do know that if I lift that cup there'll be a sugar cube under it." His hand moved to the cup at the opposite end of the line. "And if I choose this one, it'll probably be there?"

Cletus said nothing. He only smiled back.

13

DeCastries nodded. The customary easiness of his manner had returned to him. "In fact," he said, "the only cup I can be sure doesn't have a sugar cube under it is the one that we all know must have a cube—the one in the middle. Am I right?"

Cletus still only smiled.

"I am right," said deCastries. He extended his hand out over the central cup for a second, watching Cletus' eyes, then withdrew the hand. "And that was what you were after, in this demonstration with the cups and sugar cubes, wasn't it, Colonel? Your aim was to make me figure out the situation just the way I have—but also to make me so unsure of myself after being wrong three times in a row, that I'd still have to turn the center cup over to prove to myself it really was empty. Your real purpose was to strike at my confidence in my own judgment according to these *tactics of mistake* of yours, wasn't it?"

He reached out and snapped the central cup with his fingernail so that it rang with a sound like that of a small, flat-toned bell.

"But I'm not going to turn it over," he went on, looking at Cletus. "You see, having reasoned it out, I've gone one step further and worked out your purpose in trying to make me do it. You wanted to impress me. Well, I am impressed—but only a little. And in token of just how little, suppose we leave the cup sitting there, unturned? What do you say?"

"I say your reasoning's excellent, Mr. Secretary." Cletus reached out and gathered in the other two cups upside down, covering the mouth of each briefly with his hand before turning them right-side-up to expose their empty, open mouths to the lounge ceiling. "What else can I say?"

"Thank you, Colonel," said deCastries, softly. He had leaned back in his chair and his eyes had narrowed down to slits. He reached out now with his right hand to take the stem of his wineglass and rotate it once more between thumb and forefinger with precise quarter turns, as if screwing it delicately down into the white tablecloth. "Now, you said something earlier about taking this flight to Kultis only because you knew I'd be on it. Don't tell me you went to all that trouble just to show me your tactical shell game?"

"Only partly," said Cletus. The tension in the atmosphere around the table had suddenly increased, although the voices of both Cletus and deCastries remained pleasant and relaxed. "I wanted to meet you, Mr. Secretary, because I'm going to need you to arrange things so I can finish my work on tactics."

"Oh?" said deCastries, "And just how did you expect me to help?"

"Opportunities ought to present themselves to both of us, Mr. Secretary"—Cletus pushed back his chair and stood up—"now that you've met me and know what I'm after. With that much done it's probably time for me to apologize for intruding on your dinner party and leave—"

"Just a moment, Colonel . . ." purred deCastries.

A small sound of breaking glass interrupted them. Melissa's wineglass lay spilled and shattered against a saucer before her, and she was pushing herself unsteadily to her feet, one hand holding her forehead.

3

"No, no—it's all right!" she said to her father. "I'm just a little dizzy, suddenly, that's all. I'll go lie down. . . . No, Dad, you stay here! Colonel Grahame, you can help me to my cabin, can't you—as long as you are leaving anyway."

"Of course," said Cletus.

He came quickly around the table and she took hold of his arm. She was tall, and she leaned the not inconsiderable weight of her healthy young body heavily against him. Almost irritably, she waved her father and deCastries back into their seats.

"Really!" she said. Her voice sharpened. "I'm all right. I just want to lie down for a bit. Will you please not make a fuss about it? Colonel . . ."

"Right here," said Cletus. They moved off together slowly, she still leaning against him as they crossed the lounge and went out into the corridor turning left.

She continued to lean on him until they had made a turn in the corridor that hid them from the lounge entrance, then she stopped abruptly, straightened up and pulled away turning to face him.

15

"I'm all right," she said. "I just had to do something to get you out of there. You aren't drunk at all!"

"No," said Cletus, good-humoredly. "And not a very good actor either, evidently."

"You couldn't have fooled me, if you were! I can feel . . ." She half-raised her hand, fingers spread out as if to touch him on the chest; and then dropped the hand abruptly as he looked curiously at it. "I can see right through people like you. Never mind that. It would have been bad enough if you *were* drunk. Trying to play games with a man like Dow deCastries!"

"I wasn't exactly playing games," said Cletus, soberly.

"Oh, don't tell me!" she said. "Don't you think I know what kind of idiots professional soldiers can make of themselves when they try to deal with people outside their own special military world? But a Medal of Honor means something to me, even if most civilians don't know what it is!" Her eyes had slipped into line with his again. She almost wrenched her gaze away. "And that's why I helped get you away from him just now. The only reason! . . . And I'm not going to do it again!"

"I see," said Cletus.

"So you get back to your cabin now, and stay there! Stay away from Dow deCastries from now on. From Dad and me, too. . . . Are you listening?"

"Of course," said Cletus. "But I'll see you the rest of the way to your cabin, at least."

"No thanks. I can get there by myself."

"What if someone sees you doing just that and the word gets back to the Secretary that your dizziness cleared up this quickly, once you were out of the lounge?"

She glared at him, turned and stalked off down the corridor. Cletus caught up with her in two long strides and fell into step.

"About professional soldiers," he said, mildly. "One isn't just like another . . ."

She stopped and faced him abruptly, forcing him to stop also. "I suppose," she said, grimly, "you think my father never was anything but a mercenary."

"Of course not," Cletus said. "A lieutenant-general in the Royal Army of Afghanistan, wasn't he, up until ten years or so ago?"

She stared at him. "How did you know?" Her tone was accusing.

"Military history—even recent military history—is part of my field," he said. "The University Revolution at Kabul twelve years ago, which ended up by taking over the

16

government at Kabul, is part of it. The Afghanistani Army wouldn't have had more than one General Eachan Khan. He must have emigrated from Earth not more than a couple of years after the takeover."

"He didn't have to leave!" she said. "They still wanted him in the Army, even after Afghanistan gave up its independence to become a sector area of the Coalition. But there were other things . . ." She broke off.

"Other things?" asked Cletus.

"You wouldn't understand!" She turned and began walking once more down the corridor. But, after a few steps, the words came from her as if she could not keep them in. "My mother had died . . . and . . . *Salaam Badshahi Daulat Afghanistan*—when they began enforcing the death penalty for anyone singing the old Afghanistani anthem, he resigned. So he emigrated—to the Dorsai."

"It's a new world full of soldiers there, I understand," said Cletus. "It shouldn't have been too—"

"They found him work as a captain—a *captain* in a mercenary battalion!" she flashed at him. "And since then, in ten years, he's managed to work his way just back up to colonel—and there he'll stay. Because the Dorsai mercenaries can't find employment for anything larger than a short regiment—and after his expenses are paid we don't have enough left over from what he makes to visit Earth, let alone live there again, unless the Exotics or someone pay our way there on official business."

Cletus nodded. "I see," he said. "But it's a mistake for you to try to mend things through deCastries. He's not capable of being influenced the way you hope."

"Mend things . . ." She turned her head and stared at him, meeting his eyes this time in unthinking shock, her face suddenly pale.

"Of course," said Cletus. "I'd been wondering what you were doing at his table. You'd have been underage at the time your father emigrated to the Dorsai, so you must have dual Coalition–Dorsai citizenship. You have the right to go back and live on Earth any time you want to take up your Coalition citizenship. But your father can't be repatriated except by special political dispensation, which is almost impossible to get. Either you or he must think you can get deCastries to help you with that—"

"Dad's got nothing to do with it!" Her voice was fierce. "What kind of a man do you think he is?"

He looked at her. "No. You're right of course," he said. "It must have been your idea. He's not the type. I grew up in a military family back on Earth, and he reminds

17

me of some of the generals I'm related to. In fact, if I hadn't wanted to be a painter—"

"A painter?" She blinked at the sudden change of topic.

"Yes," said Cletus, smiling a little wryly. "I was just starting to make a living at it when my draft number came up, and I decided to go into the Alliance Military Academy after all, the way my family had wanted me to from the beginning. Then I got wounded, of course, and discovered I liked the theory of military art. So painting got left behind."

While he was talking she had come to a halt automatically before one of the stateroom doors lining the long, narrow corridor. But she made no attempt to open it. Instead she stood, staring at him.

"Why did you ever leave teaching at the Academy, then?" she asked.

"Someone," he said, humorously, "has to make the worlds safe for scholars like myself."

"By making a personal enemy out of Dow deCastries?" she said, incredulously. "Didn't it teach you anything when he saw through your game with the teacups and the sugar cubes?"

"But he didn't," said Cletus. "Oh, I ought to admit he did a very good job of covering up the fact he hadn't."

"He covered up?"

"Certainly," Cletus answered. "He lifted the first cup out of over-confidence, feeling sure he could handle whatever came of my shell game. When he turned up the first cube he thought I had blundered, not he. With the second cube, he revised his ideas, but was still over-confident enough to try again. When he turned up the third cube he finally woke to the fact that the game was completely under my control. So he had to find an excuse for stopping it and refusing to choose a fourth time."

She shook her head. "This is all the wrong way around," she said, unbelievingly. "You're twisting what happened to make it look the way you want it."

"No," said Cletus. "DeCastries was the one who twisted it, with his actually very clever explanation of why he wouldn't lift a cup a fourth time. The only trouble was, it was a false explanation. He knew he'd find a sugar cube under any cup he lifted."

"How could he?"

"Because I had cubes under all three cups, of course," said Cletus. "When I lifted one cube from the bowl, I

18

palmed two others. By the time he got around to the fourth choice, deCastries had probably figured that out. The fact that the game turned out to be the avoiding of finding a cube, instead of trying to find one, misled him at first. But pointing it out by then would have been too late to keep him from looking foolish at having played the game three times already. People like deCastries can't afford to look foolish."

"But why did you do it?" Melissa almost cried. "Why do you want to make an enemy like that?"

"I need to get him involved with me," said Cletus, "so I can make use of him. Unless I can make him annoyed enough to thrust, I can't parry. And only by successfully continuing to parry every attempt he makes can I finally get his whole attention. . . . Now you see," he went on, a little more gently, "why you ought to be worrying about your own involvement with Dow deCastries instead of mine. I can handle him. On the other hand, you—"

"*You* . . ." Suddenly blazing with anger, she turned and jerked open the door. "You absolute—go mix yourself up with Dow. Get yourself chewed up to mincemeat. I hope you do. But stay away from me. . . . And from Dad! Do you hear me?"

He looked at her, and a slight shadow of something like pain passed through him. "Of course," he said, stepping back. "If that's what you want."

She went in, slamming the door behind her. He stood for a second, looking at its blank surface. For a moment with her there, the self-imposed barrier of isolation he had set up around himself many years ago, when he found others did not understand him, had almost melted. But it was back now.

He drew a short, deep breath that was almost a sigh. Turning, he went off down the corridor in the direction of his own stateroom.

4

For the next four days Cletus punctually avoided Melissa
and her father—and was ignored in turn by deCastries
and Pater Ten. Mondar, on the other hand, grew to be
almost a close acquaintance, a circumstance Cletus found
not only pleasant, but interesting.

The fifth day out from Earth, the spaceliner went into
parking orbit around Kultis. Like its sister planet Mara,
Kultis was a green, warm world with transient icecaps
and only two major continental masses, north and south,
as it had been true with Earth during the Gondwanaland
period of the home planet's geological past. The shuttleboats from the chief cities of the various Kultan colonies
began to come up to take off passengers.

On a hunch, Cletus tried to phone down to Alliance
Headquarters in Bakhalla for reporting and billeting information. But the space-to-surface circuits were all tied
up by the party for Neuland, in the forward evacuation
lounge. Which meant, Cletus discovered with a little quiet
inquiry, Pater Ten speaking for Dow deCastries. This,
of course, was blatant favoritism on the part of a vessel
of supposedly neutral registry. Cletus' hunch flowered into
suspicion. One of those calls could well be concerned
with him.

Glancing around as he turned from the phone, Cletus
caught sight of the blue robe of Mondar, who was standing by the closed hatch of the midship lounge, only a
few steps from Melissa and Eachan Khan. Cletus limped
briskly over to the Exotic.

"Phones tied up," Cletus said. "Thought I'd ask Alliance Forces HQ for instructions. Tell me, is there much
activity in close to Bakhalla by Neuland guerrillas these
days?"

"Right up to our front doors," answered Mondar. He
looked at Cletus shrewdly. "What's the matter? Just now
remembering how you impressed Dow at dinner, that
first day on board here?"

"That?" Cletus lifted an eyebrow. "You mean de-

20

Castries goes to the trouble of making special guerrilla targets out of every light colonel he meets?"

"Not every one, of course," said Mondar, and smiled. "But in any case there's no cause for alarm. You'll be riding into Bakhalla with Melissa, Eachan and myself in a command car."

"That's reassuring," said Cletus. But his thoughts were already halfway elsewhere. Clearly, whatever effect he had achieved with Dow deCastries had been at least partly transparent to Mondar. Which was all right, he thought. The trail he had laid out toward his announced goal was baited along its length for just the sort of subtle mind that could envision purposes at work invisible to less perceptive men. It was that sort of mind deCastries possessed, and Mondar's was complex and deep enough in its own way to prove a useful control subject.

A gong rang through the lounge, cutting through the sounds of conversation.

"Shuttleboat for Bakhalla, now docking," droned the first officer's voice from a wall speaker. *"Now docking, midships lounge hatch, the shuttleboat for Bakhalla. All passengers for Bakhalla should be ready to board . . ."*

Cletus found himself swept forward as the hatch opened, revealing the bright metal connecting tunnel to the shuttleboat. He and Mondar were separated by the crowd.

The shuttleboat was little more than a cramped, uncomfortable, space- and atmosphere-going bus. It roared, dropped, plunged, jerked and finally skidded them all to a halt on a circle of scarred brown concrete surrounded by broad-leaved jungle—a green backdrop laced with what seemed to be threads of scarlet and bright yellow.

Shuffling out of the shuttleboat door into the bright sunlight, Cletus stepped a little aside from the throng to get his bearings. Other than a small terminal building some fifty yards off, there was no obvious sign of man except the shuttleboat and the concrete pad. The jungle growth towered over a hundred feet high in its surrounding circle. An ordinary, rather pleasant tropical day, Cletus thought. He looked about for Mondar—and was abruptly jolted by a something like a soundless, emotional thunderclap.

Even as it jarred him, he recognized it from its reputation. It was "reorientation shock"—the abrupt impact of a whole spectrum of differences from the familiar experienced all at once. His absentmindedness as he had stepped out into this almost Earth-like scene had heightened its effect upon him.

21

Now, as the shock passed, he recognized all at once that the sky was not blue so much as bluish-green. The sun was larger and a deeper golden yellow than the sun of Earth. The red and yellow threads in the foliage were not produced by flowers or vines, but by actual veins of color running through the leaves. And the air was heavily humid, filled with odors that intermingled to produce a scent something like that of a mixture of grated nutmeg and crushed grass stems. Also, it was vibrant with a low-level but steady chorus of insect or animal cries ranging from the sounds like the high tones of a toy tin flute to the mellow booming of an empty wooden barrel being thumped—but all with a creakiness foreign to the voices of Earth.

Altogether the total impact of light, color, odor and sound, even now that the first shock was passed, caught Cletus up in a momentary immobility, out of which he recovered to find Mondar's hand on his elbow.

"Here comes the command car," Mondar was saying, leading him forward. The vehicle he mentioned was just emerging from behind the terminal building with the wide shape of a passenger float-bus behind it. "Unless you'd rather ride the bus with the luggage, the wives and the ordinary civilians?"

"Thanks, no. I'll join you," said Cletus.

"This way, then," said Mondar.

Cletus went with him as the two vehicles came up and halted. The command car was a military, plasma-powered, air-cushion transport, with half-treads it could lower for unusually rough cross-country going. Over all, it was like an armored version of the sports cars used for big game hunting. Eachan Khan and Melissa were already inside, occupying one of the facing pair of passenger seats. Up front on the open seat sat a round-faced young Army Spec 9 at the controls, with a dally gun beside him.

Cletus glanced at the clumsy hand weapon with interest as he climbed aboard the car over the right-side treads. It was the first dally gun he had seen in use in the field—although he had handled and even fired one back at the Academy. It was a crossbreed—no, it was an out-and-out mongrel of a weapon—designed originally as a riot-control gun and all but useless in the field, where a speck of dirt could paralyze some necessary part of its complex mechanism inside the first half hour of combat.

Its name was a derivative from its original, unofficial

22

designation of "dial-a-gun," which name proved that even ordnance men were capable of humor. With proper adjustment it could deliver anything from a single .29 caliber pellet slug to an eight-ounce, seeker-type canister shell. It was just the sort of impractical weapon that set Cletus' tactical imagination perking over possible unorthodox employments of it in unexpected situations.

But he and Mondar were in the car now. With a hiss from its compressor, the command car's heavy body rose ten inches from the concrete and glided off on its supporting cushion of air. An opening in the jungle wall loomed before them; and a moment later they were sliding down a narrow winding road of bonded earth, with two deep, weed-choked ditches on each side unsuccessfully striving to hold back the wall of jungle that towered up on either side to arch thinly together, at last, over their heads.

"I'm surprised you don't burn back or spray-kill a cleared area on each side of the road," said Cletus to Mondar.

"On the important military routes, we do," said the Exotic. "But we're short-handed these days and the local flora grows back fast. We're trying to variform an Earth grain or grass to drive out the native forms, and plant it alongside our roads—but we're short-handed in the laboratories, too."

"Difficult—the services and supply situation," jerked out Eachan Khan, touching the right tip of his waxed gray mustache protectively as the command car came unexpectedly upon a giant creeper that had broken through the bonded earth of the roadway from below, and was forced to put down its treads to climb across.

"What do you think of the dally gun?" Cletus asked the Dorsai mercenary, his own words jolted from his lips by the lurching of the command car.

"Wrong sort of direction for small arms to go . . ." The creeper left behind, the car rose smoothly onto its supporting air cushion again. "Nagle sticks—dally guns —ultrasonics to set off, jam or destroy the components in your enemy's weapons—it's all getting too complicated. And the more complicated, more difficult the supply situation, the tougher to keep your striking forces really mobile."

"What's your idea, then?" Cletus asked. "Back to crossbows, knives and short swords?"

"Why not?" said Eachan Khan, surprisingly, his flat, clipped voice colored with a new note of enthusiasm.

23

"Man with a crossbow in the proper position at the proper time's worth a corps of heavy artillery half an hour late and ten miles down the road from where it should be. What's that business about '. . . *for want of a nail a horseshoe was lost . . .'?*"

" '*For want of a horseshoe a horse was lost. For want of a horse a rider was lost . . .*' " Cletus quoted it through to the end; and the two men looked at each other with a strange, wordless but mutual, respect.

"You must have some training problems," said Cletus, thoughtfully. "On the Dorsai, I mean. You must be getting men with all sorts of backgrounds, and you'd want to turn out a soldier trained for use in as many different military situations as possible."

"We concentrate on basics," said Eachan. "Aside from that, it's our program to develop small, mobile, quick-striking units, and then get employers to use them as trained." He nodded at Mondar. "Only real success in use so far's been with the Exotics, here. Most employers want to fit our professionals into their classical tables of organization. Works, but it's not an efficient use of the men, or the units. That's one reason we've had some arguments with the regular military. Your commanding officer here, General Traynor—" Eachan broke off. "Well, not for me to say."

He dropped the subject abruptly, sat up and peered out through the open window spaces in the metal sides of the command car at the jungle. Then he turned and called up to the driver on the outside seat.

"Any sign of anything odd out there?" he asked. "Don't like the feel of it, right along in here."

"No sir, Colonel!" called the driver back down. "Quiet as Sunday din—"

A thunderclap of sound burst suddenly all around them. The command car lurched in the same moment and Cletus felt it going over, as the air around them filled with flying earth. He had just a glimpse of the driver, still holding the dally gun but now all but headless, pitching into the right-hand ditch. And then the car went all the way over on its side and there was a blurred moment in which nothing made sense.

Things cleared again, suddenly. The command car was lying on its right side, with only its armored base and its left and rear window spaces exposing them to the outside. Mondar was already tugging the magnesium shutter across the rear window and Eachan Khan was pulling the left window-space shutter closed overhead. They were

24

left in a dim metal box with only a few narrow, sunlit apertures toward the front and around the armored section behind the driver's seat.

"You armed, Colonel?" asked Eachan Khan, producing a flat, little, dart-thrower sidearm from under his tunic and beginning to screw a long sniper's barrel onto it. Solid pellets from sporting guns—theoretically civilian weapons, but deadly enough at jungle ranges—were already beginning to whang and yowl off the armor plating of the car surrounding them.

"No," said Cletus, grimly. The air was already close in the car and the smell of crushed grass and nutmeg was overwhelming.

"Pity," said Eachan Khan. He finished screwing on the sniper barrel, poked its muzzle through one of the aperture cracks and squinted into the daylight. He fired —and a big, blond-bearded man in a camouflage suit came crashing out of the jungle wall on the far side of the road, to lie still.

"The bus will hear the firing as it comes up behind us," said Mondar out of the dimness behind Cletus. "They'll stop and phone ahead for help. A relief squad can get here by air in about fifteen minutes after Bakhalla hears about us."

"Yes," said Eachan Khan, calmly, and fired again. Another body, invisible this time, could be heard crashing down out of a tree to the ground below. "They might get here in time. Odd these guerrillas didn't let us pass and wait for the bus in the first place. Bigger package, less protection, and more prizes inside. . . . I'd keep my head down, Colonel."

This last sentence was directed at Cletus, who was heaving and wrenching in a fury at the shutter on the down side of the car. Half-propped off the road surface as the car was by the bulge of that same surface under it, opening the shutter gradually produced a space facing on the ditch into which the dead driver had pitched— a space large enough for Cletus to crawl out.

The jungle-hidden riflemen became aware of what he was up to, and a fusillade of shots rang against the armored underside of the car—though, because of the narrow angle it made with the ground, none came through the opening Cletus had produced. Melissa, suddenly recognizing what was in his mind, caught at his arm as he started through the opening.

"No," she said. "It's no use! You can't help the driver. He was killed when the mine went off—"

25

"The hell . . . with that . . ." panted Cletus, for a fire-fight did not encourage the best in manners. "The dally gun went with him when he fell."

Wrenching himself free of her grasp, he wriggled out from under the armored car, jumped to his feet and made a dash for the ditch where the body of the driver lay unseen. An explosion of shots from the surrounding jungle rang out, and he stumbled as he reached the ditch edge, tripped, spun about and plunged out of sight. Melissa gasped, for there was the sound of thrashing from the ditch, and then an arm was flung up into sight to quiver for a second and then hang there in plain view, reaching up like a last and desperate beckoning for help.

In response, a single shot sounded from the jungle and a slug blew away half the hand and wrist. Blood spattered from it, but the hand was not withdrawn; and almost immediately the bleeding dwindled, with none of the steady spurt and flow that would have signaled a still-pumping, living heart behind it.

Melissa shuddered, staring at the arm, and a shivering breath came from her. Glancing about for a minute, her father put his free hand for a moment on her shoulder.

"Easy, girl," he said. He squeezed her shoulder for a second and then was forced back to his loophole as a new burst of shots rang against the body of the car. "They'll rush us—any minute now," he muttered.

Sitting cross-legged in the dimness like a figure meditating and remote, Mondar reached out and took one of the staring girl's hands in his own. Her gaze did not move from the arm in the ditch, but her own grip tightened, tightened, on Mondar's hand with a strength that was unbelievable. She did not make a sound, but her gaze never moved and her face was as white and still as a mask.

The shots from the jungle stopped suddenly. Mondar turned to look at Eachan.

The Dorsai looked back over his own shoulder and their eyes met.

"Any second now," said Eachan, in businesslike tones. "You're a fool if you let them take you alive, Outbond."

"When there is no more point in living, I can always die," answered Mondar, serenely. "No man commands this body but myself."

Eachan fired again.

"The bus," said Mondar, calmly, "ought to have gotten close enough to hear the firing and phoned, by this time."

"No doubt," said the Dorsai. "But help'd have to be on top of us right now to do any good. Any second,

26

as I said, they'll give up sniping at us and make a rush. And one pistol won't hold off a dozen or more. . . . Here they come now!"

Through the aperture, over the soldier's shoulder strap, Mondar could see the two waves of camouflaged-overalled figures that erupted suddenly from both sides of the jungle trail and came pouring down upon the car. The little handgun in Eachan's hand was speaking steadily, and, magically—for its voice was almost lost in the general din and uproar—figures in the front of the rush were going down.

But there was only a matter of fifteen meters or so for the attackers to cover; and then the jungle and the little patch of sunlight Mondar could see were blotted out by camouflaged overalls.

The gun in Eachan's hand clicked empty—and in that second, just as the shape of the first guerrilla darkened the opening through which Cletus had gotten out, the wild yammer of a dally gun roared from behind the attackers, and they melted like sand figures under the blow of a heavy surf.

The dally gun yammered on for a second longer, and then stopped. Stillness flowed in over the scene like water back into a hole made in a mountain lake by a falling stone. Eachan pushed past the frozen figures of Mondar and Melissa and crawled out from the car. Numbly, they followed him.

Limping on his artificial left knee joint, Cletus was climbing out of the ditch, dragging the shape of the dally gun behind him. He got to his feet on the roadway just as Eachan came up to him.

"Very well done," said the Dorsai, with a rare note of warmth back in his usually stiff voice. "Thank you, Colonel."

"Not at all, Colonel," said Cletus, a little shakily. Now that the excitement was over, his one knee that was still flesh and blood was trembling with reaction, invisibly but perceptibly under his uniform trouser leg.

"Very well done, indeed," said Mondar, as quietly as ever, joining them. Melissa had halted and was staring down into the ditch where the dead driver lay. It was his arm that had been upflung, obviously with intention by Cletus, as he lay thrashing about like a deeply wounded man, unseen in the ditch. Melissa shivered and turned away to face the rest of them.

She stared at Cletus out of her white face, in which

27

a strange mixture of emotions were now intermingled. Mondar spoke:

"Here come our relief forces," commented the Exotic, gazing skyward. A couple of battle aircars, with a squad of infantry aboard each, were dropping down to the roadway. A hiss of a braking airjet sounded behind them and they turned to see the bus slide into view around a turn in the road. "As well as our signal section," he added, smiling a little.

5

The command car, its compressor damaged by guerrilla fire, was left behind. One of the battle aircars carried its four surviving passengers the rest of the way into the port city of Bakhalla. The aircar dropped the four of them off at the transport section of Alliance Headquarters in Bakhalla. Eachan Khan and Melissa said goodbye and left by autocab for their own residence in the city. Mondar opened the door of another autocab and motioned Cletus inside.

"You'll need to go to Alliance HQ for your assignment and billeting, and that's on my way. I'll drop you off."

Cletus got in; Mondar reached to punch out a destination on the control board of the autocab. The cab rose on its air cushion and slid smoothly off between the rows of white-painted military buildings.

"Thanks," said Cletus.

"Not at all," said Mondar. "You saved all our lives back in the jungle just now. I want to do more than just thank you. I take it you might like to talk to Dow deCastries again?"

Cletus looked at the Outbond curiously. All his life he had enjoyed watching people of strong aims at work to achieve them; and in the five days since he had met Mondar he had become aware of a purposefulness in the Exotic that might well be as dedicated as his own.

"I thought deCastries went down to Capital Neuland."

"He did," said Mondar, as the autocab made a right

turn into a somewhat broader boulevard and began to approach a large building of white concrete with the Alliance flag flying on top of it. "But Neuland's only twenty-five minutes from here by air. The Coalition hasn't any direct diplomatic relations with our Exotic government here on Kultis, and neither our people nor Dow want to pass up a chance to talk. After all, it's really the Coalition we're fighting—Neuland couldn't last six weeks without them. So I'm giving an unofficial little party at my home this evening—with a buffet supper and general conversation. Eachan and Melissa will be there. I'd appreciate having you, too."

"Be happy to come," said Cletus. "May I bring my aide?"

"Aide?"

"A second lieutenant named Arvid Johnson, if I'm lucky enough to find him still unassigned," Cletus said. "One of my former students at the Academy. He came to visit me when he was home from here on leave a couple of months ago. It was what he told me that got me interested in Bakhalla."

"Was it? Well, bring him by all means." The autocab slid to a halt before the walkway leading up to the entrance of the large white building. Mondar pressed a button and the autocab door next to Cletus swung open. "Bring anyone you think might enjoy it. About eight o'clock."

"We'll be there," said Cletus. He turned and let the walkway carry him up into the Headquarters building.

"Colonel Cletus Grahame?" echoed the narrow-faced, young second lieutenant at the cluttered desk behind the glass door of the billeting and assignments office, when Cletus confronted him. "You're to report to General Traynor immediately—*immediately* when you arrive."

He had a high tenor voice and he grinned unpleasantly as he spoke. Cletus smiled agreeably, asked directions to the general's office and left.

The glass door he finally found marked *Brigadier General John Houston Traynor* led him first into an outer office where a square-set, half-bald colonel in his early fifties stood, evidently just completing the giving of some directions to an overweight, thirtyish captain behind the room's single desk. Finishing, the colonel turned around and eyed Cletus.

"You're Grahame?" he asked abruptly.

"That's right, Colonel," said Cletus pleasantly, "and you . . . ?"

"Dupleine," said the other, ungraciously. "I'm chief of staff to General Traynor. You're not going into the officers pool, then?"

"I'm on special assignment from Geneva, Colonel," said Cletus.

Dupleine grunted, whirled around and went out the door Cletus had just entered. Cletus looked back at the fat captain behind the desk.

"Sir," said the captain. His voice held the hint of a note of sympathy. His face was not unkind, and even intelligent, in spite of the heavy dewlap of the double chin supporting it from beneath. "If you'll just sit down a moment, I'll tell General Traynor you're here."

Cletus sat down and the captain leaned forward to speak into the intercom grille of his desk. The reply he received was inaudible to Cletus, but the captain looked up and nodded.

"You can go right in, Colonel," he said, nodding to another door behind his desk.

Cletus rose and obeyed. . . . As he stepped through the door into the farther office, he found himself directly facing a much larger desk, behind which sat a bull-like man in his mid-forties with a heavy-boned face decorated by a startling pair of thick, black eyebrows. "Bat" Traynor, the general had been nicknamed, Cletus recalled, because of those brows. Bat Traynor stared now, the brows pulled ominously together as Cletus walked forward toward his desk.

"Colonel Cletus Grahame reporting, sir," Cletus said, laying his travel orders on the desk. Bat shoved them aside with one big-knuckled hand.

"All right, Colonel," he said. His voice was a rough-edged bass. He pointed to a chair facing him at the left side of his desk. "Sit down."

Cletus limped gratefully around to the chair and dropped into it. He was beginning to feel the fact that he had strained one or more of the few remaining ligaments in his bad knee during the episode in the ditch outside of town. He looked up to see Bat still staring point-blank at him.

"I've got your dossier here, Colonel," Bat said after a moment. He flipped open the gray plastic folder that lay on the desk before him and looked down at it. "You come from an Academy family, it says here. Your uncle was General Chief of Staff at Geneva Alliance HQ just before he retired eight years ago. That right?"

"Yes, sir," said Cletus.

"And you"—Bat flipped papers with a thick forefinger, scowling a little down at them—"got that bad knee in the Three-Month War on Java seven years ago? . . . Medal of Honor, too?"

"Yes," said Cletus.

"Since then"—Bat flipped the folder shut and raised his eyes to stare unwaveringly once more across it at Cletus' face—"you've been on the Academy staff. Except for three months of active duty, in short, you've done nothing in the Army but pound tactics into the heads of cadets."

"I've also," said Cletus, carefully, "been writing a comprehensive 'Theory of Tactics and Strategical Considerations.' "

"Yes," said Bat, grimly. "That's in there, too. Three months in the field and you're going to write twenty volumes."

"Sir?" said Cletus.

Bat threw himself back heavily in his chair.

"All right," he said. "You're supposed to be here on special assignment to act as my tactical adviser." The black eyebrows drew together in a scowl and rippled like battle flags in the wind. "I don't suppose I've got you because you heard some rumor they were going to clean out all the dead wood at the Academy and you pulled strings to be sent to some nice soft job where there's nothing for you to do?"

"No, sir," said Cletus, quietly. "I may have pulled a string or two to get sent here. But, with the General's permission, it wasn't because I thought this a soft job. I've got to do a great deal out here."

"I hope not, Colonel. I hope not," said Bat. "It just happens I put in a request for a dozen jungle-breaker tanks three months ago. . . . You're what I got instead. Now, I don't give a damn what the Academy wants to do with its Tactics Department. The kids just have to come out here into the field and relearn it all over again under practical conditions, anyway. But I needed those tanks. I still need them."

"Possibly," said Cletus, "I can come up with some means to help the General get along without them."

"I don't think so," said Bat, grimly. "What I think is that you're going to hang around here for a couple of months or so and turn out not to be particularly useful. Then I'm going to mention that fact to Alliance HQ back on Earth and ask for my jungle-breakers again. I'll get them, and you'll be transferred back to Earth—

31

if with no commendations, at least without any black marks on your record. . . . That's if everything goes smoothly, Colonel. And"—Bat reached across to a corner of his desk and pulled a single sheet of paper toward him—"speaking of the way things go, I've got a report here that you got drunk your first night out, on the ship headed here, and made a fool of yourself in front of the Outworld's Secretary for the Coalition, who was aboard."

"That's fast reporting," said Cletus, "considering that, when our party for Bakhalla left the ship, the phones aboard were all still tied up by Coalition people. I take it this report to the General comes from one of them?"

"It's none of your business who made the report!" rumbled Bat. "As a matter of fact, it comes from the captain of the spaceship."

Cletus laughed.

"What's the joke, Colonel?" Bat's voice rose.

"The idea, sir," said Cletus, "of a civilian ship commander reporting on the fitness of an Alliance officer."

"You won't find it all that funny if I have the information entered in your record, Colonel," said Bat. He stared at Cletus, at first grimly, and then a trifle disconcertedly, when Cletus did not seem greatly sobered by this threat. "But, never mind the Coalition or any civilian shipmaster. I'm your commanding officer, and *I'm* asking for an explanation of your drunkenness."

"There isn't any explanation . . ." began Cletus.

"Oh?" said Bat.

"No explanation, I was going to say," continued Cletus, "because no explanation's necessary. I've never been drunk in my life. I'm afraid the ship's captain was wrongly advised—or drew the wrong conclusion."

"Just made a mistake, eh?" said Bat, ironically.

"As it happens," said Cletus, "I think I've got a witness who'll testify I wasn't drunk. He was at the table. Mondar, the former Outbond from here to St. Louis Enclave."

Bat's mouth, opened to retort before Cletus was half done, closed instead. The general sat silent for several seconds. Then his eyebrows quivered and the frown line between his eyes smoothed somewhat.

"Then why this report?" he asked in a more neutral voice.

"The ship's people, from what I saw," said Cletus, "seemed partial to the Coalition people aboard."

"Well, then, damn it!" exploded Bat, "if you saw them

jumping to the wrong conclusion, why didn't you set them straight?"

"As a matter of elementary strategy," said Cletus, "I thought it wouldn't do any harm to let the Coalition people pick up as low an opinion of me as possible—of me, and my usefulness to you, as a tactical expert."

Bat looked balefully at him. "Their opinion couldn't be any lower than mine, anyway," he said. "You're no use to me, Colonel. This is a dirty, little, hole-in-the-wall war, with no room for strategical mysteries. This Exotic colony's got brains, money, technical developments and a seacoast. The Neulanders've got no seacoast, no industry and too much population for their back-country farms to support—because of his multiple-wife religious cult of theirs. But that same excess population's just fine for supplying guerrillas. So, the Neulanders want what the Exotics've got and the Coalition's trying to help them get it. We're here to see they don't. That's the whole situation. What the Neuland guerrillas try to do, and what we do to stop them from doing it, is just plain obvious. I need a book-strategy and tactics expert like I need a hundred-piece symphony orchestra. And I'm sure deCastries and the other Coalition people on that ship knew it as well as I do."

"Maybe I won't be quite as useless as the General thinks," said Cletus, unperturbed. "Of course, I'll have to survey and study the situation, starting by setting up a plan for trapping those guerrillas they'll be infiltrating through Etter's Pass, up country, in the next few days."

Bat's eyebrows shot up into flag position again. "New guerrillas? Who told you anything about Etter's Pass?" he snapped. "What kind of a rabbit is this you're trying to pull out of your hat?"

"No rabbit," said Cletus, "not even a professional judgment, I'm afraid. Just common sense. With Dow deCastries here, the Neulanders have to try to put on some sort of spectacular during his visit. . . . Have you got a map handy?"

Bat jabbed a button on the surface of his desk, and the wall of the room to Cletus' left lit up suddenly with the projection of a large map showing the long, narrow coastline country of the Exotic colony, and the interior range of mountains that divided it from the Neuland colony inland. Cletus stepped over to the projection, looked it over and reached up to tap with his left forefinger at a point in the middle of the mountain range running down the left side of the map.

33

"Here's Etter's Pass," he said to Bat. "A good, broad cut through the mountains, leading from Neuland down to Bakhalla—but according to reports, not much used by the Neulanders, simply because there's nothing much worth raiding on the Exotic side for over a hundred miles in any direction. On the other hand, it's a fairly easy pass to get through. There's nothing but the small town of Two Rivers down below it, here. Of course, from a practical standpoint, the Neulanders are better off sending their guerrillas into the country through passes closer to the larger population centers. But if they aren't after profit so much as spectacle, it'd pay them to infiltrate a fairly good-sized force through here in the next few days, so that a week from now they can hit one of the smaller coastal towns in force—maybe even capture and hold it for a few days."

Cletus turned, limped back to his chair and sat down. Bat was frowning at the map.

"At any rate," Cletus said, "it shouldn't be too difficult to set up a net to sweep most of them in, as they try to pass Two Rivers. In fact, I could do it myself. If you'd let me have a battalion of jump troops—"

"Battalion! *Jump troops!*" Bat started suddenly out of his near-trance and turned a glare on Cletus. "What do you think this is? A classroom, where you can dream up whatever force you need for a job? There're no jump troops on Kultis. And as for giving you a battalion of any kind of troops—even if your guess has something going for it . . ." Bat snorted.

"The guerrillas are coming, all right. I'd bet my reputation on it," said Cletus, undisturbed. "In fact, you might say I've already bet it, come to think of it. I remember talking to some of my fellow staff members at the Academy, and a friend or two down in Washington, and forecasting that infiltration, just as soon as Dow deCastries reached Neuland."

"You forecast . . ." Bat's tone became thoughtful—almost cunning—suddenly. He sat behind his desk, pondering Cletus with knitted brows. Then his dark eyes sharpened. "So you bet your reputation on this, did you, Colonel? But spare troops are something I haven't got, and in any case, you're here as a technical adviser. . . . Tell you what. I'll pull a company off Rest and Retraining and send them out with a field officer in charge. He'll be junior to you, of course, but you can go along if you want to. Officially, as an observer only, but I'll tell

34

the officer commanding that he's to keep your advice in mind. . . . Good enough?"

The last two words were barked sharply at Cletus, in a put-up-or-shut-up tone of voice.

"Certainly," said Cletus. "If the General wishes."

"All right!" Bat beamed suddenly, showing his teeth in a hearty, wolfish grin. "You can go on and see about your quarters, then, Colonel. But stay on call."

Cletus rose to his feet. "Thank you, sir," he said, and took his leave.

"Not at all, Colonel. Not at all," he heard Bat's voice saying, with almost a chuckle in it, as Cletus closed the door of the office behind him.

Cletus left the Headquarters building and went to see about establishing himself. Once set up in the Bachelor Officers' Quarters, he strolled over to the Officers' Pool HQ with a copy of his orders and checked to see if that Second Lieutenant Arvid Johnson, of whom he had spoken to Mondar, was still unattached. Informed that he was, Cletus filed a request for the lieutenant to be assigned to him as a research staff member and requested that he get in touch with him at the BOQ immediately.

He returned to the BOQ. Less than fifteen minutes later, the signal outside his room buzzed to announce a visitor. Cletus rose from his chair and opened the door.

"Arvid!" he said, letting the visitor in and closing the door behind him. Arvid Johnson stepped inside, turned and smiled happily down at Cletus as they shook hands. Cletus was tall, but Arvid was a tower, from the soles of his black dress boots to the tips of his short-cropped, whitish-blond hair.

"You came after all, sir," Arvid said, smiling. "I know you said you'd come, but I couldn't believe you'd really leave the Academy for this."

"This is where things are going on," said Cletus.

"Sir?" Arvid looked incredulous. "Away out here on Kultis?"

"It's not the locality so much," said Cletus, "as the people in it that makes things happen. Right now we've got a man among us named Dow deCastries and the first thing I want from you is to go with me to a party for him tonight."

"Dow deCastries?" Arvid said, and shook his head. "I don't think I know—"

"Secretary to the Outworlds for the Coalition," said Cletus. "He came in on the same ship from Earth as I did. . . . A gamesman."

Arvid nodded. "Oh, one of the Coalition bosses," he said. "No wonder you say things might start to happen around here. . . . What did you mean by gamesman, sir? You mean he likes sports?"

"Not in the usual sense," said Cletus. He quoted, "*'Whose game was empires and whose stakes were thrones. Whose table, earth—whose dice were human bones . . .'*"

"Shakespeare?" asked Arvid, curiously.

"Byron," said Cletus, "in his 'The Age of Bronze,' referring to Napoleon."

"Sir," said Arvid, "you don't really mean this deCastries is another Napoleon?"

"No more," answered Cletus, "than Napoleon was an earlier deCastries. But they've got points in common."

Arvid waited for a moment longer, but Cletus said nothing more. The big young man nodded again.

"Yes, sir," he said. "What time are we supposed to go to this party, Colonel?"

6

Thunder, deeper toned than Earth's, muttered beyond the ridge of hills inland from Bakhalla like a grumbling of giants, as Cletus and Arvid arrived at the residence of Mondar. But above the city the sky was clear. Out over the rooftops of the buildings leading down the harbor, the yellow sun of Kultis was filling the sky and sea alike with pinkish gold.

Mondar's home, surrounded by trees and flowering shrubs, both native and Earth variform, sat alone on a small hill in the eastern suburbs of the city. The building itself was made up of an assortment of basic building units put together originally with an eye more toward utility than appearance. However, utility no longer controlled any but the basic forms of the house. In everything else an artistic and gentle influence had been at work.

The hard white blocks of the building units, now tinted by the sunset, did not end abruptly at the green lawn, but were extended into arbors, patios and half-rooms walled with vine-covered trellises. Once Cletus and Arvid had left their car and passed into the first of these outer structures of the house, it became hard for them to tell at any time whether they were completely indoors or not.

Mondar met them in a large, airy half-room with solid walls on three sides only, and an openwork of vines on the fourth. He led them deeper into the house, to a long, wide, low-ceilinged room deeply carpeted and scattered with comfortably overstuffed chairs and couches. A number of people were already there, including Melissa and Eachan Khan.

"DeCastries?" Cletus asked Mondar.

"He's here," said Mondar. "He and Pater Ten are just finishing their talk with some of my fellow Exotics." As he spoke he was leading the two of them toward the small bar in one corner of the room. "Punch for whatever you'd like to drink. I've got to see some people right now—but I'd like to talk to you later, Cletus. Is that all right? I'll look you up just as soon as I'm free."

"By all means," said Cletus. He turned toward the bar as Mondar went off. Arvid was already picking up the glass of beer for which he had punched.

"Sir?" asked Arvid. "Can I get you . . ."

"Nothing right now, thanks," said Cletus. He was glancing around again and his eye lit upon Eachan Khan, standing alone with a glass in his hand next to a wide window screen. "Stay around here, will you, Arvid? So I can find you easily when I want you?"

"Yes, sir," said Arvid.

Cletus went toward Eachan Khan. The older man glanced around with a stony face, as though to discourage conversation, as he came up. Then, seeing who it was, Eachan's face relaxed—insofar as it could ever be said to be relaxed.

"Evening," Eachan said. "I understand you've met your commanding officer."

"News travels fast," said Cletus.

"We're a military post, after all," said Eachan. His gaze went past Cletus for a moment, and then returned. "Also, I hear you suggested something about a new infiltration of Neulander guerrillas through Etter's Pass?"

"That's right," said Cletus. "You don't think it's likely?"

"Very likely—now you've pointed it out," said Eachan. "By the way—I got hold of those three volumes on tactics you've already published. The Exotic library here

37

had copies. I've only had time to glance through them, so far"—his eyes suddenly locked with Cletus'—"but it looks like sound stuff. Very sound. . . . I'm still not sure I follow your tactics of mistake, though. As deCastries said, combat's no fencing match."

"No," said Cletus, "but the principle's applicable, all the same. For example, suppose a simple tactical trap you lay for an enemy consists of enticing his forces to strike at what seems to be a weak section of your line. But when they do, your line pulls back and draws them into a pocket, where you surround them and pinch them off with hidden, superior forces of your own."

"Nothing new about that," said Eachan.

"No," Cletus said, "but apply the tactics of mistake to essentially the same situation. Only this time, in a succession of contacts with the enemy, you entice him into picking up a series of what seem to be small, easy victories. Meanwhile, however, you're getting him to engage a larger amount of his available forces with each contact. Then, when he finally commits the greatest part of his strength for what he conceives as one more easy win—you convert that contact into a trap and he discovers that you've gradually drawn him into a field position where he's outflanked and completely at your mercy."

"Tricky," Eachan frowned. "Too tricky, perhaps . . ."

"Not necessarily," said Cletus. "Imperial China and Russia both used a crude version of this, drawing invaders deeper into their territories, until the invader suddenly realized he was too far from his supply and support bases and completely surrounded by the native enemy. . . . Napoleon and the retreat from Moscow."

"Still—" Eachan broke off suddenly. His gaze had gone past Cletus; and Cletus, turning, saw that Dow deCastries was now in the room. The tall, dark and elegant Secretary to the Outworlds for the Coalition was now standing in conversation with Melissa, by the opposite wall.

Glancing from the two figures back to Eachan, Cletus saw that the older man's face had become as cold and still as the first sheet of ice on the surface of a deep pond on a windless winter day.

"You've known deCastries awhile now?" Cletus asked. "You and Melissa?"

"The women all like him." Eachan's voice was grim. His gaze was still on Melissa and Dow.

"Yes," said Cletus. "By the way—" He broke off, and waited. With reluctance, Eachan removed his gaze from the pair across the room and looked back at him.

38

"I was going to say," said Cletus, "that General Traynor came up with something strange when I was talking to him. He said he didn't have any jump troops here in Bakhalla. That surprised me. I did some reading up on you Dorsais before I came out here, and I thought a jump course was part of the training you gave your mercenaries?"

"We do," replied Eachan, dryly. "But General Traynor's like a lot of your Alliance and Coalition commanders. He doesn't think our training's good enough to qualify the men for jump-troop work—or a lot of other combat field duties."

"Hmm," said Cletus. "Jealousy? Or do you suppose they look on you mercenaries as competitors of a sort?"

"I don't say that," said Eachan, frostily. "You draw your own conclusions, of course." His eyes showed a desire once more to wander back across the room to Melissa and Dow.

"Oh, and something else I was going to ask you," said Cletus. "The assignment sheets for Bakhalla that I looked at back on Earth listed some Navy officers, on detached duty as marine engineers—something about river-and-harbors work. But I haven't seen any Navy people around."

"Commander Wefer Linet," said Eachan, promptly, "wearing civvies, down at the end of the couch across the room there. Come along. I'll introduce you."

Cletus followed Eachan at a long slant across the room, which brought them to a couch and several chairs where half a dozen men sat talking. Here, they were less than a quarter of the distance they had been before from Dow and Melissa—but still too distant to catch the conversation going on between the two.

"Commander," said Eachan, as they reached the couch, and a short, square-faced man in his middle thirties got up promptly from the end of the couch, a drink still in his hand, "I'd like you to meet Colonel Cletus Grahame, just out from Earth, to be attached to General Traynor's staff—tactical expert."

"Happy to meet you, Colonel," said Wefer Linet, shaking Cletus' hand with a hard, friendly grip. "Dream something up for us to do besides dredging river mouths and canals and my men'll love you."

"I'll do that," said Cletus, smiling. "It's a promise."

"Good!" said Wefer energetically.

"You've got those large, underwater bulldozers, haven't you?" asked Cletus. "I read about them in the Alliance Forces Journal, seven months back, I think."

"The Mark V, yes," Linet's face lit up. "Six of them here. Care for a ride in one someday? They're beautiful pieces of machinery. Bat Traynor wanted to take them out of the water and use them knocking down jungles for him. Do it better than anything you Army people have, of course. But they're not designed for land work. I couldn't tell the general no, myself, but I insisted on direct orders from Earth and kept my fingers crossed. Luckily, they turned him down back there."

"I'll take you up on that ride," said Cletus. Eachan was once more watching Melissa and Dow with a stony concentration. Cletus glanced about the room and discovered Mondar, standing talking to a pair of women who looked like the wives of diplomatic personnel.

As if Cletus' gaze had an actual physical touch to it, the Exotic turned toward him just then, smiled and nodded. Cletus nodded back and turned once more to Wefer, who had launched into an explanation of how his Mark V's worked, at depths down to a thousand feet or in the teeth of thirty-knot currents and tides.

"It looks as if I may be tied up for the next few days, out of the city," Cletus said. "But after that, if for some reason I shouldn't leave town . . ."

"Give me a ring, anytime," Wefer said. "We're working on the main harbor here at Bakhalla right now. I can have you off the docks and down inside my command unit in ten minutes, if you'll just phone me half an hour or so ahead of time to make arrangements. . . . Hello, Outbond. The Colonel here's going to take a ride with me one of these days in a Mark V."

Mondar had come up while Wefer had been speaking.

"Good," said the Exotic, smiling. "He'll find that interesting." His gaze shifted to Cletus. "But I believe you wanted to talk to Dow deCastries, Cletus? His business with my people's over for the evening. You can see him, right across the room there, with Melissa."

"Yes . . . I see," said Cletus. He looked around at Wefer and Eachan. "I was just going over there. If you gentlemen will excuse me?"

He left Wefer with a promise to phone him at the earliest opportunity. As he turned away, he saw Mondar touch Eachan lightly on the arm and draw him off to one side in conversation.

Cletus limped over to where Dow and Melissa were still standing together. As Cletus came up they both turned to look at him, Melissa with a sudden, slight

40

frown line between her darkened eyebrows. But Dow smiled genially.

"Well, Colonel," he said. "I hear all of you had a close call coming in from the spaceport earlier today."

"Only the sort of thing to be expected here on Bakhalla, I suppose," said Cletus.

They both laughed easily, and the slight frown line between Melissa's eyes faded.

"Excuse me," she said to Dow. "Dad's got something to say to me, I guess. He's beckoning me over. I'll be right back."

She left. The gazes of the two men met and locked.

"So," said Dow, "you came off with flying honors—defeating a guerrilla band single-handed."

"Not exactly. There was Eachan and his pistol." Cletus watched the other man. "Melissa might have been killed, though."

"So she might," said Dow, "and that would have been a pity."

"I think so," said Cletus. "She deserves better than that."

"People usually get what they deserve," said deCastries. "Even Melissas. But I didn't think scholars concerned themselves with individuals?"

"With everything," said Cletus.

"I see," said deCastries. "Certainly with sleight-of-hand. You know, I found a sugar cube under that middle cup after all? I mentioned it to Melissa and she said you'd told her you'd had cubes under all three cups."

"I'm afraid so," Cletus said.

They looked at each other.

"It's a good trick," said deCastries. "But not one that'd work a second time."

"No," said Cletus. "It always has to be different, a second time."

DeCastries smiled, an animal smile.

"You don't sound much like a man in an ivory tower, Colonel," he said. "I can't help thinking you like theory less, and action more, than you admit. Tell me"—his eyes hooded themselves amusedly under his straight brows—"if it comes down to a simple choice, aren't you tempted to practice rather than preach?"

"No doubt about it," said Cletus. "But one drawback to being a scholar is you're likely to be an idealist, too. And in the long run, when these new worlds are free to work out their own destinies without Earth's influence, one man's theories could have a longer and more useful effect than one man's practice."

"You mentioned that, back aboard ship," deCastries said. "You talked about Alliance and Coalition influence being removed from worlds like Kultis. Do you still feel as safe talking like that here, with your Alliance superiors all around the place?"

"Safe enough," said Cletus. "None of them would believe it—any more than you do."

"Yes. I'm afraid I don't." deCastries picked up a wineglass from the small table beside which he was standing and held it briefly up to the light, twisting it slowly between thumb and forefinger. He lowered the glass and looked back at Cletus. "But I'd be interested in hearing how you think it's going to happen."

"I'm planning to help the change along a little," said Cletus.

"Are you?" said deCastries. "But you don't seem to have anything to speak of in the way of funds, armies or political influence to help with. Now, for example, I've got those things, myself, which puts me in a much stronger position. If I thought a major change could be accomplished—to my benefit, of course—I'd be interested in altering the shape of things to come."

"Well," said Cletus, "we can both try."

"Fair enough." deCastries held the wineglass, looking over it at Cletus. "But you haven't told me how you'd do it. I told you what my tools are—money, armed troops, political power. What have you got? Only theories?"

"Theories are enough, sometimes," said Cletus.

DeCastries slowly shook his head. He put the wineglass back down on the small table and lightly dusted against one another fingertips of the hand that had held the glass, as if to get rid of some stickiness.

"Colonel," he said, quietly, "you're either some new kind of agent the Alliance is trying to fasten on me— in which case I'll find out about you as soon as I can get word back from Earth—or you're a sort of interesting madman. In which case, events will take care of you in not much more time than it takes to establish the fact you're an agent."

He watched Cletus for a second. Cletus met his eye expressionlessly.

"I'm sorry to say," deCastries went on, "you're beginning to sound more and more like a madman. It's too bad. If you'd been an agent, I was going to offer

42

you a better job than the one you have with the Alliance. But I don't want to hire a madman—he'd be too unpredictable. I'm sorry."

"But," said Cletus, "if I turned out to be a successful madman . . : ?"

"Then, of course, it'd be different. But that's too much to hope for. So all I can say is, I'm sorry. I'd hoped you wouldn't disappoint me."

"I seem to have a habit of disappointing people," said Cletus.

"As when you first decided to paint instead of going on to the Academy and then gave up painting for a military life, after all?" murmured deCastries. "I've been a little disappointing to people in my life that way. I've got a large number of uncles and cousins about the Coalition world—all very successful managers, business chiefs, just as my father was. But I picked politics—" He broke off, as Melissa rejoined them.

"It wasn't anything. . . . Oh, Cletus," she said, "Mondar said if you wanted to find him he'd be in his study. It's a separate building, out behind the house."

"Which way do I go?" asked Cletus.

She pointed through an arched entrance in a farther wall of the room. "Just go straight through there and turn left," she said. "The corridor you'll be in leads to a door that opens on the garden. His study building's just beyond it."

"Thank you," said Cletus.

He found the corridor, as Melissa had said, and followed it out into the garden, a small, terraced area with paths running to a line of trees, the tops of which tossed sharply in a hot, wet wind against a sky full of moonlight and torn cloud ends. There was no sign of any building.

At that moment, however, just as Cletus hesitated, he caught sight of light glimmering through the trees ahead of him. He went out across the garden and through the trees. Past their narrow belt he came into the open before a low-roofed, garage-like structure so comfortably fitted in among the vegetation surrounding it that it gave the impression of being comfortably half-sunk in the earth. Low, heavily curtained windows let out the small amount of light he had seen just now. There was a door before him; and as he approached, it slid noiselessly open. He stepped inside and it closed behind him. He stopped, instinctively.

He had walked into a softly but clearly lit room, more

library than study in appearance, although it had something of both about it. It's air tasted strangely thin and dry and clean like air on some high mountain peak. Bookshelves inset in all four of the walls held a surprisingly large collection of old-fashioned, printed volumes. A study console and a library retrieval system each occupied a corner of the room. But Mondar, the only other person in the room besides Cletus, was seated apart from these devices on a sort of wide-surfaced and armless chair, his legs up and crossed before him, so that he sat like a Buddha in the lotus position.

There was nothing except this to mark the moment and place as anything out of the ordinary—but as Cletus stepped through the door, a deep, instinctive warning shouted loudly at him, checking him just inside the threshold. He sensed an impalpable living tension that held the very air of the room—a feeling as of a massive, invisible force in delicate, temporary balance. For a second his mind recoiled.

Then it cleared. For one fleeting but timeless moment he saw that which was in the room—and that which was not.

What his eyes registered were like two versions of the same scene, superimposed on each other, but at the same time distinct and separate. One was the ordinary room, with Mondar seated on his chair, and all things ordinary.

The other was the same room, but filled with a difference. Here, Mondar did not sit on his chair but floated, in lotus position, a few inches above its seat cushion. Stretching out before and behind him was a succession of duplicating images, semitransparent, but each clearly identifiable—and while those closest to him, before and behind him, were duplicates of himself, those farther from him wore different faces—faces still Exotic, but of different men, different Outbonds. Before and behind him, these stretched away until they were lost to sight.

Cletus, too, he became aware, had his images in line with him. He could see those before and he was somehow conscious of those behind him. Before him was a Cletus with two good knees, but beyond this and two more Cletuses were different men, bigger men. But a common thread ran through them, tying the pulses of their lives to his, and continuing back through him to a man with no left arm, on and on, through the lives of all those others behind him until it ended, at last, with a

44

powerful old man in half-armor sitting on a white horse with a baton in hand.

Nor was this all. The room was full of forces and currents of living pressures coming from vast distances to this focal point, like threads of golden light they wove back and forth, tying each other together, connecting some of Cletus' images with Mondar's, and even Cletus, himself, with Mondar, himself. They two, their forerunners and their followers, hung webbed in a tapestry of this interconnecting pattern of light during that single moment in which Cletus' vision registered the double scene.

Then, abruptly, Mondar turned his gaze on Cletus, and both tapestry and images were gone. Only the normal room remained.

But Mondar's eyes glowed at Cletus like twin sapphires illuminated from within by a light identical in color and texture to the threads that had seemed to fill the air of the room between both men.

"Yes," said Mondar. "I knew . . . almost from the moment I first saw you in the spaceship dining lounge. I knew you had potential. If it'd only been part of our philosophy to proselytize or recruit in the ordinary way, I'd have tried to recruit you from that minute on. Did you talk to Dow?"

Cletus considered the unlined face, the blue eyes, of the other, and slowly nodded.

"With your help," he said. "Was it actually necessary to get Melissa away, too? DeCastries and I could have talked over her head."

"I wanted him to have every advantage," Mondar said, his eyes glowing. "I wanted no doubt left in your mind that he'd been able to bid as high for you as he wanted to go. . . . He did offer you a job with him, didn't he?"

"He told me," said Cletus, "that he couldn't—to an interesting madman. From which I gathered he was extremely eager to hire one."

"Of course he is," said Mondar. "But he wants you only for what you can do for him. He's not interested in what you could make of yourself. . . . Cletus, do you know how we Exotics came about?"

"Yes," said Cletus. "I looked you up before I put in my request for transfer to here. The Association for the Investigation and Development of Exotic Sciences—my sources say you developed out of a black-magic cult of the early twenty-first century called the Chantry Guild."

"That's right," Mondar said. "The Chantry Guild was the brainchild of a man named Walter Blunt. He was a brilliant man, Cletus, but like most of the people of his time, he was reacting against the fact that his environment had suddenly been enlarged from the surface of one world to the surfaces of any number of worlds spread out through light-years of interstellar space. You probably know the history of that period as well as I do—how that first, instinctive, racial fear of space beyond the solar system built up and erupted in a series of bloody social eruptions. It spawned any number of societies and cults for people attempting to adjust psychologically to feelings of vulnerability and insignificance, deep down on the unconscious level. Blunt was a fighter, an anarchist. His answer was revolution—"

"Revolution?" asked Cletus.

"Yes. Literally—revolution," Mondar answered. "Blunt wanted to destroy part of actual, objective physical reality as well—by using primitive psychic leverage. He called what he wanted to do 'creative destruction.' He called on people to *Destruct!* But he couldn't quite push even the intense neurotics of his time all the way over the emotional brink. And then he was deposed as head of the Guild by a young mining engineer who'd lost an arm in a mine accident—"

"Lost an arm?" said Cletus sharply. "Which arm?"

"The left—yes, I think it was the left that was gone," said Mondar. "Why?"

"Nothing," said Cletus. "Go on."

"His name was Paul Formain—"

"Fort-Mayne?" Cletus interrupted a second time.

"No *t*," answered Mondar, "F-o-r-m-a-i-n." He spelled it out, looking curiously at Cletus. "Something about this interests you particularly, Cletus?"

"Only the coincidences," said Cletus. "You said he had only one arm, so the right arm he had left would have been overmuscled from compensation development. And his name sounds almost like *fort-mayne*, which are the words used by the Norman French to describe their policy to the conquered English after they took over England in the eleventh century. *Fort-mayne*—literally, 'strong-hand.' It described a policy of using whatever force was necessary to keep the native English under control. And you say he took over the Chantry Guild, deposing this Blunt?"

"Yes." Mondar frowned. "I see the coincidences, Cletus, but I don't see why they're important."

"Maybe they aren't," said Cletus. "Go on. Formain took

46

over the Chantry Guild and started your Exotic Association?"

"He almost had to wreck the Chantry Guild to do it," said Mondar. "But he did. He changed its aim from revolution to evolution. The evolution of man, Cletus."

"Evolution." Cletus repeated the word thoughtfully. "So, you don't think the human race is through evolving? What comes next, then?"

"We don't know, of course," said Mondar, folding his hands in his lap. "Can an ape imagine a man? But we're convinced the seeds of further evolution are alive in man, still—even if they aren't already germinating. We Exotics are dedicated to searching for those seeds, and protecting them once we've found them, so that they can flourish and grow until evolved man is part of our community."

"Sorry." Cletus shook his head. "I'd make a poor Exotic, Mondar. I've got my own job to do."

"But this is part of your job—and your job is part of it!" Mondar leaned forward, and his hands slid apart. "There's no compulsion on our members. Each one searches and works for the future the way he thinks best. All we ask is that when the skills of anyone are needed by the community, he makes them available to it. In return the community offers him its skills to improve *him*, physically and mentally, so he can be that much more effective in his own work. You know what you can do now, Cletus. Think what you might be able to do if you could make use of all we can teach you!"

Cletus shook his head again.

"If you turn us down," said Mondar, "it signals a danger to you, Cletus. It signals an unconscious desire on your part to go the deCastries way—to let yourself be caught up by the excitement of directly manipulating people and situations instead of dealing with what's much more valuable, but less emotionally stimulating—the struggle with ideas to find principles that'll lift people eventually above and beyond manipulation."

Cletus laughed, a little grimly. "Tell me," he said, "isn't it true that you Exotics won't carry or use weapons yourself, even in self-defense? And that's why you hire mercenaries like the Dorsai, or make agreements with political groups like the Alliance to defend yourselves?"

"Yes—but not for the reason most people think, Cletus," said Mondar, swiftly. "We haven't any moral objection to fighting. It's just that the emotions involved interfere with clear thinking, so people like myself prefer not to touch weapons. But there's no compulsion on our people on this. If you want to write your work on military tactics, or even keep and carry guns—"

"I don't think you follow me," said Cletus. "Eachan Khan told me something. You remember when you were in the command car after it overturned, earlier today, and he suggested you not let yourself be taken alive by the Neulander guerrillas—for obvious reasons? You answered that you could always die. *'No man,'* you said, *'commands this body but myself.'* "

"And you think suicide is a form of violence—"

"No," said Cletus. "I'm trying to explain to you why I'd never make an Exotic. In your calmness in the face of possible torture and the need to kill yourself, you were showing a particular form of ruthlessness. It was ruthlessness toward yourself—but that's only the back side of the coin. You Exotics are essentially ruthless toward all men, because you're philosophers, and by and large, philosophers are ruthless people."

"Cletus!" Mondar shook his head. "Do you realize what you're saying?"

"Of course," said Cletus, quietly. "And you realize it as well as I do. The immediate teaching of philosophers may be gentle, but the theory behind their teaching is without compunction—and that's why so much bloodshed and misery has always attended the paths of their followers, who claim to live by those teachings. More blood's been spilled by the militant adherents of prophets of change than by any other group of people down through the history of man."

"No Exotic spills blood," said Mondar, softly.

"Not directly, no," said Cletus. "But to achieve the future you dream of means the obliteration of the present as we know it now. You may say your aim's changed from revolution to evolution, but your goal is still the destruction of what we have now to make room for something different. You work to destroy what presently is—and that takes a ruthlessness that's not my way—that I don't agree with."

He stopped speaking. Mondar met his eyes for a long moment.

"Cletus," said Mondar at last, "can you be that sure of yourself?"

"Yes," said Cletus. "I'm afraid I can." He turned toward the door. As he reached the door and put his hand on its button, he turned back.

"Thanks all the same, Mondar," he said. "You and

your Exotics may end up going my way. But I won't go yours. Good night."

He opened the door.

"Cletus," said Mondar, behind him, "if you refuse us now, you do it at your own risk. There are larger forces at work in what you want to do than I think you understand."

Cletus shook his head. "Good night," he said again, and went out.

Back in the room where he had left Arvid, he found the young lieutenant and told him they were leaving. As they reached the parking area together and Cletus opened the door of their aircar, the sky split open above them in a wild explosion of lightning and thunder, with raindrops coming down like hailstones.

They bolted for the interior of the car. The rain was icy and the few seconds of being exposed to it had left their jackets soaked and clinging to their shoulders. Arvid put power on the vehicle and lifted it out of the lot.

"All hell's broke loose tonight," he murmured, as they swung back across the city. Then, startled, he looked at Cletus, sitting beside him.

"Now, why did I say that?" he asked. Cletus did not answer and after a second Arvid answered himself.

"All the same," he said, half to himself, "it has."

7

Cletus woke to the sensation that his left knee was being slowly crushed in a heavy vise. The dull, unyielding pain of it had roused him from his sleep, and for a moment he was its captive—the sensation of pain filling the whole universe of his consciousness.

Then, practically, he took action to control the crippling sensation. Rolling over on his back, he stared up at the white ceiling seven feet above him. One by one, starting with his thigh muscles, he commanded the large muscles of his arms and legs to lose their tensions and relax. He moved on to the neck and face muscles, the belly muscles, and finally into a feeling of relaxation pervading him completely.

His body was heavy and limp now. His eyes were drooping, half-closed. He lay, indifferent to the faint noises that filtered to him from other parts of the BOQ. He drifted, sliding gently away, like a man lax upon the surface of some warm ocean.

The state of relaxation he had induced had already muffled the dull-jawed, relentless grip of the pain upon his knee. Slowly, so as not to reawaken an alertness that would allow tension to form in him once more, he propped the pillow behind and pulled himself up in the bed. Half-sitting, he folded the covers back from his left leg and looked at it.

The knee was puffed and swollen to stiffness. There was no darkness or bruise-shade of discoloration about it, but it was swollen to the point of immobility. He fastened his gaze steadily on the swollen knee, and set about the larger job of bringing it back down to normal size and movement.

Still drifting, still in that more primitive state of mind known as regression, he connected the pain response in his knee with the pain message in his mind, and began to convert the message to a mental equivalent of that same physical relaxation and peace which held his body. Drifting with it, he felt the pain message lose its color. It faded, like an instruction written in evaporating ink, until it was finally invisible.

He felt what he had earlier recognized as pain, still present in his knee. It was a sensation only, however, neither pain nor pressure, but co-equal with both. Now that he had identified this former pain as a separate sensation-entity, he began to concentrate upon the actual physical feeling of pressure within the blood and limb, the vessels now swollen to the point of immobilizing his leg.

He formed a mental image of the vessels as they were. Then, slowly, he began to visualize them as relaxing, shrinking, returning their fluid contents to those pipe systems of the leg to which they were severally connected.

For perhaps as much as ten minutes there was no visible response from the knee area. Then gradually he began to be aware of a yielding of the pressure and a sensation of faint warmth within the knee itself. Within another five minutes it was possible to see that the swelling was actually going down. Ten minutes later, he had a knee that was still swollen, but which he could bend at a

50

good sixty-degree angle. It was good enough. He swung good leg and bad out of bed together, got up and began to dress.

He was just buckling on a weapons belt over his jungle suit, when there was a knock at his door. Cletus glanced over at the clock beside his bed. It showed eight minutes before 5 A.M.

"Come on in," he said.

Arvid stepped into the room.

"You're up early, Arv," Cletus said, snapping the weapons belt shut and reaching for his sidearm on top of the chest of drawers beside him. He slid the weapon into its holster, hanging from the belt. "Did you get the things I wanted?"

"Yes, sir," said Arvid, "the loudspeaker horn and the singleton mines are tucked away out of sight in duffle packs. I couldn't get the rifle into a pack, but it's with the packs, clipped onto the electric horse you asked for."

"And the horse, itself?"

"I've got it in the back of a courier car, outside . . ." Arvid hesitated. "I asked to go with you, sir, but the orders just called for you and the field officer in charge of the company. I want to tell you about him. They've given you a first lieutenant named Bill Athyer."

"And this Bill Athyer is no good, is that it?" asked Cletus, cheerfully, picking up his communications helmet and leading the way out of the room.

"How did you know?" Arvid stared down at Cletus, following him as they went out down the long center aisle of the BOQ.

Cletus smiled back at him, limping along, but delayed his answer until they had stepped out the front door into the misty, predawn darkness where the courier car waited for Cletus. They got in, Arvid behind the controls. As the big young lieutenant sent the vehicle sliding off on its air cushion, Cletus went on:

"I rather thought the general'd be giving me someone like that. Don't worry about it, Arv. You're going to have your hands full enough today, as it is. I want you to find office space for me and line me up a staff—a warrant officer, if you can get one for office manager, a couple of clerical tech fives and a file clerk tech two with a research specialty. Can you get right to work on that?"

"Yes, sir," answered Arvid. "But I didn't know we had authority for something like that—"

"We don't, yet," said Cletus. "But I'll get it for you. You just find the premises and the people, so we know

51

where to lay hands on them as soon as we have authorization."

"Yes, sir," said Arvid.

Having arrived at the transport area, Cletus found his company, under the command of First Lieutenant William Athyer, standing at ease in ranks, equipped, armed and apparently ready to take off. Cletus assumed that the men had had breakfast—not being the field officer in command of them, it was not up to him to see that they had; and asking Athyer about it would be impolitic, not to say insulting. Cletus descended a little stiffly from the courier car and watched as Arvid unloaded the electric horse, with its equipment.

"Colonel Grahame?" a voice said behind him. "I'm Lieutenant Athyer, in command of this company. We're ready to take off . . ."

Cletus turned. Athyer was a short, dark, fairly slim man, in his mid-thirties, with a beak-like nose. A vaguely sour expression sat on his features, as if habit had made it permanent there. His speech was abrupt, even aggressive, but the words at the end of each speech tended to thin out into a whine.

"Now that you're finally here, sir," he added.

The extra, unnecessary statement verged on impertinence. But Cletus ignored it, looking past Athyer's shoulder at the men behind the lieutenant. Their tanned skin and the mixture of old and new equipment and clothing about them suggested experience. But they were more silent than they should be; and Cletus had little doubt about the reason for this. To be put back under weapons and flown off into combat in the middle of Rest and Retraining was not likely to make soldiers happy. He looked back at Athyer.

"I imagine we'll start loading right away, then. Won't we, Lieutenant?" he said pleasantly. "Let me know where you want me."

"We're taking two atmosphere support ships for transport," growled Athyer. "I've got my top sergeant in the second. You'd better ride with me in the first, Colonel—"

He broke off to stare at the electric horse, as its overhead vanes whined into movement. Arvid had just switched its satchel turbine on, and the single-person vehicle had lifted into the air so that it could be moved easily under its own power to the support ship. Evidently, Athyer had not connected the horse with Cletus until this moment. In truth, it was an unlikely little contraption for such an outing—designed for spaceport inspection work,

52

mainly, and looking like a wheel-less bicycle frame suspended fore and aft from metal rods leading down from a side-by-side pair of counter-rotating ducted vanes driven by a nuclear-pack, satchel turbine just below them. Cletus' cone rifle and duffle bags were hung before its saddle on the crossbar.

It was not pretty, but that was no reason for Athyer to scowl at it as he was doing.

"What's this?" he demanded.

"It's for me, Lieutenant," said Cletus, cheerfully. "My left knee's half-prosthetic, you know. I didn't want to hold you and your men up if it came to moving someplace along the ground in a hurry."

"Oh? Well . . ." Athyer went on scowling. But the fact that the sentence he had begun trailed off was evidence enough that his imagination was failing him in its search for a valid excuse to forbid taking the electric horse. Cletus was, after all, a lieutenant-colonel. Athyer turned, snapping at Arvid. "Get it on board, then! Quick, Lieutenant!"

He turned away to the business of getting the company of perhaps eighty men into the two atmosphere support ships waiting on the transport area pad some fifty feet distant.

The boarding of the ships went smoothly and easily. Within twenty minutes they were skimming northward over the tops of the jungle trees toward Etter's Pass—and the sky beyond the distant mountain range was beginning to grow pale with the dawn.

"What're your plans, Lieutenant?" began Cletus, as he and Athyer sat facing each other in the small, forward passengers' compartment of the ship.

"I'll get the map," said Athyer, ducking away resentfully from Cletus' gaze. He dug into the metal command case on the floor between his boots and came up with a terrain map of the Exotic side of the mountains around Etter's Pass. He spread the map out on the combined knees of himself and Cletus.

"I'll set up a picket line like this," Athyer said, his finger tracing an arc through the jungle on the mountain slopes below the pass, "about three hundred yards down. Also, place a couple of reserve groups high up, behind the picket line on either side of the pass mouth. When the Neulanders get through the pass and far enough down the trail to hit the lower curve of the picket line, the reserve groups can move in behind them and we'll have them

53

surrounded. . . . That is, if any guerrillas do come through the pass."

Cletus ignored the concluding statement of the lieutenant's explanation. "What if the guerrillas don't come straight down the trail?" Cletus asked. "What if they turn either right or left directly into the jungle the minute that they're on this side of the mountains?"

Athyer stared at Cletus at first blankly, and then resentfully, like a student who has been asked an exam question he considers unfair.

"My support groups can fall back ahead of them," he said at last, ungraciously, "alerting the rest of the picket line as they go. The other men can still close in behind them. Anyway, we've got them enclosed."

"What's visibility in the jungle around there, Lieutenant?" asked Cletus.

"Fifteen—twenty meters," Athyer answered.

"Then the rest of your picket line is going to have some trouble keeping position and moving upslope at an angle to enclose guerrillas who're probably already beginning to split up into groups of two and three and spread out for their trek to the coast. Don't you think?"

"We'll just have to do the best we can," said Athyer, sullenly.

"But there're other possibilities," said Cletus. He pointed to the map. "The guerrillas have the Whey River to their right as they come out of the pass, and the Blue River to their left, and both those rivers meet down at Two Rivers Town, below. Which means that any way the Neulanders turn, they've got to cross water. Look at the map. There're only three good crossing spots above the town on the Blue River, and only two on the Whey —unless they'd want to go right through the town itself, which they wouldn't. So, any or all of those five crossings could be used."

Cletus paused, waiting for the junior officer to pick up on the unspoken suggestion. But Athyer was obviously one of those men who need their opportunities spelled out for them.

"The point is, Lieutenant," Cletus said, "why try to catch these guerrillas in the jungle up around the pass, where they've got all sorts of opportunities to slip past you, when you could simply be waiting for them at these crossings, and catch them between you and the river?"

Athyer frowned reluctantly, but then bent over the map to search out the five indicated crossing points that Cletus had mentioned.

"The two Whey River crossings," Cletus went on, "are closest to the pass. Also they're on the most direct route to the coast. Any guerrillas taking the passes on the Blue River are going to have to circle wide to get safely around the town below. The Neulanders know you know this. So I think it's a fairly safe bet that they'll count on your trying to stop them—if they count on anyone trying to stop them at all—at those two passes. So they'll probably merely feint in that direction and make their real crossing at these three other fords over on the Blue River."

Athyer stared at Cletus' finger as it moved around from point to point on the map in time with his words. The lieutenant's face tensed.

"No, no, Colonel," he said, when Cletus had finished. "You don't know these Neulanders the way I do. In the first place, why should they expect us to be waiting for them, anyway? In the second place, they're just not that smart. They'll come through the pass, break up into twos and threes going through the jungle and join up again at one, maybe two, of the Whey River crossings."

"I wouldn't think so—" Cletus was beginning. But this time, Athyer literally cut him short.

"Take my word for it, Colonel!" he said. "It's those two points on the Whey River they'll be crossing at."

He rubbed his hands together. "And that's where I'll snap them up!" he went on. "I'll take the lower crossing with half the men, and my top sergeant can take the upper crossing with most of the rest. Put a few men behind them to cut off their retreat, and I'll bag myself a nice catch of guerrillas."

"You're the field officer in command," said Cletus, "so I don't want to argue with you. Still, General Traynor did say that I was to offer you my advice, and I'd think you'd want to play safe, over on the Blue. If it was up to me . . ."

Cletus let his voice trail off. The lieutenant's hands, with the map already half-folded, slowed and ceased their movement. Cletus, looking at the other's lowered head, could almost see the gears turning over inside it. By this time Athyer had left all doubts behind about his own military judgment. Still, situations involving generals and colonels were always touchy for a lieutenant to be involved in, no matter who seemed to be holding all the high cards.

"I couldn't spare more than a squad, under a corporal," muttered Athyer to the map, at last. He hesitated, plainly thinking. Then he lifted his head and there was a craftiness in his eyes. "It's your suggestion, Colonel. Maybe if you'd like to take the responsibility for diverting part of my force over to the Blue . . . ?"

"Why, I'd be perfectly willing to, of course," said Cletus. "But as you pointed out, I'm not a field officer, and I can't very well take command of troops under combat conditions . . ."

Athyer grinned. "Oh, that!" he said. "We don't stick right with every line in the book out here, Colonel. I'll simply give orders to the corporal in charge of the squad that he's to do what you say."

"What I say? You mean—*exactly* what I say?" asked Cletus.

"Exactly," said Athyer. "There's an authority for that sort of thing in emergencies, you know. As commanding officer of an isolated unit I can make emergency use of any and all military personnel in whatever manner I feel is necessary. I'll tell the corporal I've temporarily allowed you status as a field officer, and of course your rank applies."

"But if the guerrillas do come through the Blue River crossings," said Cletus, "I'll have only a squad."

"They won't, Colonel," said Athyer, finishing his folding of the map with a flourish. "They won't. But if a few stray Neulanders *should* show up—why, use your best judgment. An expert on tactics like yourself, sir, ought to be able to handle any little situation like that, that's liable to turn up."

Leaving the barely concealed sneer to linger in the air behind him, he rose and went back with the map into the rear passenger compartment where the soldiers of half his command were riding.

The support ship in which they were traveling set Cletus down with his squad at the uppermost of the three crossing points on the Blue River, and took off into the dawn shadows, which still obscured this western slope of the mountain range dividing Bakhalla from Neuland Athyer had sorted out a weedy, nineteen-year-old corporal named Ed Jarnki and six men to be the force Cletus would command. The moment they were deshipped, the seven dropped automatically to earth, propping their backs comfortably against nearby tree trunks and rocks that protruded from the unbroken, green ferny carpet of the jungle floor. They were in a little clearing surrounded by tall trees that verged on a four-foot bank over the near edge of the river; and they gazed with some curiosity at Cletus as he turned about to face them.

He said nothing. He only gazed back. After a second, Jarnki, the corporal, scrambled to his feet. One after the other the rest of the men rose also, until they all stood facing Cletus, in a ragged line, half at attention.

Cletus smiled. He seemed a different man entirely, now, from the officer the seven had glimpsed earlier as they were boarding and descending from the support ship. The good humor had not gone from his face. But in addition, now, there was something powerful, something steady and intense, about the way he looked at them, so that a sort of human electricity flowed from him to them and set all their nerves on edge, in spite of themselves.

"That's better," said Cletus. Even his voice had changed. "All right, you're the men who're going to win the day for everyone, up here at Etter's Pass. And if you follow orders properly, you'll do it without so much as skinning your knuckles or working up a sweat."

8

They stared at him.

"Sir?" said Jarnki, after a moment.

"Yes, Corporal?" said Cletus.

"Sir . . . I don't understand what you mean." Jarnki got it out, after a second's struggle.

"I mean you're going to capture a lot of Neulanders," said Cletus, "and without getting yourselves hurt in the process." He waited while Jarnki opened his mouth a second time, and then slowly closed it again.

"Well? That answer your question, Corporal?"

"Yes sir."

Jarnki subsided. But his eyes, and the eyes of the rest of the men, rested on Cletus with a suspicion amounting to fear.

"Then we'll get busy," said Cletus.

He proceeded to post the men—one across the shallow ford of the river, which here swung in a lazy curve past the clearing, two men down below the bank on each side of the clearing, and the four remaining in treetop positions strung out away from the river and upslope of the direction from which any guerrillas crossing the ford would come.

The last man he posted was Jarnki.

"Don't worry, Corporal," he said, hovering on the electric horse in midair a few feet from where Jarnki swayed in the treetop, clutching his cone rifle. "You'll find the Neulanders won't keep you waiting long. When you see them, give them a few cones from here, and then get down on the ground where you won't get hit. You've been shot at before, haven't you?"

Jarnki nodded. His face was a little pale, and his position in a crotch of the smooth-barked, variform Earth oak he perched in was somewhat too cramped to be comfortable.

"Yes, sir," he said. His tone left a great deal more unsaid.

"But it was under sensible conditions, with the rest of the men in your platoon or company all around you, wasn't it?" said Cletus.

"Don't let the difference shake you, Corporal. It won't matter once the firing starts. I'm going to check the two lower crossings. I'll be back before long."

He swung the electric horse away from the tree and headed downriver. . . . The vehicle he rode was almost silent in its operation, producing nothing much more than the kind of hum a room exhaust fan makes. Under conditions of normal quiet it could be heard for perhaps fifteen meters. But this upland Kultan jungle was busy with the sounds of birds and animals. Among these was a cry like the sound of an ax striking wood, which sounded at intervals; and another sound that resembled heavy snoring, which would go on for several seconds, only to break off, pause, and then begin again. But most of the woodlife noises were simply screams of different pitches and volumes and musical character.

Altogether these made an unpredictable pattern of sound, among which the low hum of the electric horse could easily be lost to ears not specifically listening for it —such as the ears of a guerrilla from Neuland who was probably both unfamiliar with the noise and not expecting it in any case.

Cletus flew downriver and checked both the lower crossings, finding them empty of all human movement. He turned from the lowest crossing to move through midair into the jungle from the river, upslope, in the direction of the pass. With luck, he thought, since they had the longest distance to cover if several crossings were being used. Undoubtedly a rendezvous point and time would have been set up for all groups on the far side of the river.

He drifted forward just under treetop level, some forty to sixty meters above the ground, at a speed of not more than six kilometers per hour. Below him, the upland jungle flora showed less of the yellow veining than there had been in the greenery near the shuttleboat landing pad; but the threads of scarlet ran everywhere, even through the outsize leaves of the variform Earth trees—oak, maple and ash—with which Kultis had been seeded twenty years back.

The Earth flora had taken more strongly in these higher altitudes. But there was still a majority of the native plants and trees, from fern-like clumps reaching ten meters into the air, to a sprawling tree-type with purple fruits that were perfectly edible but exhaled a faint but sickening scent through their furry skins as they ripened.

Cletus was about eight hundred meters away from the river crossing before he spotted his first sign of movement, a waving of fern tops below him. He checked his forward movement and drifted downward.

A second later the foreshortened figure of a man in a brown- and green-splashed jungle suit moved into sight from under the fern.

The infiltrator was unequipped except for the pack on his back, a soft camouflage-cloth cap on his head and the pellet-gun sporting firearm he carried by its strap over his right shoulder. This was to be expected where the guerrillas were concerned. The convention that had grown up on the newer worlds in fifty years of intercolony disputes was that, unless a man carried military weaponry or equipment, he was subject only to civil law—and civil law had to prove damage to property, life or limb before any action could be taken against an armed man, even from another colony. A guerrilla caught with nothing but a sporting gun was usually only deported or interned. One with any kind of military equipment, however—even as little as a military-issue nail file—could be taken by the military courts, which usually adjudged him a saboteur and condemned him to prison or death. If this man below him was typical of the infiltrators in his group, then Jarnki and his men with their cone rifles would have a massive advantage in weapons to make up for their scarcity of numbers, which was a relief.

Cletus continued to watch the man for several minutes. He was making his way through the jungle with no real regard for silence or cover. As soon as Cletus had a line of march estimated for this individual, he turned off to one side to locate the other members of the same guerrilla force.

The rapidly rising sun, burning through the sparse leaves at treetop level, heated the back of Cletus' neck. He was sweating from his armpits, all across his chest and back under his jungle suit, and his knee was threatening to revive its ache once more. He took a moment out to force his muscles to relax and push the knee discomfort from him. There was not time for that—not yet. He went back to searching the jungle for more guerrillas.

Almost immediately he found the second man, moving along parallel to and perhaps thirty meters from the infiltrator Cletus had spotted first. Cletus continued looking, and within the next twenty minutes he ranged out to both ends of the skirmish line that was pushing through the jungle below him and counted twenty men moving abreast over a front perhaps three hundred meters in width. If the Neulanders had split their forces equally between the three crossings, which would be only elementary military precaution, that would mean an infiltration force of sixty men. Sixty men, assuming they lost something like 20 per cent of their group's strength in getting through the jungle from here to the coast, would leave about forty-eight men available for whatever assault the Neulanders planned to celebrate deCastries' visit.

Forty-eight men could do a lot in the way of taking over and holding the small coastal fishing village. But a good deal more could be done with double that number. Perhaps there was a second skirmish line behind the first.

Cletus turned the electric horse in midair and drifted it back under the treetops behind the man he had just spotted advancing. Sure enough, about eighty meters back, he discovered a second skirmish line—this time with fifteen men in it, including at least a couple who looked like officers, in that they carried more in the way of communication and other equipment and wore sidearms rather than rifles. Cletus turned the electric horse about, slid quietly through the air just below the treetops and back toward the outside lower end of the approaching skirmish line. He located it, and saw that—as he had expected—the guerrillas were already beginning to close up so as to come into the crossing point together. Having estimated the line along which their lower edge would be drawing in, he went ahead on the electric horse, stopping to plant singleton personnel mines against the trunks of trees not more that four inches thick at intervals of about twenty meters. He planted the last of these right at the water's edge, about twenty meters below the crossing. Then he swooped back to make contact with the end of the second skirmish line.

He found the end of the line just coming level with the first mine he had planted, the end man some ten meters away from it in the jungle. Cletus swooped out and around to come up behind the center of the line. Careful not to approach any closer than twenty meters, he halted the electric horse, unlimbered his rifle and sprayed a long burst up and down the line through about a sixty-degree angle.

The sound of a cone rifle firing was not the sort of noise that went unnoticed. The tiny, self-propelled cones, leaving the muzzle of the rifle at relatively low velocity but accelerating as they went, whistled piercingly through the air until their passage was concluded by the dull, abrupt thud of the impact explosion that ended their career. A man not in body armor, as these guerrillas were not, could be torn in half by one of those explosions—so that it was no wonder that, for a second after the sound of his firing had ceased, there was utter silence in the jungle. Even the birds and beasts were still. Then, somewhat laggardly, but bravely enough, from immediately in front of Cletus and all up and down the invisible skirmish line of the infiltrators, pellet guns began to snap back, like a chorus of sprung mousetraps.

The firing was blind. The pellets, zipping through the leaves of the trees about Cletus like so many hailstones, went wide. But there was an uncomfortable amount of them. Cletus had already flung the electric horse about and was putting distance between himself and those who were shooting. Fifty meters back, he turned once more around the downriver end of the line and reached for the remote trigger that set off the first of his singleton personnel mines.

Up ahead of him and to his left, there was a single loud explosion. A tree—the tree to which the land mine had been stuck—leaned like a sick giant among its fellows, and slowly at first, then faster, came toppling down among the underbrush.

By now, the jungle was alive with sound. The guerrillas were apparently firing in every direction, because the wildlife were screaming at the tops of their lungs. Cletus

61

moved in at an angle to the end of the line, fired another long burst from his weapon and quickly moved up level with his second mine.

The heavy vegetation of the jungle hid the actions of the individual guerrillas. But they were shouting to each other now; and this, as well as the wild life sounds, gave Cletus a rough idea of what was going on. Clearly, they were doing the instinctive, if not exactly the militarily wise, thing. They were beginning to draw together for mutual support. Cletus gave them five minutes in which to get well clumped, so that what had been two spread-out skirmish lines was now a single group of thirty-five individuals within a circle of jungle no more than fifty meters in diameter.

Then he swung around to the rear of this once more, set off his second singleton mine ahead of them and once more commenced firing into them from behind.

This time he evoked a veritable cricket chorus of answering pellet-gun fire—what sounded like all thirty-five weapons snapping at him at once, in every direction. The nearby Kultan wild life burst out in a cacophony of protest; and the toppling of a tree cut down by a third singleton mine added its crash to the general uproar just as the firing began to slack off. By this time, Cletus was once more around behind his line of remaining unfired mines, downriver from the guerrillas. . . . He waited.

After a few minutes commands were shouted and the guerrilla firing ceased. Cletus did not have to see into the center of the hundred-meter-wide area to know that the officers among the infiltrators were talking over the situation they had encountered. The question in their minds would be whether the explosions and cone-rifle firing they had heard had been evoked from some small patrol that just happened to be in this area, or whether they had—against all normal expectations and reason—run head-on into a large enemy force set here directly to bar their route to the coast. Cletus let them talk it over.

The obvious move by a group such as these guerrillas in a situation such as this was to sit tight and send out scouts. The infiltrators were by this time less than eight hundred meters from the river's edge clearing of the crossing point and scouts would easily discover that the point was actually undefended, which would not be good. Cletus set off a couple more of his mines and commenced firing upon the downriver side of the guerrilla area. Immediately the guerrillas answered.

But then this fire, too, began to dwindle and become

more sporadic, until there was only a single gun snapping from moment to moment. When it, at last, fell silent, Cletus took the electric horse up and swung wide, away from the river into a position about five hundred meters upriver. Here he hovered, and waited.

Sure enough, within a very few minutes, he was able to make out movement in the jungle. Men were coming toward him, cautiously, and once more spread out in a skirmish line. The Neulander guerrillas, having encountered renewed evidence of what they thought was at least a sizable force at the lowest crossing, had chosen discretion over valor. They were withdrawing to the next higher crossing, where either their passage would not be barred or they would have the comfort of joining forces with that other group of their force which had been sent to cross at the middle ford.

Cletus swung wide once more, circled in, away from the river, and headed upstream toward the second crossing. As he approached this general area, he slowed the electric horse, to minimize the noise of its ducted fans, and crept along, high up, just under treetop level.

Shortly, he made contact with a second group of the guerrilla force, also in two skirmish lines, but a good nine hundred meters yet from the middle of the three river crossings. He paused long enough to plant another row of singleton personnel mines on trees in a line just downriver from the crossing, then slipped upriver again.

When he reached the area inland of the ford, highest up on the Blue River, where Jarnki and the others waited, he found that the third group of guerrillas, approaching this highest crossing, were not on schedule with the two other groups below. This upper group was already almost upon the crossing—less than 150 meters from it.

There was no time here for a careful reconnaissance before acting. Cletus swept across thirty meters in front of their first skirmish line, firing one long whistling burst from his cone rifle when he judged he was opposite the line's center.

Safely beyond the farther end of it, he waited until the snapping of answering fire from the guerrillas had died down, and then slipped back across their front once more, this time pausing to plant four singleton mines in their path. Once he was back beyond the downriver end of their lines, he set off a couple of these mines and began firing again.

The results were gratifying. The guerrillas opened up all along their front. Not only that, but, fortunately, the men he had left at the crossing, spooked by the guerrilla firing, began instinctively returning it with their cone rifles. The result, as far as the ear could tell, was a very good impression of two fair-sized groups in a fire-fight.

There was only one thing wrong with these additional sound effects Cletus was getting from his own men. One of the heavily whistling guns belonged to Jarnki; and evidently, from the sounds of it, the corporal was on the ground within fifteen meters of the front guerrilla lines—up where the exchange of shots could well prove lethal to him.

Cletus was tempted to swear, but stifled the urge. He pulsed a sharp message over his throat mike communicator to Jarnki to fall back. There was no response, and Jarnki's weapon went on speaking. This time Cletus did swear. Dropping his electric horse to just above the ground, he threaded the vehicle through the jungle cover up to right behind the corporal's position, led to it easily by the sound of Jarnki's firing.

The young soldier was lying in the prone position, legs spread out, his rifle barrel resting upon a rotting tree trunk, firing steadily. His face was as pale as the face of a man who has already lost half the blood in his body, but there was not a mark on him. Cletus had to dismount from the horse and shake the narrow shoulder above the whistling rifle before Jarnki would wake to the fact that anyone was beside him.

When he did become conscious of Cletus' presence, the convulsive reaction sent him scrambling to get to his feet like a startled cat. Cletus held him down against the ground with one hand and jerked the thumb of the other toward the crossing behind them.

"Fall back!" whispered Cletus harshly.

Jarnki stared, nodded, turned about and began to scramble on hands and legs toward the crossing. Cletus remounted the electric horse. Swinging wide again, he approached the guerrillas from their opposite side to ascertain their reaction to these unexpected sounds of opposition.

He was forced, in the end, to dismount from the electric horse and wriggle forward on his stomach after all, for perhaps ten meters, to get close enough to understand some of what was being said. Happily, what he heard was what he had hoped to hear. This group, like the group farthest downriver, had decided to stop and talk over these sounds of an unexpected opposition.

Painfully, Cletus wriggled back to the electric horse,

mounted it and flew a wide curve once more back to the crossing itself. He reached it just as Jarnki, by this time back on his feet, also reached it. Jarnki had recovered some of his color, but he looked at Cletus apprehensively, as if expecting a tongue-lashing. Instead, Cletus grinned at him.

"You're a brave man, Corporal," Cletus said. "You just have to remember that we like to keep our brave men alive, if possible. They're more useful that way."

Jarnki blinked. He grinned uncertainly.

Cletus turned back to the electric horse and took one of his boxes of singleton mines. He handed it to Jarnki.

"Plant these between fifty and eighty meters out," Cletus said. "Just be sure you don't take any chances on getting shot while you're doing it. Then hang back in front of those Neulanders as they advance, and keep them busy, both with the mines and with your weapon. Your job is to slow those Neulanders down until I can get back up here to help you. At a guess, that's going to be anywhere from another forty-five minutes to an hour and a half. Do you think you can do it?"

"We'll do it," said Jarnki.

"I'll leave it to you, then," said Cletus.

He mounted the electric horse, swung out over the river and headed down to make contact with the group of guerrillas moving toward the middle ford.

They were doing just that when he found them. The Neulanders were by this time fairly close to the middle crossing, and right in among his mines. There was no time like the present—Cletus set them off, and compounded the situation by cruising the Neulander rear and firing a number of bursts at random into them.

They returned his fire immediately; but, shortly after that, their return shooting became sporadic and ceased. The silence that followed lengthened and lengthened. When there had been no shots for five minutes, Cletus circled downriver with the electric horse and came up behind where the middle-crossing group had been when it was firing back at him.

They were not there, and, following cautiously just under treetop level, he soon caught up with them. They were headed upriver, and their numbers seemed to have doubled. Clearly, the group from the lower crossing had joined up with them and with common consent both groups were now headed for the highest crossing and a reunion with the group scheduled to cross there.

It was as he had expected. These infiltrators were sabo-

65

teurs rather than soldiers. They would have been strictly ordered to avoid military action along the way to their destination if it was at all possible to avoid it. He followed them carefully until they were almost in contact with the group of their fellows pinned down at the highest crossing, and then swung out over the river to reconnoiter the situation at that crossing.

He came in from above and cautiously explored the situation of the upper guerrilla group. They were strung out in a ragged semicircle the ends of which did not quite reach the riverbanks some sixty meters above and thirty meters below the crossing. They were laying down fire but making no real effort to fight their way across the river—as he listened, the sound of their firing dwindled and there was a good deal of shouting back and forth as the two groups from downriver joined them.

Hovering above ground level, Cletus produced a snooper mike from the equipment bar of the horse and slipped its earphone to his right ear. He swung the snooper barrel, scanning the undergrowth, but the only conversations he could pick up were by ordinary members of the guerrilla force, none by officers discussing the action they would take next. This was unfortunate. If he had been up to crawling fifty meters or so to make a personal reconnaissance—but he was not, and there was no point considering it. Reconnaissance on the electric horse would by now be too risky. There remained the business of putting himself in the shoes of the guerrilla force commander and trying to second-guess the man's thoughts. Cletus half-closed his eyes, relaxing in the same fashion as he had relaxed that morning in order to conquer the pain of his knee. Eyelids drooping, slumping bonelessly in the saddle of the horse, he let his mind go free.

For a long moment there was nothing but a random sequence of thoughts flowing across the surface of his consciousness. Then his imagination steadied down, and a concept began to form. He felt as though he was no longer sitting on the seat of the electric horse, but standing on the soft, spongy surface of the jungle floor, his camouflaged suit glued to his body by sweat as he squinted up at the sun, which was already past its zenith, moving into afternoon. An irritation of combined frustration and apprehension filled his mind. He looked back down at the circle of guerrilla under-officers gathered about him and realized that he had to make an immediate decision. Two-thirds of his force had already failed to get across the Blue River at the time and places they were

66

supposed to cross. Now, already behind schedule, he was faced with the last opportunity for a crossing—but also with the opposition of enemy forces, in what strength he did not know.

Clearly, at least one thing was true. The infiltration of this group he commanded had turned out to be not the secret from the Exotics that it had been expected it would be. To that extent, his mission was already a failure. If the Exotics had a force here to oppose him, what kind of opposition could he expect on the way to the coast?

Clearly, the mission now stood little or no chance of success. Sensibly, it should be abandoned. But could he turn back through the paths now without some excuse to give his superiors so that he would not be accused of abandoning the mission for insufficient reason?

Clearly, he could not. He would have to make an attempt to fight his way across the river, and just hope that the Exotic forces would oppose him hard enough so that he would have an excuse to retreat. . . .

Cletus returned to himself, opened his eyes and straightened up in the saddle once more. Lifting the electric horse up just under treetop level once more, he tossed three singleton mines at different angles toward the guerrilla position, and then set them off in quick succession.

Immediately, also, he opened up with both his rifle and sidearm, holding the rifle tucked against his side and firing it with his right hand while firing his sidearm with the left.

From the crossing, and from the two other sides of the guerrilla position, came the sound of the gunfire of his soldiers upon the Neulanders.

Within seconds the guerrilla force was laying down answering fire. The racket was the worst to disturb the jungle so far this day. Cletus waited until it began to die down slightly, so that he could be heard. Then he took the loudspeaker horn from the crossbar of the electric horse. He lifted the horn to his lips and turned it on. His amplified voice thundered through the jungle:

"CEASE FIRING! CEASE FIRING! ALL ALLIANCE FORCES CEASE FIRING!"

The cone rifles of the men under Cletus' command fell silent about the guerrilla area. Gradually, the answering voice of the guerrilla weapons also dwindled and silence filled the jungle again. Cletus spoke once more through the loudspeaker horn:

"ATTENTION NEULANDERS! ATTENTION NEULANDERS! YOU ARE COMPLETELY SURROUNDED BY THE ALLIANCE EXPEDITIONARY FORCE TO BAKHALLA. FURTHER RESISTANCE CAN ONLY END IN YOUR BEING WIPED OUT. THOSE WHO WISH TO SURRENDER WILL BE GIVEN HONORABLE TREATMENT IN ACCORDANCE WITH THE ESTABLISHED RULES GOVERNING THE CARE OF PRISONERS OF WAR. THIS IS THE COMMANDER OF THE ALLIANCE FORCE SPEAKING. MY MEN WILL HOLD THEIR FIRE FOR THREE MINUTES, DURING WHICH YOU WILL BE GIVEN A CHANCE TO SURRENDER. THOSE WISHING TO SURRENDER MUST DIVEST THEMSELVES OF ALL WEAPONS AND WALK INTO THE CLEARING AT THE CROSSING IN PLAIN SIGHT WITH THEIR HANDS CLASPED ON TOP OF THEIR HEAD. I REPEAT, THOSE WISHING TO SURRENDER MUST DIVEST THEMSELVES OF ALL WEAPONS AND WALK INTO PLAIN SIGHT IN THE CLEARING AT THE CROSSING WITH THEIR HANDS CLASPED ON TOP OF THEIR HEAD. YOU HAVE THREE MINUTES TO SURRENDER IN THIS FASHION STARTING FROM WHEN I SAY NOW."

Cletus paused for a moment, then added:

"ANY MEMBERS OF THE INVADING FORCE WHO HAVE NOT SURRENDERED BY THE TIME THREE MINUTES IS UP WILL BE CONSIDERED AS INTENDING TO CONTINUE RESISTANCE, AND MEMBERS OF THE ALLIANCE FORCE ARE INSTRUCTED TO OPEN FIRE UPON SUCH INDIVIDUALS ON SIGHT. THE THREE MINUTES IN WHICH TO SURRENDER WILL NOW BEGIN. NOW!"

He clicked off the loudspeaker horn, replaced it on the horse and quickly swung toward the river, out and around to where he had a view of the clearing without being visible himself. For a long moment nothing happened. Then there was a rustle of leaves, and a man in a Neulander camouflage suit, his hands clasped over his head and some jungle grass still stuck in his bushy beard, stepped into the clearing. Even from where Cletus watched, the whites of the guerrilla's eyes were visible and he looked about him apprehensively. He came forward hesitantly until he was roughly in the center of the clearing, then stopped, looking about him, his hands still clasped on top of his head.

A moment later another guerrilla appeared in the clearing; and suddenly they were coming from every direction.

Cletus sat watching and counting for a couple of minutes. By the end of the time, forty-three men had entered the clearing to surrender. Cletus nodded, thoughtfully.

Forty-three men out of a total of three groups of thirty guerrillas—or ninety—all told. It was as he had expected.

He glanced down along the riverbank to the place, less than ten meters from him, where Jarnki crouched with the two other men who had been left here to defend this crossing and were now covering the growing mass of prisoners.

"Ed," Cletus transmit-pulsed at the young corporal. "Ed, look to your right."

Jarnki looked sharply to his right, and jerked a little in startlement at seeing Cletus so close. Cletus beckoned to him. Cautiously, still crouching low to keep under the ridge of the riverbank, Jarnki ran up to where Cletus hovered on the electric horse a few feet off the ground.

As Jarnki came up, Cletus set the vehicle down on the ground and, safely screened from the clearing by the jungle bushes before him, stepped stiffly off the horse and stretched himself gratefully.

"Sir?" said Jarnki, inquiringly.

"I want you to hear this," said Cletus. He turned to the horse again and set its communications unit for the channel number of Lieutenant Athyer, over on the Blue River.

"Lieutenant," he pulse-messaged, "this is Colonel Grahame."

There was a short pause, and then the reply came, crackling not only in the earphones plug in Cletus' ear but over the small speaker built into the electric horse, which Cletus had just turned on.

"Colonel?" said Athyer. "What is it?"

"It seems the Neulander guerrillas attempted to infiltrate across the Blue River crossings here, after all," Cletus said. "We were lucky and managed to capture about half of them—"

"Guerrillas? Captured? Half . . ." Athyer's voice faltered in the earphones and over the speaker.

"But that isn't why I messaged," Cletus went on. "The other half got away from us. They'll be headed back toward the pass, to escape back into Neuland. But you're closer to the pass than they are. If you get there with even half your men, you ought to be able to round up the rest of them without any trouble."

"Trouble? Look . . . I . . . how do I know the situation's the way you say it is? I . . ."

"Lieutenant," said Cletus, and for the first time he put a slight emphasis on the word, "I just told you. We've captured half their force, here at the upper crossing on the Blue."

"Well . . . yes . . . Colonel. I understand that. But—"

Cletus cut him short. "Then get going, Lieutenant," he said. "If you don't move fast, you may miss them."

"Yes, sir. Of course. I'll message you again, shortly, Colonel. . . . Maybe you'd better hold your prisoners there, until they can be picked up by support ship. . . . Uh, some of them might get away if you try to move them through the jungle with only your six men." Athyer's voice was strengthening as he got control of himself. But there was a bitter note in it. Clearly, the implications of the capture of a large group of enemy infiltrators by a desk-bound theoretician, when Athyer himself was the sole field officer in command of the capturing force, was beginning to register on him. There was little hope that General Traynor would overlook this kind of a failure on his part.

His voice was grim as he went on.

"Do you need a medic?" he asked. "I can spare you one of the two I've got here and send him right over by one of the support ships, now that secrecy's out and the Neulanders know we're here."

"Thanks, Lieutenant. Yes, we could use a medic," said Cletus. "Good luck with the rest of them."

"Thanks," said Athyer, coldly. "Out, sir."

"Out," replied Cletus.

He cut transmission, stepped away from the electric horse and lowered himself stiffly to the ground into a sitting position, with his back to a nearby boulder.

"Sir?" said Jarnki. "What do we need a medic for? None of the men got hurt. You don't mean you, sir . . . ?"

"Me," said Cletus.

He extended his left leg, reached down and took his combat knife from its boot sheath. With its blade he ripped open his left pants leg, from above the knee to the top of his boot. The knee he revealed was extremely swollen and not pretty to look at. He reached for the first-aid kit at his belt and took out a spray hypo. He put the blunt nose of the spray against his wrist and pulled the trigger. The cool shock of the spray being driven through his skin directly into his bloodstream was like the touch of a finger of peace.

"Christ, sir," said Jarnki, white-faced, staring at the knee.

Cletus leaned back gratefully against the boulder, and let the soft waves of the narcotic begin to fold him into unconsciousness.

"I agree with you," he said. Then darkness claimed him.

9

Lying on his back in the hospital bed, Cletus gazed thoughtfully at the stiff, sunlit form of his left leg, upheld in traction above the surface of the bed.

"So," the duty medical officer, a brisk, round-faced, fortyish major had said with a fiendish chuckle when Cletus had been brought in, "you're the type who hates to take time out to give your body a chance to heal, are you, Colonel?" The next thing Cletus had known he was in the bed with his leg balanced immovably in a float cast anchored to the ceiling.

"But it's been three days now," Cletus remarked to Arvid, who had just arrived, bringing, as per orders, a local almanac, "and he promised that the third day he'd turn me loose. Take another look out in the corridor and see if he's been in any of the other rooms along here."

Arvid obeyed. He returned in a minute or two, shaking his head.

"No luck," he said. "But General Traynor's on his way over, sir. The nurse on the desk said his office just phoned to see if you were still here."

"Oh?" said Cletus. "That is right. He'd be coming, of course." He reached out and pressed the button that tilted the bed to lift him up into a sitting position. "Tell you what, Arv. Take a look up and down the other rooms for me and see if you can scrounge me some spacepost covers."

"Spacepost covers?" replied Arvid, calmly unquestioningly. "Right, I'll be back in a minute."

He went out. It took him more like three minutes than one; but when he returned he had five of the flimsy yellow envelopes in which mail sent by spaceship was ordinarily carried. The Earth Terminal postmark was square and black on the back of each. Cletus stacked them loosely together and laid them in a face-down pile on the table surface of his bedside console. Arvid watched him.

"Did you find what you wanted in the almanac, sir?" he asked.

"Yes," said Cletus. Seeing Arvid still gazing at him curiously, he added, "There's a new moon tonight."

"Oh," said Arvid.

"Yes. Now, when the general comes, Arv," Cletus said, "stay out in the corridor and keep your eyes open. I don't want that doctor slipping past me just because a general's talking to me, and leaving me hung up here for another day. What time was that appointment of mine with the officer from the Security Echelon?"

"Eleven hundred hours," said Arvid.

"And it's nine-thirty, already," said Cletus, looking at his watch. "Arv, if you'll step into the bathroom there, its window should give you a view of the drive in front of the hospital. If the general's coming by ground car, you ought to be able to see him pulling up about now. Take a look for me, will you?"

Arvid obediently disappeared into the small bath cubicle attached to Cletus' hospital room.

"No sign, sir," his voice came back.

"Keep watching," Cletus said.

Cletus relaxed against the upright slope of the bed behind him, half-closing his eyes. He had been expecting the general—in fact, Bat would be merely the last in a long line of visitors that had included Mondar, Eachan Khan, Melissa, Wefer Linet—and even Ed Jarnki. The gangling young noncommissioned officer had come in to show Cletus the new sergeant's stripes on his sleeve and give Cletus the credit for the fact they were there.

"Lieutenant Athyer's report tried to take all the credit for himself," Jarnki said. "We heard about it from the company clerk. But the rest of the squad and me—we spread the real story around. Maybe over at the Officers' Club they don't know how it was, but they do back in the barracks."

"Thank you," said Cletus.

"Hell . . ." said Jarnki, and paused, apparently at somewhat of a loss to further express his feelings. He changed the subject. "You wouldn't be able to use me yourself, would you, Colonel? I haven't been to clerks' school, but I mean—you couldn't use a driver or anything?"

Cletus smiled. "I'd like to have you, Ed," he said, "but I don't think they'd give you up. After all, you're a line soldier."

"I guess not, then," said Jarnki, disappointed. He went

off, but not before he extracted from Cletus a promise to take him on if he should ever become available.

Jarnki had been wrong, however, in believing that Athyer's report would be accepted at face value among the commissioned ranks. Clearly, the lieutenant was known to his fellow officers for the kind of field commander he was—just as it had been fairly obvious that Bat had not by chance chosen an officer like him to test Cletus' prophecy of guerrilla infiltration. As Arvid had reported to him, after that night at Mondar's party, the word was that Bat Traynor was out to get Cletus. In itself this information had originally meant merely that Cletus would be a good person for his fellow officers to avoid. But now, since he had pulled his chestnut out of the fire up on the Blue River without burning his fingers, there was plainly a good deal of covert sympathy for him among all but Bat's closest supporters. Eachan Khan had dryly hinted as much. Wefer Linet, from his safe perch inside the Navy chain of command, had blandly alluded to it. Bat could hardly be unaware of this reaction among the officers and men he commanded. Moreover, he was a conscientious commanding officer in the formal sense. If anything, it was surprising that he had not come to pay a visit to Cletus at the hospital before this.

Cletus relaxed, pushing back the tension in his body that threatened to possess it in impatience at being anchored here on the bed when so many things were yet to be done. What would be, would be. . . .

The sound of the door opening brought his eyes open as well. He raised his head and looked to his right and saw Bat Traynor entering the hospital room. There had been no warning from Arvid, still in the bathroom. Fleetingly, Cletus permitted himself the hope that the young lieutenant would have the sense to stay out of sight now that his chance discreetly to leave the hospital room was barred.

Bat strode up to the edge of the bed and stared down at Cletus, his expressive eyebrows drawing together in a faint scowl.

"Well, Colonel," he said, as he pulled a nearby chair close to the bed and sat down so that he stared into Cletus' face. He smiled, in hard, genial fashion. "Still got you tied up, I see."

"I'm supposed to be turned loose today," Cletus answered. "Thank you for dropping by, sir."

"I usually drop by to see one of my officers who's in the hospital," said Bat. "Nothing special in your case—

73

though you did do a good job with those six men up on the Blue River, Colonel."

"The guerrillas weren't very eager to make a fight of it, sir," said Cletus. "And then I was lucky enough to have them do just what I'd guessed they'd do. The General knows how unusual it is when everything works out in the field just the way it's planned."

"I do. Believe me, I do," answered Bat. Under the heavy brows, his eyes were hard but wary upon Cletus. "But that doesn't alter the fact you were right in your guess about where they'd come through and what they'd do once they were through."

"Yes, I'm happy about that," said Cletus. He smiled. "As I told the General, I pretty much bet my reputation on it to my friends back on Earth just before I left."

He glanced, as if unthinkingly, at the loose pile of face-down spaceship covers. Bat's eyes, following the direction of Cletus' gaze, narrowed slightly at sight of the yellow envelopes.

"You've been getting congratulations, have you?" Bat asked.

"There've been a few pats on the back," Cletus said. He did not add that these had been only from such local people as Eachan, Mondar and newly made Sergeant Ed Jarnki. "Of course, the operation wasn't a total success. I heard the rest of the guerrillas managed to get back through the pass before Lieutenant Athyer could contain them."

Bat's eyebrows jerked together into a solid angry line of black. "Don't push me, Colonel," he rumbled. "Athyer's report said he got word from you too late to take his men up into position to bar the pass."

"Was that it, sir?" said Cletus. "I'd guess it was my fault, then. After all, Athyer's an experienced field officer and I'm just a desk-jockey theoretician. I'm sure everybody realizes it was just luck that the contact my squad had with the enemy was successful and the contact the lieutenant and the rest of his company had wasn't."

For a moment their eyes locked.

"Of course," said Bat, grimly. "And if they don't understand it, I do. And that's what's important—isn't it, Colonel?"

"Yes, sir," said Cletus.

Bat sat back in his chair, and his brows relaxed. "Anyway," he said, "I didn't come here just to congratulate you. A suggestion by you came through to my office that you set up a staff to make regular weekly forecasts of

74

enemy activity. There was also your request for personnel and office space to facilitate your making such forecasts. . . . Understand, Colonel, as far as I'm concerned, I still need you like I need a fifty-man string ensemble. But your success with the guerrillas has got us some good publicity back at Alliance HQ, and I don't see how you can do any harm to the rest of the war effort here on Kultis by setting up this forecast staff. So, I'm going to approve it." He paused, then shot the words at Cletus. "That make you happy?"

"Yes, sir," said Cletus. "Thank you, General."

"Don't bother," said Bat, grimly. "As for Athyer—he had his chance, and he fell on his face. He'll be coming up for a Board of Inquiry into his fitness as an Alliance officer. Now—anything else you want?"

"No," said Cletus.

Bat stood up abruptly. "Good," he said. "I don't like having my arm twisted. I prefer handing out favors before they're asked. Also, I still need those tanks, and you're still going back to Earth at the first opportunity, Colonel. Tuck that fact into your prognostications and don't forget it!"

He turned on his heel and went toward the door.

"General," said Cletus. "There is a favor you could do me . . ."

Bat checked and swung about. His face darkened. "After all?" His voice was hard. "What is it, Colonel?"

"The Exotics have quite a library here in Bakhalla," said Cletus. "With a good deal of military text and information in it."

"What about it?"

"If the General will pardon me," said Cletus, slowly, "Lieutenant Athyer's main problems are too much imagination coupled with not enough confidence in himself. If he could get away and season himself for a while—say, as Information Officer for the Expeditionary Forces, to that Exotic library—he might turn out highly useful, after all."

Bat stared at Cletus. "Now why," said Bat softly, "would you want something like that for Athyer instead of a Board of Inquiry?"

"I don't like to see a valuable man wasted," said Cletus.

Bat grunted. He turned on his heel and went out without a further word. Looking a little sheepish, Arvid emerged from the bathroom.

"I'm sorry, sir," he said to Cletus. "The General must've come by air and landed on the roof."

"Think nothing of it, Arv," said Cletus, happily. "Just get out in that corridor and find me that doctor. I've got to get out of here."

Twenty minutes later, Arvid having finally located and produced the medical officer, Cletus was finally out of his cast and on his way to the office space Arvid had located for him. It was one of a set of three office suites, each consisting of three rooms and a bath, that had originally been erected by the Exotics for housing VIP guests. The other two suites were empty, so that, in essence, they had the building to themselves—a point Cletus had stipulated earlier when he had sent Arvid out to search. When they reached the office, Cletus found it furnished only with some camp chairs and a temporary field desk. A lean major in his early forties, with a white scar across his chin, was examining these in disparaging fashion.

"Major Wilson?" asked Cletus, as the officer turned to face them. "I'm Colonel Grahame."

They shook hands.

"Security sent me over," Wilson said. "You said you were expecting some special problem here, Colonel?"

"I'm hoping for one," replied Cletus. "We're going to be handling a good deal of material here, from the classified category 'on up. I'm going to be making weekly forecasts of enemy activity for General Traynor. Sooner or later the Neulanders are bound to hear of this and take an interest in this office. I'd like to set it up as a trap for anyone they send to investigate."

"Trap, sir?" echoed Wilson, puzzled.

"That's right," said Cletus, cheerfully. "I want to make it possible for them to get in, but, once in, impossible for them to get back out."

He turned to indicate the walls around them.

"For example," he said, pointing, "heavy steel mesh on the inside of the windows, but anchored so that it can't be pried loose or cut through with ordinary tools. An obvious lock on the outer door that can be easily picked—but a hidden lock that fastens the door securely once the open lock has been picked and the door opened and shut once. Metal framing and center panel for the door frame and door itself, so that they can't break out once the hidden lock has closed the door. . . . Possibly a wiring system to electrify the doors, windows and ventilator system just to discourage any attempt to break loose."

Wilson nodded slowly, but doubtfully. "That's going to add up to a good bit in the way of work-time and ma-

76

terials," he said. "I suppose you have authorization for this, Colonel . . . ?"

"It'll be forthcoming," said Cletus. "But the thing is for your division to get to work on this right away. The general was just talking to me less than an hour ago in the hospital about getting this office set up."

"The general—oh!" said Wilson, becoming brisk. "Of course, sir."

"Good, then," said Cletus. "That's settled."

After discussion of a few details, and after Wilson had taken a few measurements, the security officer left. Cletus set Arvid to getting Eachan Khan on the field telephone, which, with the table and chairs, was the office's only equipment. The Dorsai colonel was finally located out in the training area set aside for his mercenary troops.

"Mind if I come out?" asked Cletus.

"Not at all." In the small vision screen of the field phone, Eachan's face looked faintly curious. "You're welcome anytime, Colonel. Come along."

"Right," said Cletus. "I'll be there in half an hour."

He broke the connection. Leaving Arvid to see about getting the office supplied with furniture and staff, Cletus went out and took the staff car in which Arvid had driven him here to the training area of the Dorsai troops.

He found Eachan Khan standing at the edge of a field with a ten-meter metal tower in its center, from which what looked like a company of the tanned Dorsai professionals were practicing jump-belt landings. The line of those waiting their turn stretched out behind the tower, from the top of which mercenaries were going off, one by one, the shoulder jets of the jump belts roaring briefly and kicking up a cloud of whitish-brown dust as each one fell earthward. For men not trained exclusively as jump troops, Cletus noted with satisfaction as he limped up to the watching Eachan Khan, there were a great many more soft, upright landings than might have been expected.

"There you are," said Eachan, without turning his head, as Cletus came up behind him. The Dorsai colonel was standing with his legs slightly spread, his hands clasped behind him as he watched. "What do you think of our level of jump training, now you see it?"

"I'm impressed," answered Cletus. "What do you know about guerrilla traffic on the Bakhalla River?"

"Fair amount. Bound to be, of course, with the river running right through the city into the harbor here." Eachan Khan stared at him curiously. "Not so much infiltrators as sabotage materials, I understand, though. Why?"

"There's a new moon tonight," explained Cletus.

"Eh?" Eachan stared at him.

"And according to the local tide tables," said Cletus, "we're having an unusually high tide—all the tributaries and canals will be running deeper than usual as much as twenty miles inland. A good time for the Neulanders to smuggle in either large amounts of supplies or unusually heavy equipment."

"Hm . . ." Eachan fondled the right tip of his mustache. "Still . . . if you don't mind a word of advice?"

"Go right ahead," said Cletus.

"I don't think there'd be anything you could do about it," said Eachan. "River security is maintained by a half-dozen Army amphibs with half a dozen soldiers and light weapons on each one. That's not enough to do any good at all, and everybody knows it. But your General Traynor opts for dryfoot war equipment. About six months back he got five armored personnel carriers by swearing to your Alliance HQ that his river defenses were perfectly adequate and that, instead of sending him a couple of patrol boats, they could give him the personnel carriers instead. So if you go pointing out probable trouble on the river, you're not going to be making Traynor very happy. My advice would be to let any Neulander activity there go by on your blind side."

"Maybe you're right," said Cletus. "How about lunch?"

They left the training ground and drove in to the Officers' Club for lunch, where Melissa joined them in response to a telephone call from her father at Cletus' suggestion. She was somewhat reserved, and did not often meet Cletus' eye. She had come with her father for one brief visit to Cletus in the hospital, during which she stood back and let Eachan do most of the talking. She seemed inclined to let him do most of the talking now, although she glanced at Cletus from time to time when his attention was on her father. Cletus, however, ignored her reactions and kept up a steady, cheerful flow of conversation.

"Wefer Linet's been after me," Cletus said to her when they were having coffee and dessert, "to take one of his underwater tours in one of the Mark V submarine dozers. How about joining us this evening, and we can come back into Bakhalla afterward for a late supper?"

Melissa hesitated, but Eachan broke in, almost hastily.

"Good idea, girl," he said, almost gruffly. "Why don't you do that? Do you good to get out for a change."

The tone of Eachan's voice made his words sound like a command. But the naked voice of appeal could be heard beneath the brusqueness of the words. Melissa surrendered.

"Thank you," she said, raising her eyes to meet those of Cletus, "that sounds like fun."

10

Stars were beginning to fill the Bakhallan sky as Cletus and Melissa reached the gates to the Navy Yard and were met by an ensign attached to Wefer Linet's staff. The ensign conducted them inside to the ramp where the massive, black, two-story-tall shape of a Mark V squatted on its treads just above the golden-tinged waters of the Bakhallan harbor. Cletus had phoned Wefer immediately on parting from Eachan and Melissa to set up the evening's excursion.

Wefer had been enthusiastic. Navy regulations, he gleefully informed Cletus, absolutely forbade his allowing a civilian such as Melissa aboard a duty Navy vehicle like the Mark V. But, personally, he did not give a damn. For the record, he had caught only the words "Dorsai" and "Khan" when Cletus had phoned him earlier—and to whom, of course, could those words apply but to a mercenary colonel of his acquaintance, who was certainly no civilian? So he would be waiting for Colonel Grahame and Colonel Khan aboard the Mark V at 7 P.M.

Awaiting them he was. Moreover, he seemed to have shared the joke of his little deception of Navy regulations with his under-officers and crew. The ensign meeting Cletus and Melissa at the Navy Yard gate had gravely addressed Melissa as "Colonel"; and they were hardly aboard the Mark V before three of the seamen, grinning broadly, had found occasion to do the same.

This small and ridiculous joke, however, turned out to be just the straw needed to break the back of Melissa's stiffness and reserve. On the fourth occasion of being addressed as "Colonel," she laughed out loud—and began from then on to take an honest interest in the outing.

"Any place in particular you'd like to see?" asked Wefer, as the Mark V put itself into motion and rumbled slowly down its ramp into the bay.

"Up the river," said Cletus.

"Make it so, Ensign."

"Aye, sir," said the ensign who had met them at the gate. "Balance all tanks fore and aft, there!"

He was standing at the con, a little to the left of Wefer, Cletus and Melissa, who were placed before the large, curved shape of the hemispherical screen, which looked through the muddy water ahead and about them as though it were clear as glass, to pick up the shapes of ships' undersides and other solid objects below water level in the harbor.

There was a faint hissing and rumbling noise all around them. The vibration and sound of the heavy treads on the ramp suddenly ceased, and the water line shown on the hemispherical screen moved up above the horizon mark as the huge vehicle balanced out its ballast, replacing water with compressed air where necessary, and vice versa, so that the submarine dozer—its hundreds of tons of land weight now brought into near balance with an equal volume of water—floated as lightly as a leaf in air down to the muddy bottom of the harbor, sixty feet below.

"All forward, right thirty degrees horizontal," ordered the ensign; and they began their underwater tour upriver from Bakhalla.

"You'll notice," said Wefer in the fond tone of a father pointing out the talents of his first newborn, "our treads aren't touching the bottom here. There's nearly ten feet of loose silt and muck underneath us before we hit anything solid enough for the Mark V to walk on. Of course, we could settle down into it and do just that, if we wanted to. But why bother? We're as much at home and a lot more mobile to staying up in the water itself and simply swimming with the treads. . . . Now look there . . ."

He pointed to the screen, where, some two hundred yards ahead of them, the bottom dipped abruptly below their level of sight for a space of perhaps fifty yards before it rose again.

"That's the main channel—the main current line to the sea," Wefer said. "We clean that out daily—not because there're any ships here with draft enough to need a hundred and ten feet of water under them, but because that

80

trench provides a channel for the current that helps keep the harbor from silting up. Half of our work's understanding and using existing patterns of water movement. By keeping that channel deep, we cut our normal silt-removal work in half. Not that we need to. It's just the Navy way to do it as efficiently as possible."

"You mean you've got enough Mark V's and crews to keep the harbor clear even if the channel wasn't there?" Cletus asked.

Wefer snorted good-humoredly. "Got enough . . ." he echoed. "You don't know what these Mark V's can do. Why I could keep the harbor clean, even without the current channel, with this one machine alone! . . . Let me show you around here."

He took Cletus and Melissa on a tour of the Mark V's interior, from the diver's escape chamber down between the massive treads to the arms turret at the top of the vehicle, which could be uncovered to allow the Mark V to fire either its two heavy energy rifles or the underwater laser with which it was provided.

"You see why Traynor wanted these Mark V's for use in the jungles," concluded Wefer, as they ended their tour back in the control room before the hemispherical screen. "It hasn't got the fire power of the Army's jungle-breaker tanks, but in every other respect, except land speed, it's so far superior that there's no comparison—"

"Sir," interrupted the ensign behind him, "deep-draft surface vessel coming down the channel. We're going to have to get down and walk."

"Right. Make it so, Ensign," answered Wefer. He turned to the screen and pointed at the V-shaped object cutting the line of the river surface some two hundred yards ahead of them. "See that, Cletus? . . . Melissa? It's a boat drawing nine or ten feet of water. The channel here's less than fifty feet deep and we're going to have to get right down on the bottom to make sure that boat goes over with a good couple of fathoms of clearance."

He squinted at the V shape growing on the screen. Suddenly, he laughed. "Thought so!" he said. "That's one of your river patrol boats, Cletus. Want to have a look at its topside?"

"You mean, with a sensor float?" asked Cletus, quietly.

Wefer's jaw dropped. "How'd you know about that?" he demanded, staring.

"There was an article about it in the *Navy–Marine Journal* a little less than two years ago," answered Cletus.

"It struck me as the sort of device a sensible navy would put aboard a vehicle like this."

Wefer still stared at him, almost accusingly. "Is that so?" he said. "What else about the Mark V do you know that I don't know you know?"

"I know that with a bit of luck you might be able to capture a boatload of Neulander saboteurs and supplies bound for Bakhalla tonight, if you want to try for it. Have you got a map of the river?"

"A map?" Wefer lit up. He leaned forward and punched buttons below the hemispherical screen. The image on it vanished, to be replaced by a map showing the main river channel with its tributaries from the harbor mouth at Bakhalla to some thirty miles upstream. A barely moving red dot in the shape of a Mark V seen from above was crawling up the main channel in representation of the vehicle enclosing them. "What guerrillas? Where?"

"About six kilometers upstream from here," Cletus answered. He reached out to point with his forefinger to a spot ahead of the small, red, moving shape of the Mark V, where a tributary almost as large as the main river joined it at that spot. Up beyond the point of joining, the tributary spread itself out into a number of small streams and then marshland.

"There's an unusually high tide tonight, as you know," Cletus said. "So from this point on down there will be at least an extra eight feet of water in the main channel. Enough extra depth so that any small upriver motor launch could make it down into Bakhalla harbor towing a good load of supplies, and even personnel, behind it, safely underwater in a drogue pod. It's just a guess on my part, of course, but it hardly seems to me that the guerrillas would let a chance like this slip by without making an effort to get men and supplies to their people in the city."

Wefer stared at the map and slapped his leg in delight. "You're right!" he exploded. "Ensign, we're headed for that confluence Colonel Grahame just pointed out. Button up for noise, and get the weapons turret uncovered topside."

"Aye, sir," answered the ensign.

They reached the juncture point between the tributary point and the mainstream, which Cletus had pointed out. The Mark V crept out of the channel into the relatively shallow water near the riverbank opposite the mouth of the tributary and stopped there, its turrets less than five feet below the river surface. The sensor float was released from the upper hull of the vehicle and popped to the surface—a small, buoyant square of material with the thin metal whisker of a sensor rod rising one meter from it into the air, the two connected by a fine wire to the communications equipment of the Mark V. The sensor rod had to view the scene around it by available light only; but its resolving power was remarkable. The image of the scene it sent down to the hemispherical screen in the command room of the Mark V below was very nearly as clear as if broad daylight, rather than a fingernail paring of a moon, was illuminating the conjunction of the two streams.

"Not a hull in sight," muttered Wefer, rotating the view in the hemispherical screen to take in the full 180 degrees scanned by the sensor rod. "I suppose we'll just have to sit here and wait for them."

"You could be taking a few precautions, meanwhile," suggested Cletus.

Wefer glanced aside at him. "What precautions?"

"Against their getting away downstream if by some chance they manage to slip by you," said Cletus. "Is there anything to stop you now from moving enough material into the channel downriver so that, if they do come by, they'll run aground just below us?"

Wefer stared at him in astonishment, which slowly changed to delight. "Of course!" he exploded. "Ensign! Take her downstream!"

The Mark V moved roughly a hundred yards downstream; and, extending its massive dozer blade crosswise in front of it, began to shovel sand and silt from beneath the water near the river's edges into the main channel. Fifteen minutes work filled the channel for some fifty yards to a level even with the rest of the river bottom. Wefer was inclined to stop at that point, but Cletus suggested he further refine it into a barrier consisting of a wide, sloping ramp rising gradually to within half a dozen feet of the surface. Then, also at Cletus' suggestion, the Mark V returned, not merely upstream, but up into the tributary some fifty yards behind the point where it met with the waters of the main river.

Here the water was so shallow that the Mark V sat with its turret out in the air. But a few moments work with the dozer blade sufficed to dig a shallow depression so that they could lie in wait completely underwater.

Then the wait began. It was three hours—nearly midnight—before the sensor rod on its float, invisible against the shadow of the foliage lining the tributary's bank, picked up the image of a motor launch sliding down the main channel of the tributary, its motor turning at a speed barely sufficient to keep the drogue pod, towed behind it, underwater.

They waited, holding their breaths, until ship and drogue had passed. Then Wefer jumped for the command phone, from which he had, some hours since, displaced the ensign.

"Wait," said Cletus.

Wefer hesitated, staring at Cletus. "Wait?" he said. "What for?"

"You know that launch isn't going to be able to get past the barrier you built downstream," answered Cletus. "So why not sit here a little longer and see if another boat comes along?"

Wefer hesitated. Then he stepped back from the command phone. "You really think another one might come along?" he asked, thoughtfully.

"I wouldn't be surprised," said Cletus, cheerfully.

The answer was hardly out of his mouth before the sensor picked up another approaching motor launch with pod in tow. By the time this was well passed and out into the main river, still another launch had appeared. As Wefer stood staring with incredulous delight into the hemispherical screen, twenty boats towing pods passed within thirty yards of the submerged Mark V.

When a couple of minutes had gone by following the passage of the twenty boats and pods, Cletus suggested that probably it was time they were checking up on what had happened downstream. Wefer put the Mark V in motion. It surged up out of its shallow hole and plunged under the surface again down into the main channel of the tributary.

They reached the central channel of the main river, and turned downstream. Their infrared searchlights underwater, as well as the sensor rod being towed on its float above them, gave them a picture of wild confusion just ahead of them. Of the twenty launches that had passed them, fully half were firmly aground in the sloping ramp of river bottom that the Mark V had built. The rest, still afloat but with their drogue pods bobbing helplessly on the surface behind them, were valiantly trying to tow the stranded vessels free.

Wefer commanded the Mark V to a halt. He stared into the screen with mingled elation and dismay.

"Now what?" he muttered to Cletus. "If I charge on down there, the ones that aren't stuck are just going to turn around and beat it upriver and get away. Of course I've got the weapons in the turret. But still, a lot of them are going to get past me."

"As a suggestion," said Cletus, "how's this Mark V of yours at making a wave?"

Wefer stared at him. "A wave?" he said—and then repeated, joyously. "A *wave!*"

He barked orders into the command phone. The Mark V backed up a hundred yards along the channel of the main river and stopped. The two wings of its dozer blade, which had been folded back against its body to reduce drag while traveling, folded forward again and extended themselves to right and left until the blades' full area of twenty yards of width and ten feet of height were exposed. Delicately, Wefer tilted the front of the Mark V upward until the top half of the blade poked through the surface of the river and the treads were swimming freely in the water. Then he threw the engines into full speed, forward.

The Mark V rushed down the river in a roar of water, checked itself and sank itself to the bottom of the channel just fifty yards short of the still-floating launches. For a moment a wall of water hid the scene ahead; and then this passed, speeding like an ever-diminishing ripple farther downstream.

Left behind was a scene of wreckage and confusion.

Those launches that had already been aground had had their decks swept by the wave that the Mark V had created. In some cases they had been flipped on their sides by the wave or even turned completely upside down. But the greatest effect was to be seen upon those launches that had still had water under their keels and had been trying to tow the grounded ones loose.

Without exception these free-floating boats had been driven aground as well. In many cases they had been literally hammered into the soft soil of the piled-up river bed. One launch was standing on its nose, its prow driven half a dozen feet into the sand and silt below.

"I think they're ready for you now," Cletus said to Wefer.

If anything more was needed to complete the demoralization of the guerrillas aboard the launches it was the sight of the black shape of the Mark V roaring up into view out of the river depths, the two heavy energy rifles in its turret sweeping ominously back and forth. Almost without exception those who had managed to cling to their battered crafts dove overboard at the sight and began to swim frantically for the banks of the river.

85

"Turret—" began Wefer excitedly. But Cletus put his hand over the phone.

"Let them go," Cletus said. "The important men'll still be sealed inside the pods. Let's see about collecting them before they get too worried by all that's happened and start breaking out."

The advice was good. The Neulanders inside the pods had reached the limits of their endurance with the tossing about they had taken in the wave generated by the Mark V. Already more than one of the pods bobbing helplessly on the surface of the water, still tethered to their grounded launches, was beginning to split along the top, as those within activated their emergency exits. Wefer wheeled the Mark V into the midst of the wreckage and sent his ensign with three seamen out the Mark V's top hatch with hand weapons to cover the Neulanders as they emerged. They were ordered to swim to the Mark V, where they were searched, put in wrist restraints and herded down the hatch to be locked up in the Mark V's forward hold. Cletus and Melissa stayed discreetly out of sight.

Its forward hold crammed with prisoners, and the cargo pods filled with supplies in tow, the Mark V returned to its base at the Bakhalla Navy Yard. After disposing of their prisoners and their spoils, Cletus, Melissa and Wefer at last got into the city for that late—now early morning—supper they had planned. It was after four in the morning when Cletus took a tired but happy Melissa back to her father's residence. However, as they approached their destination, Melissa sobered and fell silent; and when they pulled up in front of the door of the house that the Exotics had put at the disposal of Melissa and Eachan, she did not offer to get out of the car right away.

"You know," she said, turning to Cletus, "you're pretty remarkable, after all. First those guerrillas on our way into Bakhalla, then the ones you captured up at Etter's Pass. And now, tonight."

"Thanks," he said, "but all I did was anticipate the optimum moves for deCastries to make, and arrange to be on the scene when they were made."

"Why do you keep talking about Dow as if he was having some sort of personal duel with you?"

"He is," said Cletus.

"The Outworlds Secretary for the Coalition—against some unknown lieutenant-colonel in an Alliance Expeditionary Force? Does that make sense?"

"Why not?" Cletus said. "He has a great deal more to

lose than an unknown lieutenant-colonel in an Alliance Expeditionary Force."

"But you're just imagining it all. You have to be!"

"No," said Cletus. "Remember I pushed him into an error of judgment with the sugar cubes in the dining lounge of the ship? The Outworlds Secretary for the Coalition can't afford to be made a fool of by an unknown Alliance lieutenant-colonel—as you describe me. It's true nobody but you knows—and only because I told you—that he did make a mistake, then—"

"Was that why you told me what you'd done?" Melissa interrupted quickly. "Just so I'd tell Dow?"

"Partly," said Cletus. She drew in her breath sharply in the darkness. "But only incidentally. Because it really didn't matter whether you told him or not. He knew I knew. And it simply wasn't good policy to let someone like me walk around thinking that I could beat him, at anything."

"Oh!" Melissa's voice trembled on the verge of anger. "You're making all this up. There's no proof, not a shred of proof for any of it."

"There is, though," said Cletus. "You remember the guerrillas on the way into Bakhalla attacked the command car, in which I was riding, instead of—as your father pointed out—the bus, which would have been a much more natural target for them. And this after Pater Ten had been burning up the ship-to-planet phone lines to Neuland before we left the ship."

"That's coincidence—stretched coincidence, at that," she retorted.

"No," said Cletus, quietly. "No more than the infiltration through Etter's Pass, which, while it was also made to provide a coup for the Neulanders, would have had the effect of discrediting me as a tactical expert before I had a chance to get my feet on the ground here and learn about the local military situation."

"I don't believe it," Melissa said vehemently. "It has to be all in your head!"

"If that's so, then deCastries shares the delusion," answered Cletus. "When I slipped out of the first trap, he was impressed enough to offer me a job with him—a job, however, which obviously would have put me in a subordinate position with regard to him. . . . That happened at Mondar's party, when you stepped over to talk to Eachan, and deCastries and I had a few moments together."

She stared at him through the night shadow of the car,

as if trying to search out the expression on his face in the little light that reached them from the lamp beside the doorway of the house and the dawn-pale sky above the aircar.

"You turned him down?" she said, after a long moment.

"I just have. Tonight," said Cletus, "after the guerrillas on landing and Etter's Pass, he couldn't delude himself that I wouldn't expect that the next obvious move for the Neulanders would be to take advantage of the high tide on the river to run in supplies and saboteurs to Bakhalla. If I'd let that infiltration take place without saying or doing anything, he'd have known that I'd become, to all intents and purposes, his hired man."

Again, she stared at him. "But you—" She broke off. "What can you expect to get out of all this, this . . . chain of things happening?"

"Just what I told you on the ship," said Cletus. "To trap deCastries into a personal fencing match with me, so that I can gradually lead him into larger and larger conflicts—until he commits himself completely in a final encounter where I can use his cumulative errors of judgment to destroy him."

Slowly, in the shadow, she shook her head. "You must be insane," she said.

"Or perhaps a little more sane than most," he answered. "Who knows?"

"But . . ." She hesitated, as though she was searching for an argument that would get through to him. "Anyway, no matter what's happened here, Dow's going to be leaving now. Then what about all these plans of yours about him? Now he can just go back to Earth and forget you—and he will."

"Not until I've caught him in an error of judgment too public for him to walk away from or hide," said Cletus. "And that's what I have to do next."

"One more—what if I tell him you're going to do that?" she demanded. "Just suppose the whole wild thing's true, and I go to Capital Neuland tomorrow and tell him what you're planning? Won't that ruin everything for you?"

"Not necessarily," said Cletus. "Anyway, I don't think you'll do that."

"Why not?" she challenged. "I told you on the ship, that first night, that I wanted help from Dow for Dad and myself. Why shouldn't I tell him anything that might make him more likely to help me?"

"Because you're more your father's daughter than you think," said Cletus. "Besides, your telling him would be a

88

waste of effort. I'm not going to let you throw yourself away on deCastries for something that'd be the wrong thing for Eachan and you anyway."

She stared at him, saying nothing, for one breathless minute. Then she exploded.

"*You* aren't going to let me!" she blazed. "*You're* going to order my life and my father's, are you? Where'd you get that kind of conceit, to think you could know what's best for people and what isn't best for them—let alone thinking you could get what you think best for them, or take it away from them if they want it? Who made you . . . king of everything . . ."

She had been fumbling furiously with the latch of the door on her side of the aircar as the words tumbled out of her. Now her fingers found it, the door swung open and she jumped out, turning to slam the door behind her.

"Go back to your BOQ—or wherever you're supposed to go!" she cried at him through the open window. "I knew there was no point going out with you tonight, but Dad asked me. I should have known better. *Good night!*"

She turned and ran up the steps into the house. The door slammed behind her. Cletus was left to silence and the empty, growing light of the pale dawn sky, unreachable overhead.

11

"Well, Colonel," said Bat, grimly, "what am I supposed to do with you?"

"The General could put me to use," said Cletus.

"Put you to use!" They were standing facing each other in Bat's private office. Bat turned in exasperation, took two quick steps away, wheeled and stepped back to glare up at Cletus once more. "First you make a grandstand play up by Etter's Pass, and it pays off so that you collect about five times as many prisoners as you had men to collect them with. Now you go out for a midnight picnic with the Navy and come back loaded with guerrillas and supplies bound for Bakhalla. Not only that, but you take a civilian along with you on this Navy spree!"

"Civilian, sir?" said Cletus.

"Oh yes, I know the official story!" Bat interrupted him, harshly. "And as long as it's a Navy matter, I'm letting it ride. But I *know* who you had with you out there, Colonel! Just as I know that wooden-headed young character, Linet, couldn't have dreamed up the idea of capturing those motor launches full of guerrillas. It was your show, Colonel, just like it was your show up at Etter's Pass! . . . And I repeat, what am I going to do with you?"

"In all seriousness, General," said Cletus, in a tone of voice that matched his words, "I mean what I say. I think you ought to put me to use."

"How?" Bat shot at him.

"As what I'm equipped to be—a tactician," said Cletus. He met the glare from under the general's expressive brows without yielding, and his voice remained calm and reasonable. "The present moment's one in which I could be particularly useful, considering the circumstances."

"What circumstances?" Bat demanded.

"Why, the circumstances that've more or less combined to trap the Military Secretary of the Coalition here on Kultis," Cletus replied. "I imagine there's little doubt, in the ordinary way of things, that Dow deCastries would be planning on leaving this planet in the next day or two."

"Oh, he would, would he?" said Bat. "And what makes you so sure that you know what a Coalition high executive like deCastries would be doing—under any circumstances?"

"The situation's easily open to deduction," answered Cletus. "The Neulander guerrillas aren't in any different situation than our Alliance forces here when it comes to the matter of getting supplies out from Earth. Both they and we could use a great many things that the supply depots back on Earth are slow to send us. You want tanks, sir. It's a safe bet the Neulander guerrillas have wants of their own, which the Coalition isn't eager to satisfy."

"And how do you make that out?" Bat snapped.

"I read it as a conclusion from the obvious fact that the Coalition's fighting a cheaper war here on Kultis than we are," said Cletus, reasonably. "It's typical of Alliance–Coalition confrontations for the past century. We tend to supply our allies actual fighting forces and the equipment to support them. The Coalition tends merely to arm and advise the opposition forces. This fits well with their ultimate aim, which isn't so much to win all these minor conflicts they oppose us in but to bleed dry the Alliance na-

90

tions back on Earth, so that eventually the Coalition can take over, back there where they believe all the important real estate is."

Cletus stopped speaking. Bat stared at him. After a second, the general shook his head like a man coming out of a daze.

"I ought to have my head examined," Bat said. "Why do I stand here and listen to this?"

"Because you're a good general officer, sir," said Cletus, "and because you can't help noticing I'm making sense."

"Part of the time you're making sense . . ." muttered Bat, his eyes abstracted. Then his gaze sharpened and he fastened it once more on Cletus' face. "All right, the Neulanders want equipment from the Coalition that the Coalition doesn't want to give them. You say that's why deCastries came out here?"

"Of course," said Cletus. "You know yourself the Coalition does this often. They refuse material help to one of their puppet allies, but then, to take the sting out of the refusal, they send a highly placed dignitary out to visit the puppets. The visit creates a great deal of stir, both in the puppet country and elsewhere. It gives the puppets the impression that their welfare is very close to the Coalition's heart—and it costs nearly nothing. Only, in this one instance, the situation's backfired somewhat."

"Backfired?" said Bat.

"The two new guerrilla thrusts that were supposed to celebrate deCastries' visit—that business up at Etter's Pass, and now last night's unsuccessful attempt to infiltrate a good number of men and supplies into the city of Bakhalla—have blown up in the Neulanders' faces," Cletus said. "Of course, officially, Dow's got nothing to do with either of those two missions. Naturally we know that he undoubtedly did know about them, and maybe even had a hand in planning them. But as I say, officially, there's no connection between him and them, and theoretically he could leave the planet as scheduled without looking backward once. Only I don't think he's likely to do that now."

"Why not?"

"Because, General," said Cletus, "his purpose in coming here was to give the Neulanders a morale boost—a shot in the arm. Instead, his visits have coincided with a couple of bad, if small, defeats for them. If he leaves now, his trip is going to be wasted. A man like deCastries is bound to put off leaving until he can leave on a note of success. That gives us a situation we can turn to our own advantage."

"Oh? Turn to our advantage, is it?" said Bat. "More of your fun and games, Colonel?"

"Sir," answered Cletus, "I might remind the General that I was right about the infiltration attempt through Etter's Pass, and I was right in my guess last night that the guerrillas would try to move men and supplies down the river and into the city—"

"All right! Never mind that!" snapped Bat. "If I wasn't taking those things into consideration I wouldn't be listening to you now. Go ahead. Tell me what you were going to tell me."

"I'd prefer to show you," answered Cletus. "If you wouldn't mind flying up to Etter's Pass—"

"Etter's Pass? Again?" said Bat. "Why? Tell me what map you want, and show me here."

"It's a short trip by air, sir," said Cletus, calmly. "The explanation's going to make a lot more sense if we have the actual terrain below us."

Bat grunted. He turned about, stalked to his desk and punched open his phone circuit.

"Send over Recon One to the roof here," he said. "We'll be right up."

Five minutes later, Cletus and Bat were en route by air toward the Etter's Pass area. The general's recon craft was a small but fast passenger vehicle, with antigrav vanes below its midsection and a plasma-thrust engine in the rear. Arvid, who had been waiting for Cletus in the general's outer office, was seated up front in the co-pilot's seat, with the pilot and the vessel's one crewman. Twenty feet behind them, in the open cabin space, Bat and Cletus conversed in the privacy provided by their distance and lowered voices. The recon craft approached the Etter's Pass area and, at Cletus' request, dropped down from its cruising altitude of eighty thousand feet to a mere six hundred. It began slowly to circle the area encompassing Etter's Pass, the village of Two Rivers and the two river valleys that came together just below the town.

Bat stared sourly at the pass and the town below it, nestled in the bottom of the V that was the conjunction of the two river valleys.

"All right, Colonel," he said. "I've taken an hour out of my day to make this trip. What you've got to tell me had better be worth it."

"I think it is," answered Cletus. He pointed at Etter's Pass and swung his fingertip from it down to the town below. "If you'll look closely there, sir, you'll see Two

92

Rivers is an ideal jump-off spot for launching an attack through the pass by our forces, as the first step in an invasion of Neuland."

Bat's head jerked around. He stared at Cletus. *"Invade Neuland . . ."* He lowered his voice hastily, for the heads of all three men up front had turned abruptly at the sound of his first words. "Have you gone completely out of your skull, Grahame? Or do you think I have, that I'd even consider such a thing? Invading Neuland's a decision that's not even for the General Staff back on Earth to make. It'd be the political boys in Geneva who'd have to decide that!"

"Of course," said Cletus, unruffled. "But the fact is, an invasion launched from Two Rivers could very easily be successful. If the General will just let me explain—"

"No!" snarled Bat, keeping his voice low. "I told you I don't even want to hear about it. If you got me all the way up here just to suggest that—"

"Not to suggest it as an actuality, sir," said Cletus. "Only to point out the benefits of the appearance of it. It's not necessary actually to invade Neuland. It's only necessary to cause the Neulanders, and deCastries, to realize such an invasion could be successful, if launched. Once they realize the possibility, they'll be under extreme pressure to take some counteraction to prevent it. Then, if after they've taken such action, we move to show that invasion was never our intention, Dow deCastries will have been involved in a local blunder from which it'll be impossible for him to detach his responsibility. The Coalition's only way of saving face for him and itself will be to cast all blame on the Neulanders and penalize them as evidence that the blame-casting isn't just rhetoric. The only form that penalizing can take is a lessening of Coalition help to Neuland. . . . Naturally, any reduction in Coalition aid to the Neulanders puts the Alliance contribution to the Exotics in that much stronger position."

Cletus stopped talking. Bat sat for a long second, gazing at him with an unusual expression—something almost like awe—below the heavy, expressive eyebrows.

"By God!" Bat said, at last, "you don't think in simple terms, do you, Grahame?"

"The complexity's more apparent than real," answered Cletus. "Everyone's more or less the prisoner of his current situation. Manipulate the situation and the individual often hasn't much choice but to let himself be manipulated as well."

Bat shook his head, slowly. "All right," he said, drawing a deep breath, "just how do you plan to signal this fake invasion attempt?"

"In the orthodox manner," answered Cletus. "By maneuvering of a couple of battalions of troops in this area below the pass—"

"Hold on. Whoa—" broke in Bat. "I told you once before I didn't have spare battalions of troops lying around waiting to be played with. Besides, if I order troops up here on anything like maneuvers, how am I going to claim later that there never was any intention to provoke Neuland in this area?"

"I realize you haven't any regular troops to spare, General," said Cletus. "The answer, of course, is not to use regular troops. Nor should you order them up here. However, the Dorsai regiment under Colonel Khan is engaged in jump-belt training right now. You could agree to a suggestion which Colonel Khan might make to the Exotics—and which the Exotics will certainly check out with you—that he bring his Dorsais up here for a week of live training jumps in this ideal terrain, which combines river valleys, jungle and hill country."

Bat opened his mouth as if to retort—then closed it sharply. His brows drew together in a thoughtful frown.

"Hmm," he said. "The Dorsais . . ."

"The Dorsais," Cletus reminded him, "don't operate out of your budget. They're financed separately by the Exotics."

Bat nodded, slowly.

"A full two battalions of men in this area," went on Cletus, "are too many for deCastries and the Neulanders to ignore. The fact that they're Dorsais rather than your own troops makes it seem all the more likely you're trying to pretend innocence, when in fact you've got some thrust into Neulander territory in mind. Add one more small factor, and you'll make suspicion of such a thrust a certainty, to deCastries at least. He knows I've been concerned with the two recent incidents when the Neulanders were frustrated. Appoint me your deputy general commander of this Dorsai unit, with authority to move them wherever I want, and nobody on the other side of the mountains will have any doubt left that the jump training's only a cover for an attack on Neuland territory."

Bat jerked his head up and stared at Cletus suspiciously. Cletus returned his gaze with the calm innocence of a man whose conscience has nothing to hide.

"But you *won't* be moving those Dorsais anywhere, except between Bakhalla and this area, will you, Colonel?" he demanded softly.

"I give you my word, sir," said Cletus. "They'll go nowhere else."

For a long moment Bat continued to stare, hard, at Cletus. But then, once again, slowly he nodded.

They returned to Bat's office in Bakhalla. As Cletus was leaving, headed for his staff car in the parking lot, a flyer settled into one of the marked spaces and Mondar got out, followed by the small, waspish shape of Pater Ten.

"There he is," said Pater Ten in a brittle voice, as he spotted Cletus. "Why don't you go ahead into the Headquarters building, Outbond? I'll stop a minute with Colonel Grahame. Dow wanted me to extend his congratulations on Grahame's success last week—and last night."

Mondar hesitated briefly, then smiled. "As you like," he said, turned and went on toward the Headquarters building.

Pater Ten walked over to face Cletus.

"Congratulate me?" asked Cletus.

"The Military Secretary," said Pater Ten, almost viciously, "is a very fair-minded man—"

In mid-sentence he broke off. For a second some inner change seemed to wipe his face clean of expression, and then it shaped itself again into a different kind of expression—an expression like that of an excellent stage mimic who has decided to impersonate the character and mannerisms of Dow deCastries. Except that Pater Ten's eyes were fixed and remote, like a man under hypnosis.

When he spoke, it was in an eerie echo of Dow's ordinary speech:

"Evidently," said those silkily urbane tones, "you're still trying to raise the ante, Grahame. Take my advice. Be warned. It's an occupation that's fraught with danger."

As abruptly as it had come, the unnatural resemblance to Dow smoothed itself from the little man's features and his gaze became normal again. He looked sharply up at Cletus.

"Very fair-minded," Pater said. "You underestimate him. I promise you, you've underestimated him—" The little man broke off, abruptly. "What're you looking at me like that for?" he snapped, acidly. "You don't believe me, is that it?"

Cletus shook his head, sadly. "I believe you," he said.

"It's just that I see I did underestimate him. It seems he's not just a dealer in other people's minds. He buys souls as well."

He turned and walked off to his car, leaving Pater Ten staring after him uncomprehendingly but with the automatic rage on his face with which the violent little man viewed nearly all things in the universe.

12

They met in Eachan Khan's office a week later—Cletus, Eachan and the four other top officers among the Dorsais. There was Eachan's second-in-command, Lieutenant-Colonel Marcus Dodds, a tall, quiet, narrow-boned man. There were also a major with a shaved head and expressionless features in a hard, round, blue-black face, with the single name of Swahili, a Major David Ap Morgan, who was thin and slightly buck-toothed and as fair-skinned as Swahili was dark; and, last, there was Captain Este Chotai, short, heavy-fleshed and handsome, with narrow eyes in a slightly mongoloid face. They sat around the long conference table in Eachan's wide office, with Eachan at the head of the table and Cletus seated at his right.

"And so, gentlemen," said Eachan Khan, winding up his explanation of Cletus' presence in their midst, "we have a new commanding officer from the Alliance Forces. I'll let Colonel Grahame speak for himself from this point on."

Eachan got up from his chair at the head of the table and stepped aside. Cletus rose, and Eachan took Cletus' former place at the table. Cletus moved over behind the chair Eachan had occupied, but he did not sit down immediately.

Instead, he turned about to look at the large map of Etter's Pass–Two Rivers area projected on the wall behind him. He looked at it and something deep, powerful and unyielding moved without warning through him. He drew in a slow deep breath and the silence of the room behind him seemed to ring suddenly in his ears. The features of the map before him seemed to leap out at him as if he saw, not the projected representation, but the actual features of jungle, hill and river that they represented.

He turned about and faced the Dorsai officers. Under his gaze they stiffened and their eyes narrowed as though something massive and unknown had stepped suddenly among them. Even Eachan stared at Cletus as though he had never seen him before.

"You're all professional soldiers," said Cletus. His voice was completely flat, without inflection or emphasis, but it rang in the room with a finality that left no room for doubt or argument in its listeners. "Your future depends on what you'll be doing in the next two weeks. Therefore I'm going to tell you what no one else on this planet yet knows, and I'm going to trust you to keep that information locked inside you."

He paused. They sat staring at him like men in a trance.

"You're going to fight a battle. My aim isn't going to be to kill the enemy in this battle, but to force him to surrender in large numbers, so if all goes according to plan you ought to win with little or no casualties. . . . I don't guarantee that. I only say that it ought to be that way. But, in any case, you'll have fought a battle."

He paused for a second, looking into their faces one by one. Then he went on.

"Behind me here," he said, "you see the upland area into which you're going to move at the end of this week for further jump-training and jungle practice. This practice isn't just to fill time. The better shape your men are in at the end of the training period, and the better they know the area, the better chance they'll have to survive in the fight, later. Colonel Khan will give you your specific orders. That's all I'll tell you now. As I say, I don't want you to tell anyone, not even the men you command, that any sort of real action's in prospect. If you're the kind of officers I think you are, and they're the kind of men I think they are, they'll absorb the feeling that something is going to happen without your having to tell them. . . . That's all."

He sat down abruptly and turned to Eachan.

"Take over, Colonel," he said to Eachan.

Eachan, unmoving, continued to gaze at him for just a fraction of a second longer before he rose, cleared his throat and began to describe the patterns of movement of the various units from Bakhalla into the Two Rivers area.

Four days later support ships of the type that had flown Cletus with Lieutenant Athyer and his troops up to Etter's Pass began ferrying the mercenary soldiers to Two Rivers. Cletus went up on one of the early flights and toured the area with Eachan Khan. Cletus' first concern was for the town or village—it was really more village than town—of Two Rivers itself.

The settlement was actually a tight little V-shaped clump of condominiums and individual homes surrounding a warehouse and business section and filling the triangular end-point of flatland where the valleys of the Blue and Whey rivers came together. This patch of flatland extended itself, with a few scattered streets and buildings, up the valley of each river for perhaps a quarter of a mile before the riverbanks became too high and steep for much building to be practical. The town was a community supported essentially by the wild-farming of a majority of its inhabitants, wild-farming being the planting, in the surrounding jungle areas, of native or mutated trees and plants bearing a cash crop without first dividing up or clearing the land. A wild-farmer owned no territory. What he owned was a number of trees or plants that he tended and from which he harvested the crops on a regular basis. Around Two Rivers a sort of native wild cherry and mutated rubber plants introduced by the Exotics four years ago were the staple wild-farm crops.

The local people took the invasion by the Dorsais in good spirits. The mercenaries were much quieter and better-mannered in their off-duty hours than were regular troops. Besides, they would be spending money in the town. The locals, in general, paid little attention to Cletus, as, with Eachan Kahn, he marked out positions for strong points with dug-in weapons on the near banks of the two rivers just above the town and down within the open land of the community itself. When Cletus had finished, he had laid out two V-shaped lines of strong points, one inside the other, covering the upriver approaches to the town and the river junction itself.

"Now," said Cletus to Eachan, when this was done, "let's go take a look up beyond the pass."

They took one of the support ships that had just discharged its cargo of Dorsai soldiers and was about to return to Bakhalla for another load. With it they flew up and over the area of Etter's Pass and made a shallow sweep over the some ten miles of mountainous territory beyond it to where the ground sloped away into the farther jungle that was Neuland territory.

"I expect the Neulanders will be coming around to see what we're doing," he said to Eachan, "as soon as their people in Bakhalla tell them the Dorsais have moved up here for training. I want this side of the mountains kept under observation by men who won't be spotted. I assume you've got people like that?"

"Of course!" said Eachan. "I'll have a watch on up here all twenty-six hours of the day. How soon do you want it to start?"

"Right away," answered Cletus.

"I'll have men started out in half an hour," Eachan answered. "Anything else?"

"Yes," Cletus said. "I want those defensive strong points, in and above the town, dug in, with an earth wall inside and sandbags outside so that it's at least six feet thick at the base and seven feet above the level of the ground outside."

Eachan frowned slightly. But his reply was laconic. "Yes, Colonel," he said.

"That's it, then," said Cletus. "I'm headed back to Bakhalla. I'll have the ship drop you back down at Two Rivers first. Are you planning on coming back to town later?"

"This evening," he answered, "as soon as I've got all the men moved in here and set up. I'm planning on commuting. Here, days—Bakhalla, nights."

"I'll see you back at the city then," said Cletus. He turned to the pilots of the support ship. "Take us back to Two Rivers."

He dropped off Eachan and went back to Bakhalla. There he found his work waiting for him—in two stacks, for, in accepting a role as Bat's deputy commanding officer of the Dorsais, he had in essence taken on another full job. The Dorsais operated with a small to nonexistent Headquarters staff, as they did in all areas requiring noncombatant personnel. In the field, each Dorsai was his own cook, launderer and bottle washer, and each officer was responsible for all paper work involving his command. Away from the field, in barracks so to speak, men were hired from the regular fighting units, at a small addition to their ordinary wages, to work as clerks, cooks, vehicle drivers and the rest, but in the field there was none of this.

Those Dorsais, therefore, who ordinarily would have lightened Cletus' paper workload concerning the mercenary soldiers were now in battle gear up at Two Rivers. It was this fact that also required Eachan to commute back to Bakhalla every night to take care of his own paper work.

Cletus, of course, had the use of the staff Arvid had collected to help in making his forecasts of enemy activity. But members of the staff, including Arvid himself, were fully occupied with their regular jobs, at least during normal working hours. Cletus had set them to functioning as a research service. They were collecting information on both Neuland and the Exotic colony, plus all the physical facts about Kultis—weather, climate, flora and fauna—that pertained to the two opposed peoples. This information was condensed and fed to Cletus as soon as it was available; at least half his working day was taken up in absorbing and digesting it.

So it was that the first five days after the Dorsais had been moved up to Two Rivers, Cletus spent at his office between the hours of seven in the morning and midnight, with very few breaks in between. About seven o'clock of the fifth evening, after the rest of the staff had already left for the day, Wefer Linet showed up unexpectedly.

"Let's go catch some more Neulander guerrillas," Wefer suggested.

Cletus laughed, leaned back in his chair and stretched wearily. "I don't know where there are any, right now," Cletus said.

"Let's go have dinner then and talk about it," said Wefer craftily. "Maybe between the two of us we can figure out how to find some."

Cletus laughed again, started to shake his head, and then let himself be persuaded. After the dinner, however, he insisted on returning to his desk. Wefer came back with him, and only reluctantly took his leave when Cletus insisted that the work yet undone required his immediate attention.

"But don't forget," Wefer said on his way out, "you'll call me if anything comes up. I've got five Mark V's, and four of them are yours on half an hour's notice. It's not just me, it's my men. Everyone who was with us out there on the river has been spreading the story around until I haven't got anyone in my command who wouldn't want to go with you if another chance comes up. . . . You'll find something for us to do?"

"It's a promise," said Cletus. "I'll turn up something for you shortly."

Wefer at last allowed himself to be ushered out. Cletus went back to his desk. By eleven o'clock he had finished the extensive and detailed orders he had been drafting to cover the actions and contingencies of the next two days. He made up a package of the orders, which were to be passed on to Eachan Khan for application to the Dorsai troops, and, going out, drove himself in a staff aircar to the Headquarters building in the Dorsai area.

He parked in front of it. There were two other cars waiting there; the one window of Eachan's office that faced him was alight. The rest of the building—a temporary structure of native wood painted a military light green that looked almost white in the pale light of the now-waxing new moon overhead—was dark, as were all the surrounding office and barracks buildings. It was like being in a ghost town where only one man lived.

Cletus got out of the car and went up the steps into the front hall of the building. Passing through the swinging gate, which barred visitors from the clerks normally at work in the outer office, he went down the corridor beyond the outer office to where the half-open door of Eachan's private office was marked by an escaping swathe of yellow light that lay across the corridor floor. Coming quietly up on that patch of light, Cletus checked, suddenly, at the sound of voices within the room.

The voices were those of Eachan and Melissa—and their conversation was no public one.

Cletus might have coughed, then, or made some other noise to warn that he had come upon them. But at that moment he heard his own name mentioned—and instantly guessed at least half of the conversation that had gone before. He neither turned and retreated nor made a sound. Instead he stood, listening.

"I thought you liked young Grahame," Eachan had just finished saying.

"Of course I like him!" Melissa's voice was tortured. "That's got nothing to do with it. Can't you understand, Dad?"

"No." Eachan's voice was stark.

Cletus took one long step forward, so that he could just see around the corner of the half-open door into the lighted room. The illumination there came from a single lamp, floating a foot and a half above the surface of Eachan's desk. On opposite sides of the desk, Eachan and Melissa stood facing each other. Their heads were above the level of the lamp, and their faces were hidden in shadow, while the lower parts of their bodies were clearly illuminated.

"No, of course you can't!" said Melissa. "Because you won't try! You can't tell me you like this better—this

101

hand-to-mouth mercenary soldiering—than our home in Jalalabad! And with Dow's help you can go back. You'll be a general officer again, with your old rank back. That's *home,* Dad! Home on Earth, for both of us!"

"Not any more," said Eachan deeply. "I'm a soldier, Melly. Don't you understand? A *soldier!* Not just a uniform with a man walking around inside it—and that's all I'd be if I went back to Jalalabad. As a Dorsai, at least I'm still a soldier!" His voice became ragged, suddenly. "I know it's not fair to you—"

"I'm not doing it for me!" said Melissa. "Do you think I care? I was just a girl when we left Earth—it wouldn't be the same place at all for me, if we went back. But Mother told me to take care of you. And I am, even if you haven't got the sense to take care of yourself."

"Melly . . ." Eachan's voice was no longer ragged, but it was deep with pain. "You're so sure of yourself . . ."

"Yes, I am!" she said. "One of us has to be. I phoned him, Dad. Yesterday."

"Phoned deCastries?"

"Yes," Melissa said. "I called him in Capital Neuland. I said we'd come anytime he sent for us from Earth. *We'd* come, I said, Dad. But I warn you, if you won't go, I'll go alone."

There was a moment's silence in the darkness hiding the upper part of Eachan's stiff figure.

"There's nothing there for you, girl," he said, hoarsely. "You said so yourself."

"But I'll go!" she said. "Because that's the only way to get you to go back, to say I'll go alone if I have to—and mean it. Right now, I promise you, Dad . . ."

Cletus did not wait to hear the end of that promise. He turned abruptly and walked silently back to the front door of the building. He opened and closed the door, banging the heel of his hand against it noisily. He walked in, kicked open the gate in the fence about the outer office area and walked soundingly down the hall toward the light of the partly opened door.

When he entered the office room, the overhead lights had been turned on. In their bright glare, Melissa and Eachan still stood a little apart from each other, with the desk in between.

"Hello, Melissa!" Cletus said. "Good to see you. I was just bringing in some orders for Eachan. Why don't you wait a few minutes and we can all go have a cup of coffee or something?"

"No, I . . ." Melissa stumbled a little in her speech. Under the overhead lights her face looked pale and drawn. "I've got a headache. I think I'll go right home to bed." She turned to her father. "I'll see you later, Dad?"

"I'll be home before long," Eachan answered.

She turned and went out. Both men watched her go. When the echo of her footsteps had been brought to an end by the sound of the outer door of the office building closing, Cletus turned back to face Eachan and threw the package of papers he was carrying onto Eachan's desk.

"What's the latest word from the scouts watching the Neulander side of the mountains?" Cletus asked, watching the older man's face and dropping into a chair on his side of the desk. Eachan sat down more slowly in his own chair.

"The Neulanders've evidently stopped moving men into the area," Eachan said. "But the scouts estimate they've got thirty-six hundred men there now—nearly double the number of our Dorsai troops. And they're regular Neulander soldiery, not guerrillas, with some light tanks and mobile artillery. My guess is that's better than 60 per cent of their fully equipped, regular armed forces."

"Good," said Cletus. "Pull all but a couple of companies back into Bakhalla."

Eachan's gaze jerked up from the packet of orders to stare at Cletus' face. "Pull back?" he echoed. "What was the point in going up there, then?"

"The point in going up there," said Cletus, "was to cause Neuland to do exactly what they've done—assemble troops on their side of the mountain border. Now we pull back most of our men, so that it looks as though we've lost our nerve. Either that, or never intended to be a threat after all."

"And was that what we intended?" Eachan looked narrowly at Cletus.

Cletus laughed cheerfully. "Our intent, just as I say," he answered, "was to make them assemble a large force on their side of the pass through the mountains. Now we can pack up and go home—but can they? No doubt you've heard the army rumor—and by this time the Neulanders will have heard it too—that General Traynor and myself were overhead discussing an invasion of Neuland, and that we made a special trip up to Etter's Pass to survey it with that in mind."

"You mean," said Eachan, "that deCastries and the Neulanders will be sure that we really meant to invade them?"

"I mean just the opposite," said Cletus. "There's a great

103

deal of truth to the fact that a liar is always going to sus-pect you of lying and a thief'll always suspect your hon-esty. DeCastries is a subtle man, and the weakness of subtle men is to suspect any straightforward action of being a screen for some kind of trick. He'll be sure to have concluded the rumor was leaked specifically for the purpose of causing him—and Neuland—to move a lot of troops into position on a false invasion scare, which would evaporate then and leave them looking foolish. Con-sequently, being the man he is, he'll have resolved to play along with our game and take advantage of us at the very moment we plan to be chuckling over his embar-rassment."

Eachan frowned. "I don't believe I follow you," he said.

Cletus nodded at the package of papers. "It's all in the orders, there," he said. "You'll start withdrawing men from the Two Rivers area early tomorrow, a shipload at half hour intervals. As each shipload gets back here and gets sorted out, turn them loose on three-day passes."

Eachan stared at him, grimly. "And that's it?" Eachan said, at last.

"That's it—until I give you further orders," said Cletus, getting to his feet. He turned about and headed toward the door.

"Good night," said Eachan behind him. As Cletus went out the door and turned left to go off down the corridor, he caught a glimpse of Eachan, still standing behind the desk, looking after him.

Cletus went back to his quarters and to bed. The next morning he allowed himself the unusual luxury of sleeping late. It was 10 A.M. by the time he drifted into the Officers' Club for a late breakfast and just short of noon when he finally arrived at his office. Arvid and the staff Arvid had accumulated there were all diligently at work. Cletus smiled at them like an indulgent father and called them all together.

"I'm flying up to Two Rivers this afternoon," he said, "to supervise the windup of the Dorsai exercises up there. So there's not much point in your feeding me with a lot of information material that'll go stale between now and Monday morning anyway. I've been working you all above and beyond the call of duty. So take the rest of the day off—all of you, that is, except Arvid"—he smiled at the big young officer—"and I'll see you again at the beginning of next week."

The staff evaporated like a scattering of raindrops on
104

hot pavement after a tropical shower. Once they were gone, Cletus went carefully around the office, making sure all its security systems were in working order and ready to be put in operation. Then he came back, sat down opposite Arvid's desk and reached over to pick up Arvid's phone. He dialed the number of the Navy base.

"This is Colonel Cletus Grahame," he told the duty petty officer at the far end. "Would you try to locate Commander Linet for me, and have him call me back? I'm at my office."

He put the phone back on Arvid's desk and waited. Arvid was watching him curiously. Cletus got up and walked over to his own desk. He picked up his own phone there and brought it back to exchange it for the phone in front of Arvid. Arvid's phone he took back to his own desk.

He punched out the first two digits of the five-digit number that would connect him with Bat Traynor's office. Then, with the phone activated, but the call incompleted, he pushed the phone from him and looked over at Arvid.

"Arv," he said, "some time in the next few hours Eachan Khan's going to be calling me. If anyone but Colonel Eachan calls, I've just stepped out and you don't know when I'll be back. But if Colonel Eachan calls, tell him that I'm on the phone to General Traynor at the moment—and I will be. Ask him if you can take a message, or say I'll call him back in a few minutes."

Arvid frowned in slight puzzlement—but the frown evaporated almost immediately into his usual agreeable expression.

"Yes, sir," he said. . . . "And now?" he asked, after Cletus had made the call.

"Now, we wait."

Wait, they did—for nearly two hours, during which perhaps a dozen unimportant phone calls came in and were neatly fielded by Arvid. Then the phone Cletus had moved from his desk to that of the lieutenant buzzed abruptly and Arvid lifted the receiver.

"Colonel Grahame's office, Lieutenant Johnson speaking—" Arvid broke off, glancing over at Cletus. "Colonel Khan? Yes, sir . . ."

Cletus had already picked up Arvid's phone and was completing the punching of the proper sequence of numbers for contact with Bat's office. In the background he heard Arvid saying that he could take a message. Bat's office answered.

"This is Colonel Grahame," Cletus said into the phone.

"I'd like to talk to General Traynor right away—in fact, immediately. It's red emergency."

He waited. There was a fractional delay at the other end of the line. Arvid, meanwhile, had hung up. There was silence in the office. Cletus could see out of the corner of his eye how Arvid was standing, watching him.

"Grahame?" Bat's voice exploded suddenly against Cletus' ear. "What's all this?"

"Sir," said Cletus, "I discovered something, and I think I ought to talk to you about it right away—privately. I can't tell you over the phone. It's got to do with the Coalition and it involves not only us, here on Kultis, but the whole Alliance. I'm at my office. I've given my staff the rest of the day off. Could you make some excuse to leave your office and come over here so that we could talk privately?"

"Talk? What is all this—" Bat broke off. Cletus heard the other's voice, suddenly withdrawn from the mouthpiece of the phone, speaking distantly to someone else. "Joe, go get me that file on . . . the plans for the new military district south of town."

There were a few more seconds of pause, and then Bat's voice came back close to the phone but muted and cold in tone.

"Now you can tell me," he said.

"I'm sorry, sir," said Cletus.

"Sorry? You mean you don't even trust the phone circuits to my office?"

"I didn't say that, sir," answered Cletus evenly. "I only suggested that you make some excuse to get out of your office and meet me privately over here at mine."

His voice was almost wooden in its lack of expression. There was a long pause at the other end of the phone circuit. Then Cletus heard Bat's indrawn breath hiss sharply.

"All right, Grahame," said Bat, "but this better be as serious as you're making it sound."

"Sir," said Cletus seriously, "without exaggeration, it concerns not only the highest Coalition personnel presently on the planet, but members of our own Alliance command here in Bakhalla as well."

"See you in fifteen minutes," said Bat. The phone circuit clicked in Cletus' ear, and then went dead.

Cletus put the phone down and turned to look at Arvid, who was staring at him.

"Eachan's message?" Cletus prompted gently. With a start, Arvid came out of his trance.

"Sir, the Neulanders are attacking Two Rivers!" he burst out. "Colonel Khan says they're coming in both by air and through the pass—and there's less than three companies of Dorsais left in Two Rivers, not counting a few scouts still out in the jungle who'll have been captured or bypassed by the Neulander troops by this time."

Cletus picked up the phone and punched for Lieutenant-Colonel Marcus Dodds at the landing field by the Dorsai military area.

"Colonel Dodds—sir?" said the lean, quiet face of Eachan's second-in-command, appearing in the small phone screen.

"Have you heard about the Neulander attack at Two Rivers?" Cletus asked.

"Yes, sir," Dodds answered. "Colonel Khan just messaged us to stop all release of men. We're starting to get them turned around now."

"Good," said Cletus. "I'll join you shortly."

He broke the circuit, put the phone down and crossed the room to an arms cabinet. Unlocking it, he took out a pistol belt and sidearm. He turned and tossed these to Arvid. Arvid put out one hand automatically and caught them.

"Sir?" he said, puzzled, "the Neulanders aren't attacking in the city, here, are they?"

Cletus laughed, reclosing and locking the arms cabinet. "No, Arv," he said, turning back to the tall lieutenant, "but the Neulanders have started to move up at Two Rivers, and Dow deCastries is the kind of man to want to take out insurance, even when he has a sure thing. I'd look a little strange wearing a sidearm, but you can wear it for me."

He turned back to his desk phone and punched for the Navy base.

"This is Colonel Grahame," he said. "A little while ago I put in an important call for Commander Linet . . ."

"Yes, sir," said the voice of the ensign who had answered the phone. "The commander's been trying to get you sir, but your circuits were busy just now. Just a minute, sir . . ."

Wefer's voice broke in on the line. "Cletus! What's up?"

"You offered me the use of four of your Mark V's," Cletus said. "I need only three of them. But they have to move upriver between here and the town of Two Rivers, at the confluence of the Blue and the Whey. That's nearly two hundred and thirty miles of river travel. Do you think

107

they could make it between now and, say, an hour before dawn tomorrow?"

"Two hundred and thirty miles? Between now and an hour to dawn? Nothing to it!" shouted Wefer over the phone circuit. "What's up?"

"The Neulanders have moved regular troops across the border at Etter's Pass," said Cletus, in a level voice. "They'll be attacking Two Rivers shortly after sunup tomorrow. I'll give you the details of what I want you for later. But can you move your Mark V's to within a mile downstream of where the two rivers come together and hold them there without being seen?"

"You know I can!" said Wefer. "But you'll be in touch?"

"I'll be contacting you before dawn tomorrow," said Cletus.

"Right! We're on our way!" The phone clicked dead at Wefer's end.

"Go ahead, Arv," said Cletus. "Wait for me outside at the car. I'll be along in a minute."

Arv stared. "We're leaving?" he said. "But, sir, isn't the general due . . ."

His voice ran down into silence as Cletus stood patiently waiting. "Yes, sir," he said.

He went out.

Cletus put the phone in his hand back down on the desk by which he was standing. He glanced at his watch. Some eight minutes had gone by since he had spoken to Bat, and Bat had said he would be here in fifteen minutes. Cletus made a last tour of the office to make sure all the security devices were in order. Then he let himself out the front door, pulling the door to, but leaving it slightly unlatched, with the trap spring activated. The next person to walk through that door would find it closing automatically behind him, locking him into an area from which escape was not easily possible.

Cletus turned and went out to his staff car, where Arvid waited. They drove off toward the BOQ.

13

As Cletus' command car tilted on its air cushion and slid around the corner into the short street leading toward the BOQ, Cletus saw the parking lot before the BOQ half-filled with parked cars, clustered before the main entrance of the building in two rows with a narrow aisle in between.

Both ends of the parking lot were empty; the building itself, with those other buildings of the officers' compound beyond it, seemed to slumber emptily under the afternoon sun. The BOQ's occupants for the most part would now be either at work, having a late lunch, or asleep within. As the staff car slid on its air cushion toward the entrance to the parking lot, Cletus raised his eyes and caught the glint of sunlight on something metallic just below the ridge of the roof over the BOQ's main entrance.

Cletus looked at the empty-windowed double row of cars sitting flat on the cement of the parking lot, with their air cushions turned off. His lips thinned. At that moment, as they turned into the aisle between the two rows of cars, there were sizzling sounds like the noise of enormous slices of bacon frying above them, followed by several licking dragons' breaths of superheated air, as energy weapons sliced into the metal sides and roof of his command car like the flames of acetylene torches into thin tinfoil. Arvid fell heavily against Cletus, his uniform jacket black and smoking on the upper right side, and the staff car careened out of control, to its right, into two empty parking spaces between cars, where it wedged itself, still on its air cushion between the grounded vehicles.

A bleak fury exploded inside Cletus. He turned, jerked the sidearm from its holster at Arvid's side, ducked down and punched open the door on his side of the staff car. He dove through it into the space between his car and the grounded one on the right. He rolled back under his own floating car and crawled rapidly to the back end of the grounded car on his left. Lying flat, he peered around its end. There was a man on his feet, energy rifle in hand, coming toward him between the two rows of parked vehicles at a run. Cletus snapped a shot from the sidearm and the man went tumbling, head over heels. Cletus ducked around the car to his right and into the next space between it and the car farther on.

The charge weapons now were silent. From memory of the sound and damage to the command car, Cletus guessed no more than three gunmen were involved. That left two to deal with. Glancing out, Cletus could see the man he had shot sprawled, lying still on the pavement, his energy weapon rolled out of his grasp, its transparent, rifle-like barrel reflecting the sunlight. Cletus backed up, opened the near door of the car on his right and crawled in. Lying flat on its floorboards, he raised it on its air cushion and set it backing out in reverse.

As it reached the center space between the two rows of parked cars, he dived out the opposite door, just as two beams cut into the other side and the roof of the car behind him. He snatched up the fallen charge weapon and, carrying it, scuttled behind the screen of the still-moving car until it slammed into the opposite row of cars. Then he ducked into the closest available space there, turned about and looked back around the nearest car end.

The other two gunmen were visible, standing out in the open now, back to back, by the car Cletus had last sent smashing into the ones opposite. One was facing Cletus' direction, the other in the opposite direction, both with their charge weapons up and scanning the spaces between the vehicles for any sign of movement.

Cletus pulled back, cradled the charge weapon in his left elbow and lobbed his sidearm in a high arc over the heads of the two standing men to fall with a clatter by Cletus' own cut-up command car.

Both of the gunmen spun about to face in the direction of the noise. Cletus, standing up and stepping out from between his two parked cars, cut them down with the energy weapon he still held in his hands.

Breathing heavily, Cletus leaned for a second against the back of the car by which he had emerged. Then, throwing aside the energy weapon, he limped hastily back toward the staff car in which Arvid still lay.

The lieutenant was conscious when Cletus arrived. He had taken a bad burn through the upper part of his chest and shoulder on the right side, but energy-weapon wounds were self-cauterizing; the wound was ugly, but there was no bleeding. Cletus eased him down onto the grass and went into the BOQ to call for medical aid from an astounded military hospital unit.

"Guerrillas!" Cletus said briefly, in answer to their questions. "There're three of them—all dead. But my aide's wounded. Get over here as soon as you can."

He cut the connection and went back out to see how Arvid was doing.

"How . . ." whispered Arvid, when Cletus bent over him.

"I told you deCastries would like insurance," said Cletus. "Lie still now, and don't talk."

The ambulance unit from the military hospital swooped down then, its shadow falling across them like the shadow of some hawk from the skies just before it landed softly on the grass beside them. White-uniformed medics personnel tumbled out, and Cletus got to his feet.

"This is Lieutenant Johnson, my aide," said Cletus. "Take good care of him. The three guerrillas out in the parking lot are all dead. I'll write up a full report on this later—but right now I've got to get going. You can handle things?"

"Yes, sir," said the medic in charge. He was a senior, with the gold and black bars of a warrant officer on his collar. "We'll take care of him."

"Good," said Cletus.

Without stopping to say anything further to Arvid, he turned and went up into the BOQ and down the hall to his own quarters. Swiftly, he changed into combat overalls and the straps for battle gear. When he came out, Arvid had already been taken away to the hospital and the three dead gunmen had been brought up and laid on the grass. Their clothes were the ordinary sort of civilian outfits normally seen on the streets of Bakhalla, but the lower part of the faces of each was pale in contrast to the tan of their foreheads, showing where heavy Neulander beards had been shaved off recently.

Cletus tried his command car, found it operable, and slid off in the direction of the Dorsai area.

When he arrived there, he found most of the returned Dorsai troops already marshaled by units on the exercise ground—armed, equipped and ready to be enshipped back to Two Rivers. Cletus went directly to the temporary Headquarters unit set up at one side of the field and found Lieutenant-Colonel Marcus Dodds there.

"You haven't sent any shiploads back up yet, have you?" Cletus demanded the moment Dodds saw him.

"No, Colonel," answered the tall, lean man. "But we should probably be thinking about moving men back up soon. If we try to have troops jump into Two Rivers after dark, three out of four of them are going to land in the rivers. And by daylight tomorrow, those Neulander troops will probably be in position in both river valleys above the town. They'd have a field day picking off our jump troops if we send men in then."

"Don't worry about it," Cletus said brusquely. "We aren't going to jump into the town in any case."

Marc Dodds' eyebrows raised in his narrow, brown face. "You're not going to support—"

"We'll support. But not that way," said Cletus. "How many of the men that were sent back and turned loose on pass are still out?"

"Not more than half a company, probably, all told. They've been hearing about this and coming back on their own," said Marc. "No Dorsai's going to let other Dorsais be surrounded and cut up when he can help—"

He was interrupted by the phone ringing on the field desk before him. He picked it up and listened for a moment without comment.

"Just a minute," he said, and lowered the phone, pushing in on the muffle button. "It's for you. Colonel Ivor Dupleine—General Traynor's chief of staff."

Cletus reached out his hand and Marc passed the phone into it.

"This is Colonel Grahame," Cletus said into the mouthpiece. Dupleine's choleric face, tiny in the phone screen by Cletus' thumb, glared up at him.

"Grahame!" Dupleine's voice barked in his ear. "This is Colonel Dupleine. The Neulanders've moved troops over the border at Etter's Pass and seem to be setting up around Two Rivers. Have you still got any Dorsai troops up there?"

"A couple of companies in the town itself," said Cletus.

"Only a couple? That's not so bad then!" said Dupleine. "All right, listen now. Apparently those Dorsais over there with you are getting all stirred up. You're not to make any attempt against those Neulander troops without direct orders. *That's* a direct order—from General Traynor himself. You understand? You just sit tight there until you hear from me or the general."

"No," said Cletus.

For a moment there was a dead silence at the other end of the circuit. Dupleine's face stared out at Cletus from the phone screen.

"What? What did you say?" snapped Dupleine, at last.

"I ought to remind you, Colonel," said Cletus, quietly, "that the general put me in complete command of these Dorsais with responsibility only to him."

"You . . . but I'm giving you the general's orders, Grahame! Didn't you hear me?" Dupleine's voice choked on the last word.

"I've got no proof of that, Colonel," said Cletus, in the same unvarying tone of voice. "I'll take my orders from the general, himself. If you'll have the general tell me what you've just told me, I'll be happy to obey."

"You're insane!" For a long moment, he once more stared at Cletus. When he spoke again, his voice was lower, more controlled, and dangerous. "I think you know what refusing to obey an order like that means, Colonel. I'm going to sign off here and give you five minutes to think it over. If I haven't heard from you within five minutes, I'll have to go to the general with your answer just the way you gave it. Think about it."

The little screen in the phone went dark, and the click of the disconnected circuit sounded in the earphone. Cletus put the phone back on the desk.

"Where's your map projector?" he asked Marc.

"Right over here," he answered, leading the way across the room to a horizontal table-screen, with the black shape of a projector bolted beneath it. A map of the Etter's Pass area showed on the screen. As they both reached the edge of the table-screen, Cletus put his finger on the marked position of Two Rivers town where the streams of the Whey and the Blue came together.

"By dawn tomorrow," he said to Marc, "whoever's commanding those Neulanders will want to be in a position to start his attack on our troops in the town. That means" —Cletus' finger traced horseshoe-shaped curves, their open ends facing downstream, about the valleys of both the Whey and the Blue rivers just above the town—"our men from here should be able to go in as jump troops— since they're fresh from training for it—just upriver of both those positions with comparative safety—since the Neulander forces should all be looking downriver. Now, I understand that the Neulanders don't have any real artillery, any more than we do. Is that right?"

"That's right, sir," Marc said. "Kultis is one of the worlds where we've had an unspoken agreement with the Coalition not to supply our allies, or our troops stationed with those allies, with anything more then portable weapons. So far as we know, they've kept to their part of the

113

bargain as far as Neuland's concerned. Actually, they haven't needed anything more than hand weapons, just as we haven't, since up till now all their fighting's been done with native guerrillas. We can expect their troops to have light body armor, energy weapons, rocket and fire bomb launchers . . ."

Together they plotted the probable future positions of the Neulander troops, particularly those carrying the launchers and other special weapons. While they worked, a ceaseless stream of orders came in and out of the field HQ, frequently interrupting their talk.

The sun had set several hours before one of the junior officers tapped Cletus deferentially on the elbow and offered him the phone.

"Colonel Dupleine again, sir," the officer said.

Cletus took the phone and looked at the image of Dupleine. The face of the Alliance colonel looked haggard.

"Well, Colonel?" asked Cletus.

"Grahame—" began Dupleine, hoarsely, and then broke off. "Is anyone there with you?"

"Colonel Dodds of the Dorsais," answered Cletus.

"Could I . . . talk to you privately?" said Dupleine, his eyes searching around the periphery of the screen as though to discover Marc, who was standing back to one side out of line of sight from the phone. Marc raised his eyebrows and started to turn away. Cletus reached out a hand to stop him.

"Just a minute," he said. He turned and spoke directly into the phone. "I've asked Colonel Dodds to stay. I'm afraid I'd prefer having a witness to whatever you say to me, Colonel."

Dupleine's lips sagged. "All right," he said. "The word's probably spreading already. Grahame . . . General Traynor can't be located."

Cletus waited a second before answering. "Yes?" he said.

"Don't you understand?" Dupleine's voice started to rise. He stopped, visibly fought with himself and got his tones down to a reasonable level again. "Here the Neulanders have moved not just guerrillas, but regular troops, into the country. They're attacking Two Rivers—and now the general's dis . . . not available. This is an emergency, Grahame! You have to see the point in canceling any orders to move the Dorsai troops you have there, and coming over to talk with me, here."

"I'm afraid I don't," answered Cletus. "It's Friday eve-

114

ning. General Traynor may simply have gone somewhere for the weekend and forgotten to mention he'd be gone. My responsibility's to his original orders, and those leave me no alternative but to go ahead with the Dorsais in any way I think best."

"You can't believe he'd do a thing like that—" Dupleine interrupted himself, fury breaking through the self-control he had struggled to maintain up until this point. "You nearly got gunned down by guerrillas yourself, to-day, according to the reports on my desk! Didn't it mean anything to you that they were carrying energy weapons instead of sport rifles? You know the Neulander guerrillas always carry civilian-level weapons and tools so they can't be shot as saboteurs if they're captured! Doesn't the fact that three men with energy weapons tried to cut you down mean anything to you?"

"Only that whoever's giving the orders on the Neuland side," said Cletus, "would like to have me removed as commander of the Dorsai troops. Clearly, if they don't went me commanding, the best thing I can do for our side is to command."

Dupleine glared at him wearily from the phone screen. "I warn you, Grahame!" he said. "If anything's happened to Traynor, or if we don't find him in the next few hours, I'll take emergency command of the Alliance Forces here myself. And the first thing I'm going to do is to revoke Bat's order to you and put you under arrest!"

The tiny screen in the phone went dark, the voice connection went dead. A little wearily, Cletus put the phone down on the table-screen and rubbed his eyes. He turned to Marcus Dodds.

"All right, Marc," he said. "We won't delay any longer. Let's start moving our men back up to Two Rivers."

14

Cletus went in with the first wave of six transport craft, which circled eight miles upstream from Two Rivers and dropped their jump troops on both sides of the two river valleys. A reconnaissance aircraft, swinging low over the jungle in the darkness following moon-set, two hours before, had picked up the heat images of two large bodies of Neulander troops waiting for dawn in both the river valleys, five miles above the town. Another, smaller, reserve force was camped just below the mouth of Etter's Pass—but its numbers were slight enough so that the Dorsais could disregard any counterattack from that direction. Cletus watched the flares of the jets from the jump belts of the descending men, and then ordered the pilot of his transport ship to fly low above the river, heading downstream from the town.

A quarter mile below the town, the river curved to the right, and it was just around this curve that the response came from the M5's. The transport ship came down and hovered above the water, and the turret of one of the huge submarine dozers rose blackly from the dark waters.

Cletus went down an elevator sling to the turret, and the hatch in it opened. Wefer stepped out. Together they stood on the slight slope of the wet metal casing below the tower.

"Here we are, then," Wefer said. "Three of us, just like the doctor ordered." Under his black hair, his friendly, pugnacious face was excited in the dim light. "What do you want us to do?"

"The Neulander troops—and their regular troops," said Cletus, "are concentrated in the two river valleys a few miles above the town. They'll be pushing down those valleys and into the town along the flatland below the river bluffs. But I don't think they'll be trying to come at the town from this downriver side. So you ought to be able to work without being seen."

"Sure, sure," said Wefer, sniffing the chilly dawn air like a hunting dog. "But what do you want us to do?"

"Can you plow up the bottom of the river just below the town, to raise the water level in and above the town?"

"In this little trickle of a river?" answered Wefer. "No trouble at all. We'll simply raise an underwater ridge at some point where the river bluffs on either side come straight down to the water's edge. The water has to rise to get over it. How high a dam? How much do you want to raise the water level?"

"I want the water six feet deep, a mile above the town," Cletus said.

For the first time, Wefer frowned. "Six feet? A full fathom? You'll flood the town itself. That flat spot between the rivers that the town's built on can't be more than six or eight feet above water level on both sides.

116

You'll have another four to six feet of running water in the streets. Do you want that?"

"That's exactly what I want," said Cletus.

"Well . . . of course there's plenty of solid buildings there in the warehouse district for people to climb into," said Wefer. "I just don't want to get the Navy billed for flood damage—"

"It won't be," said Cletus. "I'm still under General Traynor's direct orders as commander here. I'll take the responsibility."

Wefer peered at Cletus in the growing light, shook his head and whistled admiringly. "We'll get right at it then," he said. You ought to have your fathom of water up above the city there in about four hours."

"Good," said Cletus. He stepped into the elevator sling and waved to the transport ship to pull him back in. "Good luck."

"Good luck to you and your Dorsais!" Wefer replied. "You'll need it more than we do. We're just going to be doing our daily jobs."

Once back inside the transport, Cletus ordered it to swing back up to within line of sight of Two Rivers itself. The sky was lightening rapidly now, and the individual buildings in Two Rivers were easily picked out. Cletus had a coherent light beam trained on the curved reception mirror on the roof of the warehouse building that the Dorsais had taken over as their Two River HQ during the week of jump practice. He sent a call down the light beam and got an immediate answer from Eachan.

"Colonel?" Eachan's voice was distant, clipped and unruffled. "Been expecting to hear from you. I haven't had any reports from my scouts out in the jungle for better than three hours now. They're all either captured or lying low. But I gather the Neulanders are clustered in both river valleys above town. I've got all strong points here manned and ready."

"Fine, Colonel," said Cletus. "I just wanted to tell you to expect to get your feet wet. You might also warn the civilians in town to gather in the higher buildings of the warehouse district above the second floor."

"Oh? Thunderstorm coming?"

"We're not that lucky, I'm afraid," said Cletus. A good heavy rainstorm would have been all to the advantage of the well-trained Dorsai, both the jump troops and those in fixed positions in the city. "The weather forecast is for hot and clear. But the river's going to rise. I'm told you'll have four to six feet of water in the streets there."

117

"I see. I'll take care of it—with the troops and civilians too—" Eachan broke off. "Are we getting reinforcements here in the town?"

"I'm afraid I can't spare you any," Cletus said. "But with luck, it'll be over one way or the other before the Neulanders are really on top of you. Do the best you can with the men you have."

"Understood," said Eachan. "That's all from this end then, Colonel."

"That's all from my end for the moment, too, Colonel," replied Cletus. "Good luck."

He broke the light-beam contact and ordered the transport ship back to Bakhalla for a new load of jump troops. Now that it was open daylight over Two Rivers and there was no more secrecy to be gained by operating at low altitudes in the shadows below the peaks above the town, Cletus accompanied the next wave of jump troops riding in a courier craft, which he set to circling above the reach of hand-weapon fire from the ground.

The second wave of Dorsai troops to go down on their jump belts were harassed, but ineffectively so, by angled fire from the Neulander troops downriver.

"Good enough," commented Marc Dodds, who had accompanied Cletus in the courier ship, leaving Major David Ap Morgan to take charge of getting off the last two remaining waves and accompanying the last as its commanding officer. "They'll have aircraft hitting our next wave, though. I don't know why they haven't had Neulander ships in the air over here before now."

"Another instance of the too imaginative mind," said Cletus. Marc glanced at him inquiringly, and Cletus went on to explain. "I was telling Eachan last night that too much subtlety would lead to mistakes. The Neulanders know that the Alliance has supplied the Exotics with many more and better air-combat craft than the Coalition supplied them. So automatically they've drawn the wrong conclusion. They think our lack of air cover is only apparent—bait to tray them into putting their own ships up so our superior air power can knock them down. Also, they know that only the Dorsais were jump-training, and they'll be suspecting that the Dorsais are the only ones who're being sent against them for that reason. They know they outnumber us two or three to one on the ground, which would tend to make them complacent."

The third wave came in and jumped to the jungle below. True to Cletus' assessment of the situation, there was no appearance of Neuland aircraft to oppose the jump. Nor

118

was there with the fourth and final wave. With all four waves of Dorsai jump troops now down on the ground, the pattern of Cletus' battle plan began to make itself felt. He had set his Dorsais down in the jungle on the top of the bluffs on either side of both rivers upstream from the concentration of Neulander troops. Now, spread out in skirmish lines, the Dorsais began to open up on the rear of the Neulander troops. The Neulanders fought back, but withdrew steadily, as their force began to move down into the river valleys toward the town. They showed no tendency to turn and fight and no panic at being caught by small-arms fire from their rear. Up in their circling aircraft, Cletus and Marc kept in touch with their units on the ground by line-of-sight light-beam voice transmission.

"We aren't even slowing them down," said Marc, his mouth a straight line as he observed the scene below in the multiple reconnaissance screens set up before them.

"They'll be slowed up later," replied Cletus.

He was very busy plotting the movements of the running battle below on the reconnaissance screen, even as he issued a steady stream of orders to individual small units of the Dorsai troops.

Marc fell silent and turned back to examining the situation on the reconnaissance screens as it was developing under the impetus of Cletus' orders. Before him the two main elements of the Neulander forces were like large fat caterpillars crawling down the inner edge of the valley troughs of the two rivers, converging as the rivers converged toward the single point that was the town of Two Rivers. Behind, and inland from the rivers, the Dorsai troops, like thin lines of tiny ants, assailed these two caterpillars from the rear and the inland sides. Not that all this was visible to the naked eye below the thick screen of jungle cover. But the instruments and Cletus' plotting on the chart revealed it clearly. Under attack the caterpillars humped their rearward ends closer toward their front, bunching up under the attacks of the ants, but otherwise were undisturbed in their progress.

Meanwhile, Cletus was extending his pursuing Dorsai troops forward along the inland side of each enemy force until the farthest extended units were almost level with the foremost troops of the enemy units they harassed. Occasionally they dented the Neulander lines they faced. But in case of trouble the Neulanders merely withdrew over the edge of the steeply sloping bluff and fought the Dorsai back over, what was in effect, a natural parapet.

Not merely that, but more and more their forward-moving units were dropping below the edge of the bluff with a skirmish line along its edge to protect their march—so that fully 80 per cent of the enemy force was beyond the reach of the Dorsai weapons in any case.

Cletus broke off abruptly from his work on the screens and turned to Marc.

"They're less than two miles from the upper edge of the town," he said. "I want you to take over here and keep those Neulander forces contained all along their lines. Make them get down below the bluff and stay there, but don't expose men any more than you have to. Contain them, but hold your troops back until you get word from me."

"Where're you going, sir?" Marc asked, frowning.

"Down," said Cletus, tersely. He reached for one of the extra jump belts with which the aircraft was supplied and began strapping it on. "Put half a company of men on each river over on their jump belts and send them down the opposite side. They're to fire back across the river into any exposed elements of the enemy as they go, but they are not to stop to do it. They're to keep traveling fast until they rendezvous with me down here."

He turned and tapped with his fingernail on the bend in the river below the town beyond which Wefer and his three Mark V's were at work. "How soon do you estimate they can meet me down there?" he asked.

"With luck, an hour," answered Marc. "What're you planning to do, sir—if you don't mind my asking?"

"I'm going to try to make it look as though we've got reinforcements into that town," Cletus said. He turned and called up to the pilot in the front of the reconnaissance ship. "Cease circling. Take me down to just beyond the bend in the main river there—point H29 and R7 on the grid."

The aircraft wheeled away from its post above the battle and began to circle down toward the river bend. Cletus moved over to the emergency escape hatch and put his hand on the eject button. Marc followed him.

"Sir," he said, "if you haven't used a jump belt in a long time—"

"I know," Cletus interrupted him cheerfully, "it's a trick to keep your feet down and your head up, particularly when you're coming in for a landing. Don't worry—" He turned his head to shout to the pilot up front. "That patch of jungle just inside the bend of the river. Call 'Jump' for me."

120

"Yes, sir," the pilot called back. There was a moment's pause and then he shouted, *"Jump."*

"Jump," echoed Cletus.

He punched the eject button. The emergency door flipped open before him and the section of decking beneath his feet flipped him abruptly clear of the aircraft. He found himself falling toward the tops of the jungle treetops, six hundred feet below.

He clutched the hand control in the center of the belt at his waist, and the twin jets angling out from his shoulder tank flared thunderously, checking him in midair with a wrench that left him feeling as though his back had been broken. For a moment, before he could catch his breath, he actually began to rise. Then he throttled back to a slow fall and began the struggle to keep himself in vertical position with his feet under him.

He was not so much falling as sliding down at a steep angle into the jungle below. He made an effort to slow the rate of his fall, but the sensitive, tricky reactions of the jump belt sent him immediately into a climb again. Hastily, he returned the throttle to its first, instinctive fall-setting.

He was very near the tops of the taller trees now, and it would be necessary to pick his way between them so as not to be brained by a branch in passing or land in one of the deadly, dagger-like thorn bushes. Careful not to twist the throttle grip in the process, he shifted the control handle slightly this way and that to determine the safe limits of a change of direction. His first attempt very nearly sent his feet swinging into the air, but he checked the swing and after a moment got himself back into a line of upright descent. There was a patch of relatively clear jungle down to his right. Gingerly he inched the control handle over and was relieved as his airy slide altered toward the patch. Then, abruptly, he was among and below the treetops.

The ground was rushing at him. The tall, jagged stump of a lightning-blasted tree, which he had not seen earlier because it was partly covered with creepers blending in with the green of the ground cover, seemed to leap upward at him like a spear.

Desperately he jammed the handle over. The jets bucked. He went into a spin, slammed at an angle into the tree stump and smashed against the ground. A wave of blackness took him under.

15

When he came to—and it may have been only seconds later, he was lying twisted on the ground with his bad knee bent under him. His head was ringing, but, otherwise, he did not feel bad.

Shakily he sat up and, using both hands, gently began to straighten out his bum leg. Then there was pain, mounting and threatening unconsciousness.

He fought the unconsciousness off. Slowly it receded. He leaned back, panting against the tree trunk, to catch his breath and use his autocontrol techniques. Gradually the pain in his knee faded, and his breathing calmed. His heartbeat slowed. He concentrated on relaxing the whole structure of his body and isolating the damaged knee. After a little while, the familiar floating sensation of detachment came to him. He leaned forward and gently straightened the knee, pulled up the pants leg covering it and examined it.

It was beginning to swell, but beyond that his exploring fingers could not tell him what serious damage had been done it this time. He could sense the pain like a distant pressure off behind the wall of his detachment. Taking hold of the tree trunk and resting all his weight on his other foot, he slowly pulled himself to his feet.

Once on his feet he gingerly tried putting a little of his weight on that leg. It supported him, but there was a weakness about it that was ominous.

For a moment he considered using the jump belt to lift himself into the air once more, over the treetops and down to the river. But after a second, he dismissed the idea. He could not risk another hard landing on that knee, and coming down in the river with as much current as there was now was also impractical. He might have to swim, and swimming might put the knee completely beyond use.

He unbuckled the jump belt and let it fall. Relieved of its weight, he hopped on his good foot to a nearby sapling about two inches in diameter. Drawing his sidearm, he shot the sapling's trunk through some six feet above the ground, and again at ground level. Stripping off a few twigs from the length of wood this provided left him with a rough staff on which he could lean. With the help of the staff he began hobbling toward the river's edge. He finally reached the bank of the gray, flowing water. He took the body phone from his belt, set it for transmission limited to a hundred yards and called Wefer on the Navy wavelength.

Wefer answered, and a few minutes later one of the Mark V's poked its massive, bladed snout out of the water ten yards in front of him.

"What now?" asked Wefer, after Cletus had been assisted aboard and down into the control room of the Mark V. Cletus leaned back in the chair they had given him and stretched out his bad leg carefully.

"I'm having a company of men, half on each side of the river, meet us here in about"—he broke off to look at his watch—"thirty minutes or so from now. I want one of your Mark V's to take them, a platoon at a time, underwater up to the downriver end of the town. Can you spare one of your machines? How's the water level coming, by the way?"

"Coming fine," answered Wefer. "Those platoons of yours are going to find it knee-deep in the lower end of town by the time they get there. Give us another hour, and with only two machines I'll have the river as deep as you want it. So there's no problem about detaching one of the Mark V's for ferry purposes."

"Fine," said Cletus.

He rode into the town with the last Mark V load of the ferried Dorsais. As Wefer had predicted, the water was knee-deep in the streets near the downriver end of the town. Eachan Khan met him as he limped into the command room of the Dorsai HQ in Two Rivers.

"Sit down, Colonel," said Eachan, guiding Cletus into a chair facing the large plotting screen. "What's happening to the river? We've had to herd all the civilians into the tallest buildings."

"I've got Wefer Linet and some of those submarine dozers of his working downstream to raise the river level," answered Cletus. "I'll give you the details later. Right now, how are things with you here?"

"Nothing but some long-range sniping from the forward Neulander scouts, so far," said Eachan, coolly. "Those sandbagged strong points of yours were a fine idea. The men will be dry and comfortable inside them while the

Neulanders will be slogging through ankle-deep water to get to them."

"We may have to get out in the water and do a little slogging ourselves," said Cletus. "I've brought you nearly two hundred extra men. With these added to what you've got, do you think you could mount an attack?"

Eachan's face had never inclined to any large changes of expression, but the stare he gave Cletus now was as close to visible emotion as Cletus had seen him go.

"Attack?" he echoed. "Two and a half—three companies—at most, against six or eight battalions?"

Cletus shook his head. "I said mount an attack. Not carry one through," he replied. "All I want to do is sting those two Neulander fronts enough so that they'll pause to bring up more men before starting to go forward against us again. Do you think we can do that much?"

"Hmm." Eachan fingered his mustache. "Something like that . . . yes, quite possible, I'd think."

"Good," said Cletus. "How can you get me through, preferably with picture as well as voice, to Marc Dodds?"

"We're on open channel." Eachan answered. He stepped across the room and returned with a field phone.

"This is Colonel Khan," he said into it. "Colonel Grahame wishes to speak with Colonel Dodds."

He passed the phone to Cletus. As Cletus' hands closed about it, the vision screen in the phone's stem lit up with the image of Marc's face, the plotting screen of the aircraft behind him.

"Sir?" Marc gazed at Cletus. "You're in Bakhalla?"

"That's right," Cletus answered. "And so's that company of men I had you send to meet me at the bend of the main river. Give me a view of the board behind you there, will you?"

Marc moved aside, and the plotting screen behind him seemed to expand to fill the full screen of the phone. Details were too small to pick out, but Cletus could see that the two main bodies of Neuland troops were just beginning to join together on the sandy plain that began where the river bluffs on adjacent banks of the converging Blue and Whey rivers finally joined and ended in a sloping V-pointed bluff above the town. Behind the forward scouts, the advancing main line of the Neulanders was less than half a mile from the forward Dorsai strongpoints defending the town. Those strongpoints and the defending Dorsais would be firing into the enemy at long range, even now.

"I've got men along the tops of the bluffs all the way

above the Neulanders on both rivers," said the voice of Marc, "and I've got at least two energy-rifle companies down on the flats at the foot of the bluffs behind their rear guards, keeping up fire into them."

"Pull those rifle companies back," Cletus said. "There's no point in risking a man we don't have to risk. And I want you to have your men on top of the bluffs stay there, but slacken off on their firing. Do it gradually, cut it down bit by bit until you're just shooting into them often enough to remind them that we're there."

"Pull back?" echoed Marc. His face came back into the screen, frowning. "And slacken fire? But what about the rest of you down in the town there?"

"We're going to attack," said Cletus.

Marc stared out of the screen without answering. His thoughts were as visible as though they were printed in the air before him. He, with better than three thousand men, was being told to back off from harassing the rear of an enemy force of more than six thousand—so as not to risk casualties. Meanwhile, Cletus, with less than six hundred men, was planning to attack the enemy head on.

"Trust me, Colonel," said Cletus softly into the phone. "Didn't I tell you all a week ago that I planned to get through this battle with as few men killed as possible?"

"Yes, sir . . ." said Marc, grudgingly, and obviously still bewildered.

"Then do as I tell you," said Cletus. "Don't worry, the game's not over yet. Have your men slacken fire as I say, but tell them to stay alert. They'll have plenty of chance to use their weapons a little later on."

He cut the connection and handed the phone back to Eachan.

"All right," he said. "Now let's see about mounting that attack."

Thirty minutes later, Cletus was riding with Eachan in a battle car that was sliding along on its air cushion ten inches above the water flooding the town, water that was now ankle-deep, even here at the upper edge of the town. He could see, moving ahead of him, spaced out in twenty-yard intervals and making good use of the houses, trees and other cover they passed, the closest half dozen of his Dorsai troopers in the first line of attack. Immediately in front of him, in the center of the control panel of the battle car, he could see a small replica plotting screen being fed with information by a remote circuit from the main plotting screen under Eachan's control at Dorsai HQ in the town behind him. It showed the Neulanders forming up at the base of the vertical wall of stone and earth where adjacent river bluffs came together. Their line stretched right across the some six hundred yards of sandy soil making up the neck of the land that connected the foot of the bluffs with the broader area of slightly higher ground on which the town of Two Rivers was built.

Only the apparent width of the neck of land showed on the plotting screen, however. Its actual width was lost now in an unbroken sheet of running water stretching from the bluffs on what had been the far side of the Whey River to the opposite bluffs on what had been the far side of the Blue. Under that gray, flowing sheet of liquid it was impossible to tell, except for the few small trees and bushes that dotted the neck of land, where the water was ankle-deep and where it was deep enough for one of Wefer's Mark V's to pass by on the bottom, unnoticed. Cletus had warned the attacking men to stay well toward the center of the enemy line, to avoid blundering into deeper water that would sweep them downstream.

The attackers paused behind the cover of the last row of houses and dressed their line. The enemy was only a few hundred yards away.

"All right," said Cletus into his battle phone. "Move out!"

The first wave of attackers rose from their places of concealment and charged forward at a run, zigzagging as they went. Behind them their companions, as well as the strongpoints with a field of fire across the former neck of land, opened up on the enemy with missile weapons.

The Neuland troops still standing on the dry footing of the slightly higher ground at the foot of the bluffs stared at the wild apparition of rifle-armed soldiers racing toward them, in great clouds of spray, with apparent suicidal intent. Before they could react, the first wave was down behind whatever cover was available, and the second wave was on its way.

It was not until the third wave had moved out that the Neulanders began to react. But by this time the fire from the attackers—as well as the slightly heavier automatic fire from the strongpoints—was beginning to cut up their forward lines. For a moment, disbelief wavered on the edge of panic. The Neuland troops had been under the impression that there was no one but a token force to oppose them in Two Rivers—and that it would be a matter of routing out small pockets of resistance, no more. Instead, they were being attacked by what was clearly a much greater number of Dorsais than they had been led to believe were in the town. The front Neuland line wavered and began to back up slightly, pressing in on the troops behind them, who were now crowding forward to find out what was going on.

The confusion was enough to increase the temporary panic. The Neuland troops, who had never fought a pitched battle before, for all their Coalition-supplied modern weapons, lost their heads and began to do what any seasoned soldier would instinctively have avoided doing. Here and there they began to open up at the charging figures with energy weapons.

At the first touch of the fierce beams from the weapons, the shallow water exploded into clouds of steam—and in seconds the oncoming Dorsais were as effectively hidden as though the Neulanders had obligingly laid down a smoke screen for their benefit.

At that the panic in the first few ranks of the Neulanders broke completely into a rout. Their forward men turned and began trying to fight their way through the ranks behind them.

"Back!" Cletus ordered his charging Dorsais by battle phone. For, in spite of the temporary safety of the steam-fog that enveloped them, their mere handful of numbers was by now dangerously close to the mass soldiery of the Neulanders' force, as his plotting screen reported, even though vision was now obscured. "Get back! All the way back. We've done what we set out to do!"

Still under safety of the steam-fog, the Dorsais turned and retreated. Before they were back to the cover of the houses, the steam blew clear. But the Neulander front was still in chaos, and only a few stray shots chased the attackers back into safety.

Cletus brought them back to Dorsai HQ and climbed stiffly out of the battle car, whose air cushion hovered it above more than seven feet of water now lapping at the top of the steps leading to the main entrance of the building. He made a long step from the car to the threshold of the entrance and limped wearily inside toward the command room.

He was numb with exhaustion and he stumbled as he went. One of the younger officers in the building stepped over to take his arm, but Cletus waved him off. He limped shakily into the command room, and Eachan turned from the plotting screen to face him.

"Well done, sir," said Eachan slowly and softly. "Brilliantly done."

"Yes," replied Cletus thickly, too tired to make modest

127

noises. On the screen before him the Neulanders were slowly getting themselves back into order. They were now a solid clump around and about the foot of the bluff. "It's all over."

"Not yet," said Eachan. "We can hold them off awhile yet."

"Hold them off?" The room seemed to waver and threaten to rotate dizzily about Cletus' burning eyes. "You won't have to hold them off. I mean it's all over. We've won."

"Won?"

As if through a gathering mist, Cletus saw Eachan staring at him strangely. A little clumsily, Cletus made it to the nearest chair and sat down.

"Tell Marc not to let them up to the top of the bluffs unless they surrender," he heard himself saying, as from a long way off. "You'll see."

He closed his eyes, and seemed to drop like a stone into the darkness. Eachan's voice reached down after him.

". . . Medic, here!" Eachan was snapping. "Damn it, hurry up!"

So it was that Cletus missed the last act of the battle at Two Rivers. From the moment of the Neulanders' momentary panic at being attacked by the Dorsais under Cletus' direction, trouble began to beset the six thousand soldiers from Neuland. It took them better than half an hour to restore order and make themselves ready to move forward upon the town again. But all that time the river level, raised by the work of Wefer's Mark V's, had been rising. Now it was up over the knees of the Neulanders themselves, and fear began to lay its cold hand upon them.

Ahead of them were certainly more Dorsai troops than they had been led to expect. Enough, at least, so that the Dorsais had not hesitated to mount an attack upon them. To go forward might cause them to be caught in a trap. Besides, to go forward was to go into steadily deepening water. Even the officers were uncertain—and caution suggested itself as the better part of valor. The word was given to withdraw.

In orderly manner, the two halves of the Neuland invading force split up and began to pull back along the river flats down which they had come. But, as they backed up, in each case, the width of the flat narrowed and soon the men farthest away from the bluff found themselves stumbling off into deeper water and the current pulling them away.

128

As more and more Neuland troopers were swept out into the main river current, struggling and splashing and calling for help, a new panic began to rise in the ranks of those still standing in shallow water. They began to crowd and jostle to get close to the bluff. Soon their organization began to dissolve. Within minutes, soldiers were breaking away from the ranks and beginning to climb directly up the bluffs toward the safety of high ground overhead.

But it was at this moment that Marc, following Cletus' earlier written orders, gave the command to his Dorsais lined up along the top of the bluff to fire down into these refugees from the rising waters. . . . And it was all over but the shouting.

They did not even have to call on the Neulanders to surrender. The panic-stricken colonists in uniform from over the mountains beyond Etter's Pass threw away weapons and began climbing the slope with their hands in the air, at first only a few, then mobs. By the time the sun was touching the western horizon, more than six thousand soldiers—as it was later to turn out, better than 70 per cent of Neuland's army—sat huddled together as prisoners under the guns of their Dorsai guards.

But Cletus, still unconscious, knew none of this. Back in a room of the Dorsai HQ in Two Rivers, a prosthetic physician flown up from Bakhalla was straightening up from his examination of Cletus' swollen left knee, his face grave.

"How is it, Doctor?" asked Eachan Khan, sharply. "It's going to mend all right, isn't it?"

The physician shook his head and looked at Eachan soberly. "No, it isn't," the physician said. "He's going to lose the leg from just above the knee."

16

"Prosthetic knee and ankle joints—in fact, prosthetic lower limbs," said the physician, patiently, "are really excellent. Inside of a couple of months after you've adapted to the prosthetic unit, you'll find yourself almost as mobile as you were before with that limp. Of course, no one likes to face the thought of an amputation, but—"

"It's not the thought of an amputation that worries me," interrupted Cletus. "I've got things to do that require two flesh and blood legs. I want a surgical replacement."

"I know," answered the doctor. "But you remember we ran tests on you and you've got an absolute level of rejection. All the evidence is that it's a case of psychological, not physiological, rejection. If that's the case, all the immune-supressant drugs on the list can't help you. We can graft the leg on but your body's sure to reject it."

"You're sure it's a case of psychological rejection?" said Cletus.

"Your medical history shows you have a uniformly successful resistance to hypnosis, even under ordinary drugs," the doctor answered. "We find that kind of resistance almost always in people who exhibit psychological rejection of grafted organs, and whenever it's found we always—without exception—have psychological rejection. But just to put it to the test, I've brought along one of the new synthetic parahypnotic drugs. It leaves you conscious up to safe levels of dosage, but it absolutely anesthetizes volition. If you can resist hypnosis with that in you, then the resistance is below the levels even psychiatry can reach. It's probably a genetic matter. Do you want to try it?"

"Go ahead," said Cletus.

The doctor fastened the band of a hypnospray around Cletus' forearm, with the metered barrel of the drug poised above a large artery. The level of the liquid in the barrel of the spray was visible. Resting his thumb and little finger on Cletus' arm on either side of the band, the doctor placed the top of his forefinger on the spray button.

"I'll keep asking you your name," he said. "Try not to tell me what it is. As you continue to refuse, I'll keep stepping up the dosage level. Ready?"

"Ready," said Cletus.

"What's your name?" asked the doctor. Cletus felt the cool breath of the hypnospray against the skin of his forearm.

Cletus shook his head.

"Tell me your name?" repeated the doctor.

Cletus shook his head. The cool feeling of the spray continued. Slightly to his surprise, Cletus felt no light-headedness or any other indication that the drug was working on him.

130

"Tell me your name."

"No."

"Tell me your name . . ."

The questioning continued and Cletus continued to refuse. Abruptly, without warning, the room seemed filled with a white mist. His head whirled, and that was the last he remembered.

He drifted back into a weariness, to find the doctor standing over his bed. The hypnospray was unstrapped from his arm.

"No," said the doctor, and sighed. "You resisted right up to the point of unconsciousness. There's simply no point in trying a transplant."

Cletus gazed at him almost coldly. "In that case," he said, "will you tell Mondar the Exotic Outbond that I'd like to talk to him?"

The doctor opened his mouth as if to say something, closed it again, nodded and left.

A nurse came to the door. "General Traynor is here to see you, Colonel," she said. "Do you feel up to seeing him?"

"Certainly," said Cletus. He pressed the button on the side of the bed that raised the head section, lifting him up into a sitting position. Bat came in the door and stood beside the bed looking down at him; his face was like a stone mask.

"Sit down, sir," Cletus said.

"I'm not going to be here that long," said Bat.

He turned about to close the door of the room. Then he turned back to glare down at Cletus.

"I've just got two things to tell you," he said. "When I finally smashed the door open on the arms locker in your office and got a gun to shoot the hinges off the door, it was Sunday afternoon, so I made sure I got secretly out of town and phoned Colonel Dupleine quietly, before I made any fuss. You'll be glad to hear, then, there isn't going to be any fuss. Officially, I had a slight accident Friday afternoon a little ways outside of Bakhalla. My car went off the road. I was knocked unconscous and pinned in it. I wasn't able to get out until Sunday. Also, officially, what you did up at Two Rivers in capturing those Neulanders was done at my orders."

"Thank you, sir," said Cletus.

"Don't butter me up!" snarled Bat, softly. "You knew I was too bright to go around raising hell about your putting me out of the way until I'd found out what the score was. You knew I was going to do what I did. So

131

let's not play games. You locked me up and nobody's ever going to know about it. But you captured two-thirds of the Neuland armed forces and *I'm* the one who's going to get most of the credit back in Geneva. That's the way things stand, and that's one of the two things I came to tell you."

Cletus nodded.

"The other thing's this," Bat said. "What you pulled off up there at Two Rivers was one hell of a piece of fine generalship. I can admire it. But I don't have to admire you. I don't like the way you work, Grahame, and I don't need you—and the Alliance doesn't need you. The second thing I came to tell you is this—I want your resignation. I want it on my desk inside of forty-eight hours. You can go back home and write books as a civilian."

Cletus looked at him quietly. "I've already submitted my resignation from the Alliance Military Service," he said. "I'm also giving up my citizenship as an Earth citizen. I've already made application for citizenship on the Dorsai, and it's been accepted."

Bat's eyebrows rose. For once his hard, competent face looked almost foolish. "You're skipping out on the Alliance?" he asked. "Completely?"

"I'm emigrating, that's all," said Cletus. He smiled a little at Bat. "Don't worry, General. I've no more interest in making public the fact that you were locked in my office over part of the weekend than you have. We'll assume a Neulander spy got into the office, found himself trapped and managed to break his way out."

Their eyes met. After a second, Bat shook his head. "Anyway," he said. "We won't be seeing each other again."

He turned and left. Cletus lay gazing at the ceiling until he fell asleep.

Mondar did not show up until the following afternoon; he apologized for not coming sooner.

"The message saying that you wanted to see me was sent through the regular mail," he said, sitting down in a chair at Cletus' bedside. "Evidently your good physician didn't see any urgency in your asking for me."

"No," said Cletus, "it's outside his area of knowledge."

"I think he assumed I'd have to tell you that I—or we Exotics, that is—couldn't help you either," said Mondar, slowly. "I'm afraid he may have been right. I called the hospital after I got your message and talked to someone I know on the staff here. I was told you've got a problem

132

of almost certain psychological rejection of any organ graft."

"That's right," said Cletus.

"He said you thought that perhaps I—or perhaps some other Exotic, working with you, could succeed in overcoming such a psychological reaction long enough for a healthy leg to be grafted on you."

"It's not possible?" Cletus watched the Exotic closely as he spoke.

Mondar looked down and smoothed the blue robe covering his crossed knees. Then he looked back up at Cletus.

"It's not impossible," he said. "It'd be possible in the case, say, of someone like myself, who's trained in the areas of mental and physical self-control since he was a boy. I can ignore pain, or even consciously will my heart to stop beating, if I wish. I could also, if necessary, suppress my immune reactions—even if they included the kind of psychological rejection that afflicts you. . . . Cletus, you've got a tremendous amount of native talent, but you haven't had my years of training. Even with my assistance you wouldn't be able to control the rejection mechanism in your body."

"You're not the only one who can ignore pain," said Cletus. "I can do that too, you know."

"Can you?" Mondar looked interested. "Of course, come to think of it. Both after your first time up at Etter's Pass, and this last time at Two Rivers when you damaged the knee again, you did a good deal of moving around on it when ordinarily such movement should have been unendurable."

His eyes narrowed a little, thoughtfully. "Tell me—do you deny the pain—I mean do you refuse to admit the pain is there? Or do you *ignore* it—that is you remain conscious that the sensation is there but you don't allow the sensation to affect you?"

"I ignore it," answered Cletus. "I start out by relaxing to the point where I feel a little bit as though I'm floating. Just that much relaxation takes a lot of the sting out of the pain. Then I move in on what's left and more or less take the color out of it. What I'm left with is a little like a feeling of pressure. I can tell if it increases or decreases, or if it goes away entirely, but I'm not bothered by it in any way."

Mondar nodded slowly. "Very good. In fact, unusually good for self-trained," he said. "Tell me, can you control your dreams?"

"To a certain extent," said Cletus. "I can set up a mental problem before falling asleep, and work it out while I'm asleep—sometimes in the shape of a dream. I can also work out problems the same way while I'm awake by throwing a certain section of my mind out of gear, so to speak, and letting the rest of my body and mind run on automatic pilot."

Mondar gazed at him. Then he shook his head. But it was an admiring shake.

"You amaze me, Cletus," the Exotic said. "Would you try something for me? Look at that wall just to your left there, and tell me what you see."

Cletus turned his head away from Mondar and gazed at the flat, vertical expanse of white-painted wall. There was a small prickling sensation at the side of his neck just behind and below his right ear—followed by a sudden explosion of pain from the site of the prick, like the pain from the venom of a bee sting following the initial puncture. Cletus breathed out calmly; as the breath left his lungs, a crimson violence of the pain was washed clean and unimportant. He turned back to Mondar.

"I didn't see anything," he said, "of course."

"Of course. It was only a trick to get you to turn your head away," said Mondar, putting what looked like a miniature mechanical pencil back in his robes. "The amazing thing is, I wasn't able to measure any skin flinch, and that's a physiological reaction. Clearly your body hasn't much doubt about your ability to handle pain quickly."

He hesitated. "All right, Cletus," he said. "I'll work with you. But it's only fair to warn you that I still don't see any real chance of success. How soon do you want the transplant done?"

"I don't want it done," said Cletus. "I think you're probably quite right about the impossibility of suppressing my rejection mechanism. So we'll do something else. As long as it's a long shot anyway, let's try for a miracle cure."

"Miracle . . ." Mondar echoed the word slowly.

"Why not?" said Cletus cheerfully. "Miracle cures have been reported down through the ages. Suppose I undergo a purely symbolic operation. There's both flesh and bone missing from my left knee where the prosthetic unit was surgically implanted after I was first wounded years ago. I want that surgical implant taken out and some small, purely token portions of the flesh and bone from equivalent areas of my right knee transplanted into the

134

area where the original flesh and bone is missing in the left. Then we cover both knees up with a cast"—his eyes met Mondar's—"and you and I concentrate hard while healing takes place."

Mondar sat for a second. Then he stood up.

"Anything is eventually possible," he murmured. "I've already said I'd help you. But this is something that's going to require some thought, and some consultation with my fellow Exotics. I'll come back to see you in a day or two."

The next morning Cletus had a visit from both Eachan Khan and Melissa. Eachan came in first, alone. He sat stiffly in the chair beside Cletus' bed. Cletus, propped up in a sitting position gazed at the older man keenly.

"Understand they're going to try to do something to fix that knee of yours," Eachan said.

"I twisted some arms," answered Cletus, smiling.

"Yes. Well, good luck." Eachan looked away, out the window of the room for a moment, and then back at Cletus. "Thought I'd bring you the good wishes of our men and officers," he said. "You promised them a victory almost without a casualty—and then you delivered it."

"I promised a battle," Cletus corrected, gently. "And I was hoping we wouldn't have much in the way of casualties. Besides, they deserve a good deal of credit themselves for the way they executed their battle orders."

"Nonsense!" said Eachan brusquely. He cleared his throat. "They all know you're emigrating to the Dorsai. All very happy about it. Incidentally, seems you started a small rash of emigrations. That young lieutenant of yours is coming over as soon as his shoulder heals up."

"You accepted him, didn't you?" Cletus asked.

"Oh, of course," Eachan said. "The Dorsai'll accept any military man with a good record. He'll have to pass through our officers school, of course, if he wants to keep his commission with us, though. Marc Dodds told him there was no guarantee he'd make it."

"He will," said Cletus. "Incidentally, I'd like your opinion on something—now that I'm a Dorsai myself. If I supply the funds for subsistence, training facilities and equipment, do you suppose you could get together a regiment-sized body of officers and men who would be willing to invest six months in a complete retraining program—if I could guarantee them that at the end of that time they'd be able to find employment at half again their present pay?"

Eachan stared. "Six months is a long time for a professional soldier to live on subsistence," he said, after a moment. "But after Two Rivers, I think it just might be done. It's not just the hope of better pay, much as that means to a lot of these people who've got families back on the Dorsai. It's the better chance of staying alive to get back to the families that you might be able to give them. Want me to see about it?"

"I'd appreciate it," said Cletus.

"All right," said Eachan. "But where's the money to come from for all this?"

Cletus smiled. "I've got some people in mind," he said. "I'll let you know about that later. You can tell the officers and the men you contact that it's all conditional on my having the funds, of course."

"Of course." Eachan fingered his mustache. "Melly's outside."

"Is she?" asked Cletus.

"Yes. I asked her to wait while I had a word with you on some private matters first, before she came in . . ." Eachan hesitated. Cletus waited.

Eachan's back was as stiffly upright as a surveyor's rod. His jaw was clamped and the skin of his face was like stamped metal.

"Why don't you marry her?" he said, gruffly.

"Eachan . . ." Cletus checked himself and paused. "What makes you think Melissa would want to marry me, anyway?"

"She likes you," said Eachan. "You like her. You'd make a good team. She's mostly heart and you're nearly all head. I know you both better than you know each other."

Cletus shook his head slowly, for once finding no words ready to his tongue.

"Oh, I know she acts as if she knows all the answers when she doesn't, and acts like she wants to run my life, and yours, and everybody else's for them," went on Eachan. "But she can't help it. She does feel for people, you know—I mean, feel for what they're actually like, at core. Like her mother in that. And she's young. She feels something's so about someone and can't see why they don't do exactly what she thinks they ought to do, being who they really are. But she'll learn."

Cletus shook his head again. "And me?" he said. "What makes you think I'd learn?"

"Try it. Find out," retorted Eachan.

"And what if I made a mess of it?" Cletus looked up at him with more than a touch of grimness.

"Then at least you'll have saved her from deCastries," said Eachan, bluntly. "She'll go to him to make me follow her—to Earth. I will, too, to pick up the pieces. Because that's all that'll be left of her afterward—pieces. With some women it wouldn't matter, but I know my Melly. Do you want deCastries to have her?"

"No," said Cletus, suddenly quiet. "And he won't. I can promise you that, anyway."

"Maybe," said Eachan, getting to his feet. He swung about on his heel. "I'll send her in now," he said, and went out.

A moment or two later, Melissa appeared in the doorway. She smiled wholeheartedly at Cletus and came in to seat herself in the same chair Eachan had just vacated.

"They're going to fix your knee," she said. "I'm glad."

He watched her smile. And for a second there was an actual physical sensation in his chest, as though his heart had actually moved at the sight of her. For a second what Eachan had said trembled in his ears, and the guarded distance that life and people had taught him to keep about him threatened to dissolve.

"So am I," he heard himself saying.

"I was talking to Arvid today . . ." Her voice ran down. He saw her blue eyes locked with his, as if hypnotized and he became aware that he had captured her with his own relentless stare.

"Melissa," he said slowly, "what would you say if I asked you to marry me?"

"Please . . ." It was barely a whisper. He shifted his gaze, releasing her; she turned her head away.

"You know I've got Dad to think about, Cletus," she said, in a low voice.

"Yes," he said. "Of course."

She looked back, suddenly, flashing her smile at him, and put a hand on one of his hands, where it lay on the sheet.

"But I wanted to talk to you about all sorts of other things," she said. "You really are a remarkable man, you know."

"I am, am I?" he said, and summoned up a smile.

"You know you are," she said. "You've done everything just the way you said you would. You've won the war for Bakhalla, and done it all in just a few weeks with no one's help but the Dorsai troops. And now you're going to be a Dorsai yourself. There's nothing to stop you from writing your books now. It's all over."

Pain touched his innerself—and the guarded distance closed back around him. He was once more alone among people who did not understand.

"I'm afraid not," he said. "It's not over. Only the first act's finished. Actually, now it really begins."

She stared at him. "Begins?" she echoed. "But Dow's going back to Earth tonight. He won't be coming out here again."

"I'm afraid he will," said Cletus.

"He will? Why should he?"

"Because he's an ambitious man," said Cletus, "and because I'm going to show him how to further that ambition."

"Ambition!" Her voice rang with disbelief. "He's already one of the five Prime Secretaries of the Coalition Supreme Council. It's only a year or two, inevitably, until he'll get a seat on the Council itself. What else could he want? Look at what he's got already!"

"You don't quench ambition by feeding it any more than you quench a fire the same way," said Cletus. "To an ambitious man, what he already has is nothing. It's what he doesn't have that counts."

"But what doesn't he have?" She was genuinely perplexed.

"Everything," said Cletus. "A united Earth, under him, controlling all the Outworlds, again under him."

She stared at him. "The Alliance and the Coalition combine?" she said. "But that's impossible. No one knows that better than Dow."

"I'm planning to prove to him it is possible," said Cletus.

A little flush of anger colored her cheeks. "You're planning—" She broke off. "You must think I'm some kind of a fool, to sit and listen to this!"

"No," he said, a little sadly, "no more than anyone else. I'd just hoped that for once you'd take me on faith."

"Take you on faith!" Suddenly, almost to her own surprise, she was blindingly furious. "I was right when I first met you and I said you're just like Dad. Everybody thinks he's all leather and guns and nothing else, and the truth of the matter is, those things don't matter to him at all. Nearly everybody thinks you're all cold metal and calculation and no nerves. Well, let me tell you something—you don't fool everybody. You don't fool Dad, and you don't fool Arvid. Most of all, you don't fool me! It's people you care about, just like it's tradition Dad cares about—the tradition of honor and courage and truth and all those things nobody thinks we have any more. That's what they took away from him, back on Earth, and that's what I'm going to get back for him, when I get him back there, if I have to do it by main force—because he's just like you. He has to be made to take care of himself and get what he really wants."

"Did you ever stop to think," said Cletus, quietly, when she finished, "that perhaps he's found tradition all over again on the Dorsai?"

"Tradition? The Dorsai?" Scorn put a jagged edge on her voice. "A world full of a collection of ex-soldiers gambling their lives in other people's little wars for hardly more pay than a tool programmer gets! You can find tradition in that?"

"Tradition to come," said Cletus. "I think Eachan sees into the future further than you do, Melissa."

"What do I care about the future?" She was on her feet now, looking down at him where he lay in the bed. "I want him happy. He can take care of anyone but himself. *I* have to take care of him. When I was a little girl and my mother died she asked me—*me*—to be sure and take care of him. And I will."

She whirled about and went toward the door. "And he's all I'm going to take care of," she cried, stopping and turning again at the door. "If you think I'm going to take care of you, too, you've got another think coming! So go ahead, gamble yourself twice over on some high principle or another, when you could be settling down and doing some real good, writing and working, person to person, the way you're built to do!"

She went out. The door was too well engineered to slam behind her, but that was all that saved it from slamming.

Cletus lay back against his pillows and gazed at the empty, white and unresponsive wall opposite. The hospital room felt emptier than it had ever felt before.

He had still one more visitor, however, before the day was out. This was Dow deCastries, preceded into Cletus' hospital room by Wefer Linet.

"Look whom I've got with me, Cletus!" said Wefer, cheerfully. "I ran into the Secretary here at the Officers' Club, where he was having lunch with some of the Exotics, and he told me to bring you his congratulations for abstract military excellence—as opposed to anything affecting the Neuland–Bakhalla situation. I asked him why he didn't come along and give you the congratulations himself. And here he is!"

He stepped aside and back, letting Dow come forward. Behind the taller man's back Wefer winked broadly at Cletus. "Got to run an errand here in the hospital," said Wefer. "Back in a minute."

He ducked out of the room, closing the door behind him. Dow looked at Cletus.

"Did you have to use Wefer as an excuse?" Cletus asked.

"He was convenient." Dow shrugged, dismissing the matter. "My congratulations, of course."

"Of course," said Cletus. "Thank you. Sit down, why don't you?"

"I prefer standing," said Dow. "They tell me you're going off to bury yourself on the Dorsai now. You'll be getting down to the writing of your books then?"

"Not just yet," said Cletus.

Dow raised his eyebrows. "There's something else for you to do?"

"There're half a dozen worlds and a few billion people to be freed first," said Cletus.

"Free them?" Dow smiled. "From the Coalition?"

"From Earth."

Dow shook his head. His smile became ironic. "I wish you luck," he said. "All this, in order to write a few volumes?"

Cletus said nothing. He sat upright in his bed, as if waiting. Dow's smile went away.

"You're quite right," Dow said, in a different tone, though Cletus still had not spoken. "Time is growing short, and I'm headed back to Earth this afternoon. Perhaps I'll see you there—say in six months?"

"I'm afraid not," said Cletus. "But I expect I'll see you out here—among the new worlds. Say, inside two years?"

Dow's black eyes grew cold. "You badly misunderstand me, Cletus," he said. "I was never built to be a follower."

"Neither was I," said Cletus.

"Yes," said Dow, slowly, "I see. We probably will meet after all then"—his smile returned, suddenly and thinly— "at Phillippi."

"There never was any other place we could meet," said Cletus.

"I believe you're right. Fair enough," said Dow. He stepped backward and opened the door. "I'll wish you a good recovery with that leg of yours."

"And you, a safe trip to Earth," said Cletus.

Dow turned and went out. Several minutes later the door opened again and Wefer's head appeared in the opening.

"DeCastries gone?" Wefer asked. "He didn't talk long at all then."

"We said what we had to say," answered Cletus. "There wasn't must point in his staying, once we'd done that."

17

Three days later, Mondar made his reappearance at Cletus' bedside.

"Well, Cletus," he said, sitting down in the chair by the bed, "I've spent most of my time since I saw you last going into your situation with other members of our group who've had more experience with certain aspects of what you suggested than I have. All together we worked out a pattern of behavior that looks as if it might give the greatest possible encouragement to the miracle you're after. The main question seemed to be whether it would be better for you to be intimately acquainted with the physiology of your knees, and the process of tissue growth and regrowth, or whether it would be better for you to have as little knowledge of it as possible."

"What was the decision?" Cletus asked.

"We decided it would be best if you knew as little as possible," Mondar said. "The point is, the stimulus for what's going to be essentially an abnormal body reaction has to come from a very primitive level of the organism —you being the organism."

"You don't want me visualizing what's going on then?"

"Just the opposite," answered Mondar. "You should remove your concern with the regrowth process as completely as possible from any symbolic area. Your determination to achieve regrowth must be channeled downward into the instinctive level. To achieve that channeling you're going to need practice, and so we worked up a set of exercises that I'm going to teach you to do over the next two weeks. I'll come here and work with you daily until you can do the exercises by yourself. Then I'll observe until I think you've got complete control in the necessary areas. Then we'll recommend the symbolic operation, in which the genetic pattern of your right knee will be transferred in the form of a few cells of tissue of flesh and bone to the area of the left knee, where we want regrowth to take place."

"Good," said Cletus. "When do you want to start the exercises?"

"Right now, if you like," answered Mondar. "We start out by getting off the topic of your knees entirely and into some completely different area. Any suggestions for a topic?"

"The best one in the universe," Cletus answered. "I was intending to talk to you about it anyway. I'd like to borrow two million IMU's."

Mondar gazed at him for a second, then smiled. "I'm afraid I don't have that much with me," he said. "After all, out here away from Earth two million International Monetary Units are rather more scarce than they are back on Earth. Are you very urgent about your need for them?"

"Urgent and absolutely serious," replied Cletus. "I'd like you to talk to your fellow Exotics here in Bakhalla—and anywhere else, if necessary. I'm not wrong, am I, in thinking your organization could lend me that kind of money if you thought it was worthwhile?"

"Not wrong, no," said Mondar, slowly. "But you have to admit it's a rather unusual request from an essentially propertyless ex-colonel in the Alliance forces who's now an emigrant to the Dorsai. What do you plan doing with a sum of money like that?"

"Build an entirely new type of military unit," Cletus answered. "New in organization, training, hardware and tactical abilities."

"Using," said Mondar, "the Dorsai mercenaries, of course?"

"That's right," answered Cletus. "I'm going to produce a fighting force at least five times as effective as any comparable military unit presently in existence. Such a force will be able to underbid not only the Alliance, but the Coalition, when it comes to supplying military force to an off-Earth colony such as yours. I can raise the pay of the men and officers in it and still market an effective force for less than even the Dorsai mercenaries were charging in the past—simply because we'll need less men to do the same job."

"And you're suggesting," Mondar said, thoughtfully,

"that such a mercenary force would soon pay back a two million loan?"

"I don't think there's any doubt of it," said Cletus.

"Possibly not," said Mondar, "provided these new mercenaries of yours will do what you say they'll do. But how could anyone know that in advance? I'm afraid, Cletus, that our organization would need some kind of security before lending out such a very large amount of money."

"Security," said Cletus, "is often unnecessary where the borrower's reputation is good."

"Don't tell me you've borrowed two million IMU's on occasions before this?" Mondar raised his eyebrows quizzically.

"I was speaking of a military, not a financial, reputation," Cletus said calmly. "Your Exotics have just had the best possible proof of the military reputation in question. A small group of Dorsai mercenaries, single-handedly, have succeeded in doing what a very large and much better equipped Alliance force wasn't able to do—essentially destroy Neuland as a military power and win the local war for your colony. The conclusion to be drawn from that is that this colony of yours doesn't need the Alliance forces. It can protect itself perfectly adequately with its Dorsai mercenaries, alone. Am I right?"

"You certainly present a good argument," said Mondar.

"The security for the loan, therefore," said Cletus, "is the best sort of security in the world. It's the literal security of this colony, guaranteed by the Dorsai mercenaries until the loan is paid back."

"But what if . . . ah . . ." Mondar said, delicately, "you Dorsais should default on your bargain? I don't mean to insult you, of course, but in matters like this all possibilities are going to have to be considered. If I don't bring up the question, someone else will. What if, after we'd lent you the money and you'd retrained your troops, you refused either to pay or to continue guaranteeing the security of this colony?"

"In that case," said Cletus, spreading his hands on the sheet of the bed, "who else would hire us? Successful mercenaries, like traders in any other goods, build their business on the basis of satisfied customers. If we took your money and then welshed on our agreement, what other colony would be willing to take a chance on us?"

Mondar nodded. "A very good point," he said. He sat for a moment, his gaze abstracted, as if he communed with himself in some secret corner of his brain. Then his eyes came back to Cletus.

143

"Very well," he said, "I'll convey your request for a loan to my fellow Exotics. That's as much as I can do, you realize. It'll take some little time for the matter to be considered, and I can't promise you any great hopes of success. As I said, it's a very large amount of IMU's you're asking to borrow, and there is, after all, no great reason why we should lend it."

"Oh, I think there is," said Cletus easily. "If my estimate of you Exotics is correct, one of your eventual aims is to be completely independent of outside obligations—so that you can be free to work out your vision of the future without interference. The Alliance's military aid has been helpful to you, but it's also kept you under the Alliance's thumb. If you can buy security from mercenary soldiers without obligation, you'll have achieved a freedom that I think you all want very badly. A two million unit loan on good security is a small risk to take for the chance of gaining that freedom."

He looked significantly at Mondar. Mondar shook his head slightly; there was a touch of admiration in his face.

"Cletus, Cletus," said Mondar, "what a waste it is, your not being an Exotic!" He sighed, and sat back in the chair. "Well, I'll pass your request for a loan along. And now, I think it's time we got started with your exercises. Sit back and try to achieve that state of a floating sensation that you described to me. As you probably know, it's called a state of regression. I'm also putting myself now into such a state. Now, if you're ready, join me in concentration on that isolated pinpoint of life, that single sperm cell that was the first core and beginning of your consciousness. To that early and primitive consciousness, now, you must try to return."

Three weeks later, healing well and with both legs stiffened by a walking cast about each knee, Cletus was swinging along on wrist-crutches with Arvid in the Bak-halla in-town terminal. They were headed toward the airbus that would lift them to that same shuttleboat landing pad on which Cletus had first set down on Kultis a couple of months before—the airbus being made necessary by new construction on the road to the pad, now that guerrilla activity had been halted.

As they passed the main lounge of the terminal, an Alliance officer stepped out in front of them. He was First Lieutenant Bill Athyer, and he was drunk—not drunk enough to stumble in his speech or his walk, but

144

drunk enough to bar their way with an ugly light in his eye. Cletus halted. Arvid took half a step forward, opening his mouth, but Cletus stilled the young man with a hand on one massive arm.

"Leaving for the Dorsai, are you, Colonel?" said Athyer, ignoring Arvid. "Now that everything's nice and prettied up here, you're on your way?"

Cletus leaned on the crutches. Even bent over in this position, he had to look down to meet Athyer's bloodshot eyes.

"Thought so." Athyer laughed. "Well, sir, I didn't want to let you get away, sir, without thanking you. I might have gone up before a review board, if it hadn't been for you, sir. Thank you, sir."

"That's all right, Lieutenant," said Cletus.

"Yes, isn't it? Quite all right," said Athyer. "And I'm safely tucked away in a library instead of facing a reprimand and maybe losing one turn at an advance in grade. No danger of my getting out in the field where I might foul up again—or, who knows, might even make up for not being quite as smart as you up at Etter's Pass, sir."

"Lieutenant . . ." Arvid began in a dangerous rumble.

"No," said Cletus, still leaning on the crutches, "let him talk."

"Thank you, Colonel. Thank you, sir. . . . Damn you, Colonel"—Athyer's voice broke suddenly, raw-throated —"did your precious reputation mean so much to you that you had to bury me alive? At least you could've let me take my lumps fair and square, without any show-off kindness from you! Don't you know I'll never get another chance in the field now? Don't you know you've marked me for good? What am I supposed to do now, stuck in a library for the rest of my army life with nothing but books?"

"Try reading them!" Cletus made no attempt to hold his voice down. It carried clearly to the crowd that by now was listening, and the scorn in it was, for once in his life, cruel and unsparing. "That way, you just might learn something about the handling of troops in combat. . . . Come along, Arv."

He swung his crutches out to one side and went around Athyer. Arvid followed. Behind them, as the crowd closed in about them once more, they heard Athyer's hoarse, pursuing shout:

"I'll read, all right!" it rang behind them. "And I'll keep reading until I've got the goods on you—*Colonel!*"

18

Six months later, Cletus was not only successfully healed, but ready to begin upon the work he had anticipated, in emigrating to the Dorsai.

Entering the last two miles of his fifteen-mile daily run, he leaned into the beginning of the long slope up the hill that would bring him back to the shore of Lake Athan across from the home of Eachan Khan on the outskirts of the town of Foralie, on that world known as the Dorsai. His stride shortened, his breathing deepened, but aside from these changes there was no difference. He did not slacken speed.

It had been nearly five months now since the casts had been taken off his legs to reveal a perfectly healthy, regrown left knee. The local medical fraternity had been eager to keep him available for tests and study of the essential miracle that had occurred, but Cletus had other things to do. Within a week, tottering along on legs that had just begun to relearn how to walk, he took ship with Melissa and Eachan Khan for the Dorsai. He had been here since, his engagement to Melissa an accepted fact, as a guest in Eachan's household, and the time from his arrival until now had been spent in unrelenting physical self-training.

The methods of that training were simple, and except in one respect, orthodox. Basically, he spent his days in walking, running, swimming and climbing. It was the climbing that provided the one unorthodox element to this routine, for Cletus had caused to be built, and continually added to since its construction, a sort of adult-sized jungle gym, a maze of steel pipes interconnected at different heights and angles that was now some thirty feet high, twenty feet wide and more than fifty feet long.

Cletus' day began now, six months after his departure from the hospital on Kultis, with a vertical climb, hands only and without pause, from the ground to the top of a rope suspended from a tree limb eighty feet above ground. Having reached the limb, he then moved a dozen feet

146

farther out along its length, climbed down a shorter rope only fifty feet in length and set it swinging until the arc of his airborne travels brought him close enough to the top bar of the jungle gym for him to catch hold. The next thirty minutes or so were spent in clambering through the jungle gym by routes that had grown increasingly complex and torturous as the gym had been extended and Cletus' physical condition had improved.

At the far end of the jungle gym, his morning's run—which, as has been said, was now fifteen miles—began. It was a run that began across country of a fairly level surface, but later led him among a variety of the steep hills and slopes that this mountainous territory provided. Here the altitude was eighty-four hundred feet above sea level, and the effect upon Cletus' red blood cell count and coronary artery size had been remarkable.

It ended with this long, steady uphill slope two miles in length. Just beyond the upper end of the slope, the ground dipped down again for about fifty yards among pine-like trees, and Cletus came to the edge of Lake Athan.

He did not even break stride as he approached the bank, but went off it in a shallow dive directly into the waters of the lake. He surfaced and began swimming the half-mile distance across the lake to the shore above which the long, low-roofed, rather rustic shape of Eachan's house could be seen, small among trees.

The water of this mountain lake was cold, but Cletus was not chilled by it. His body, heated by the run, found it pleasantly cool. He swam, as he had done all the rest of his exercise, dressed in running shoes, socks, shorts and shirt; he was by now so accustomed to the weight of these water-heavy shoes and clothes upon him that he did not notice them.

He swam powerfully, arms digging deep, his head rolling rhythmically toward his right shoulder to take deep breaths of the upland air. His feet churned a steady wake behind him. Almost before he had settled to the soothing rhythm of his swimming, he drove into the shallow water at the lake's other side and got to his feet.

He glanced at his wristwatch and trotted leisurely up the slope to the ground-floor sliding window that led directly into his bedroom. Ten minutes later, showered and changed, he joined Eachan and Melissa in the sunny dining room of the long house for lunch.

"How did you do?" asked Melissa. She smiled at him with a sudden, spontaneous warmth, and a warm current of shared feeling sprang into existence between them. Six months of close association had destroyed all obvious barriers separating them. Cletus was too likable and Melissa too outgoing for them not to be drawn together under such close conditions. They had reached the stage now where what they did not say to each other was almost more important than their words.

"Under six minutes average on the fifteen-mile run," he answered. "A little over ten minutes crossing the lake." He looked over at Eachan. "I think it's time to set up that demonstration I planned. We can use the running track in the stadium at Foralie."

"I'll attend to it," said Eachan.

Three days later the demonstration took place. Present in the Foralie stadium under a warm August sun were the eighty-odd ranking Dorsai officers whom Eachan had invited. They sat down front in one section of the stand before a large screen fed by a battery of physiological monitoring equipment tuned to various transmitters on and within Cletus' body.

Cletus was in his usual running outfit. Neither the jungle gym nor a pool for swimming was in evidence, since this was to be a simple demonstration of endurance. As soon as the visiting officers were all seated, Eachan stood by to monitor the reports of various instruments onto the screen so that all could see them, and Cletus started running.

The various mercenary officers present had all been made acquainted with Cletus' history, particularly the events on Kultis, and the near miraculous regrowth of his wounded knee. They watched with interest while Cletus set a pace of nearly ten miles an hour around the half-mile track. After the first mile, he dropped back to a little better than eight miles an hour; his pulse, which had peaked at 170, dropped to about 140 and hung there.

He was running quite easily and breathing steadily as he approached the four-mile mark. But then, although his speed did not decrease, his pulse began to climb once more, slowly, until by the end of the six miles it was almost up to 180. Here it peaked again, and from that point on he began slowly to lose speed. By the time he had completed the eighth mile he was down below seven miles an hour, and by the time he finished the ninth he was barely moving at six miles an hour.

Clearly, he was approaching the exhaustion point. He pushed himself twice more around the track. Coming up toward the end of the tenth mile, he was barely jogging. Clearly, he had run himself out; but this kind of performance by anyone, let alone a man who had been a prosthetic cripple half a standard year before, was enough to waken a hum of amazement and admiration from the watchers.

Some of them stood up in their seats, ready to step down into the field and congratulate Cletus as he tottered toward the conclusion of the tenth mile, which seemed obviously intended to be the end of the race.

"Just a minute, please, gentlemen," Eachan Khan said. "If you'll hold your seats a little longer . . ."

He turned and nodded to Cletus, who was now passing the ten-mile mark directly in front of the viewers. Cletus nodded and kept on going.

Then, to the utter astonishment of the watchers, a remarkable thing happened. As Cletus continued around the track, his step became firmer and his breathing eased. He did not immediately pick up speed, but his pulse rate, as shown on the viewing screen, began slowly to fall.

At first it went down by ragged steps, dropping a few beats, holding firm, then dropping a few more. But as he continued, it began to drop more steadily. By the time he was back around in front of the watching officers, his pulse rate was again 150.

And his speed began to pick up. It did not pick up much; he gained back to just under six miles an hour. But he held steady at that pace, continuing to circle the track.

He ran six more laps of the track—three miles—and at the end of the third mile his speed and pulse rate were still constant.

At the end of that additional third mile he stopped running, walked a lap without any sign of unusual distress, and ended up in front of the watching group, breathing normally and hardly perspiring, with his pulse in the low seventies.

"That's it, gentlemen," he said, addressing them all. "Now I'm going to have to take a few moments to clean up, and the rest of you may adjourn to Eachan's house, where we'll be able to talk in more comfort and privacy. I'll join you there in about twenty minutes, and I'll leave you now to consider what you've just seen without any further explanation, except that what you've just seen me do, did, in fact, exact a penalty upon my bodily reserves greater than that ordinarily demanded by exertion. However, as you see, it was possible and practical, at that price."

He turned away toward the dressing room at the near end of the stadium. The spectators moved outside to an airbus rented by Eachan, and were flown out to Eachan's house, where the window wall along one side of the long living room had been opened up so that the living room and the patio outside became one large gathering space. Food and drink had been provided, and there, a little later, Cletus joined them.

"As you know," he said, standing facing them as they sat in a rough semicircle in chairs about him, "all of you here were officers we invited because I hoped you might be interested in joining me in forming an entirely new military unit, a military unit I intend to command, and which would pay its officers and men only subsistence during a training period of some months, but which would thereafter pay them at least double the rate they had been receiving as mercenaries up until this time. It goes without saying that I want the cream of the crop, and that I expect that cream of the crop to invest not merely their time but their wholehearted enthusiasm in this new type of organization I have in mind."

He paused. "That was one of the reasons for the demonstration you've just seen," he said. "What you saw, in the crudest terms, was a demonstration in which I was at least half again as physically effective as my bodily energy level and conditioning would allow me to be. In short, I've just given you an example of how a man can make himself into a man and a half."

He paused again, and this time he raked his eyes over every face in the audience before he continued.

"I am going to expect," he said, slowly and emphatically, "every enlisted man and officer in this military unit I'm forming to be able to multiply himself to at least that extent by the time he's finished training. This is a first prerequisite, gentlemen, to anyone wishing to join me in this venture."

He smiled, unexpectedly. "And now, relax and enjoy yourselves. Stroll around the place, look at my homemade training equipment, and ask as many questions as you like of Eachan, Melissa Khan or myself. We'll have another meeting out here in a few days time for those of you who have decided to join us. That's all."

He stepped away from the center of their attention and made his way to the buffet tables where the food and drink had been set up. The gathering broke up into small groups and the hum of voices arose. By late afternoon most of the visitors had left, some twenty-six of them having pledged their services to Cletus before leaving. A somewhat large number had promised to think it over and get in touch with him within the next two days. There remained a small group of those who had already pledged themselves to Cletus before the demonstration, and these met in the once more enclosed living room after dinner for a private conference.

Present were Arvid, now recovered from his shoulder wound, Major Swahili and Major David Ap Morgan, whose family was also a Foralie neighbor. Eachan's other officers were still back in Bakhalla commanding the force of Dorsais that remained there in Exotic pay to guard the colony, now that the Alliance had withdrawn its troops under Bat Traynor. Bat's misgivings about leaving had not been shared by Alliance HQ back on Earth, which had been overjoyed to free nearly half a division of men to reinforce its hard-pressed military commitments on half a dozen other new worlds. In addition to Arvid, Ap Morgan, Swahili and Eachan, himself, were two old friends of Eachan's—a Colonel Lederle Dark and a Brigadier General Tosca Aras. Dark was a thin, bald man who seemed to be all bone and long muscle under a somewhat dandified exterior. Tosca Aras was a small, neat, clean-shaven man with washed-out blue eyes and a gaze as steady as an aimed field rifle in its gun mount.

"By the end of the week," Cletus said to them all, "anyone who hasn't made up his mind to join us won't be worth having. From those I talked to today, I estimate we'll get perhaps fifty good officers, perhaps ten of which we'll lose in training. So there's no point in wasting time. We can start setting up a table of organization and a training schedule. We'll train the officers, and they can train their men afterward."

"Who's to be in charge of the extra energy training?" asked Lederle Dark.

"I'll have to be, to begin with," Cletus answered him. "Right now there's nobody else. And all of you will have to join the other officers in my classes on that. The rest of it you can all handle by yourselves—it's simply a matter of running them through the physical and practicing standard field problems, but from the viewpoint of the new organizational setup."

"Sir," said Arvid, "excuse me, but I still don't seem to really understand why we need to shake up the whole table of organization—unless you want it different just so the men in this outfit will feel that much more different."

"No—though the feeling of difference isn't going to do us any harm," Cletus said. "I should have gone into this with all of you before now. The plain fact of the matter is that a military body structured into squads, platoons, companies, battalions and so on is designed to fight the type of war that used to be common but which we aren't going to be encountering out here on the new worlds. Our fighting units are going to bear more resemblance to a group of athletes in a team sport than they are to the old type of fighting unit. The tactics they're going to be using—my tactics—aren't designed for structured armies in solid confrontation with each other. Instead, they're designed to be useful to what seems to be a loose group of almost independently acting units, the efforts of which are coordinated not so much by a hierarchy of command as by the fact that, like good members of a team, they're familiar with each other and can anticipate what their teammates will do in response to their own actions and the general situation."

Cletus paused and looked around him. "Are there any of the rest of you who don't understand that?" he asked.

Eachan cleared his throat. "We all understand what you say, Cletus," he said. "But what the words are going to mean when they're turned into battle units is something we've got to see before it'll make much sense. Here you cut the squad to six men—and that's divided into two teams of three men each. You make four squads to a group, with a senior or junior groupman in charge, and two groups make up a force. It's plain enough, but how's anyone going to know how it'll work until they see it in practice?"

"They aren't. You aren't—of course," answered Cletus. "But what you can do now is absorb the theory of it, and the reasoning behind the theory. Shall I go over it again?"

There was a moment of silence.

"Probably better," said Eachan.

"All right then," said Cletus. "As I think I've told you all, the basic principle is that, from the individual right up to the largest organizations within the total Dorsai military command, each unit should be capable of reacting like a single member of a team made up of other members equal in size and importance to himself. That is, any one of the three soldiers in any given half squad should be able to operate in perfect unison with the other two members of his team with no more communication than a few code words or signals that would cue the others to standard actions or responses to any given situation. Sim-

152

ilarly, the two teams in any squad should be able to work as partners with no more than a few code words or signals. Likewise, the four squads should be able to operate as a team in the group with each squad knowing its role in any one of a hundred or more group actions indentifiable by code word or signal. Just as the two groups must be able to react together almost instinctively as a single command, the commandant of which should likewise be trained to react in pattern with the commandants of the commands with which he is associated."

Cletus stopped talking. Once more there was the small silence.

"You say you'll supply the patterns?" Tosca Aras said. "I mean you'll work out all these team actions that are triggered by code words and signals and so forth?"

"I already have them worked out," said Cletus.

"You have?" Aras' voice teetered on the edge of incredulity. "There must be thousands of them."

Cletus shook his head. "Something over twenty-three thousand, to be exact," he said. "But I think you may be missing the point. The actions of a team are included within the actions of the squad, just as the actions of the squad are included within the actions of the group. In short, it's like a language with twenty-three thousand words. There are innumerable combinations, but there's also a logical structure. Once you master the structure, then the choice of words within the sentence is severely restricted. In fact, there's only one ideal choice."

"Then why have such a complicated setup anyway?" asked David Ap Morgan.

Cletus turned to look at the young major. "The value of the system," he said, "doesn't come so much from the fact that there are a large number of combinations of tactical actions ranging from the team on up through the command, but from the fact that any large choice of action implies a certain spectrum of choices of action for the lesser elements of the command, so that the individual soldier, on hearing the general code word for the command to which he belongs, knows immediately within what limits the actions of all the groups, all the squads and his own team must be."

He paused. "In short," he said, "no one, right up through the battle operator or the commander of the total military unit, simply follows orders. Instead, they all —right down to the individual line soldier—react as a team member in a common effort. The result is that breaks in the chain of command, misunderstood or incorrect orders, and all the other things that go to mess up a battle plan by mischance, are bypassed. Not only that, but from the lowest ranks on up each subordinate is ready to step into the position of his superior with 90 per cent of the necessary knowledge that his superior had at the moment the superior was put out of action."

Arvid gave a low whistle of admiration. The other officers in the room all looked at him. With the exception of Cletus, he was the only one among them who had never been a practicing Dorsai field officer. Arvid looked embarrassed.

"A revolutionary concept," said Tosca Aras. "More than revolutionary if it works out in practice."

"It's going to have to work," said Cletus. "My whole scheme of strategy and tactics is based upon troops that can operate along those lines."

"Well, we'll see." Aras picked up the thick manual Cletus had issued to each of them just after dinner and which had been lying since then in his lap. He stood up. "An old dog learning new tricks is an understatement in my case. If the rest of you gentlemen don't mind I'll be getting to my homework."

He said good night and went out, starting a general exodus. Eachan stayed behind, and Arvid—Arvid, to apologize for that whistle.

"You see, sir," he said earnestly to Cletus, "it suddenly came clear to me, all of a sudden. I hadn't seen it before. But now I see how it all ties together."

"Good," said Cletus. "That's half the learning process done for you right there."

Arvid followed the others out of the living room. Eachan alone was left. Cletus looked at him.

"Do *you* see how it all hangs together?" Cletus asked him.

"Think so," said Eachan. "But remember, I've been living with you for the last half year—and I know most of the patterns in that manual of yours already."

He reached for the decanter behind the glasses ranked on the small table beside his chair and thoughtfully poured himself a small amount of whiskey.

"Shouldn't expect too much too soon," he said, sipping at it. "Any military man's bound to be a bit conservative. In the nature of us. But they'll come through, Cletus. It's beginning to be more than just a name with us here, this business of being Dorsais."

He turned out to be correct. By the time the officers' training program got under way a week later, all of those who had sat in the living room with Cletus that night knew their manuals by heart—if not yet quite by instinct. Cletus divided the officers to be trained among the six of them, in groups of roughly ten each, and training began.

Cletus took the class that he had labled simply "Relaxation," the course that would train these officers to tap that extra source of energy he had demonstrated to them all at the Foralie stadium after running himself to the normal exhaustion point. His first class consisted of the six from the living room. Eachan was among them, although he already had more than a faint grasp of the technique involved. Cletus had been privately tutoring both him and Melissa in it for the past couple of months, and both had become noticeably capable with it. However, it was Eachan's suggestion—and Cletus found it a good one—that his inclusion in the class would be an example to the others that someone besides Cletus could achieve unusual physiological results.

Cletus began his class just before lunch, after they had completed the full day's physical training schedule, consisting of jungle gym, run and swim. They were physically unwound by the exercise, and more than a little empty because of the long hours since breakfast. In short, they were in a condition of maximum receptivity.

Cletus lined them up behind a long steel bar supported between two posts at about shoulder height off the ground.

"All right," he said to them. "Now I want you all to stand on your right legs. You can reach out and touch the bar in front of you with your fingertips to help keep your balance, but take your left feet off the ground and keep them off until I tell you you can put them down again."

They complied. Their pose was a little on the ridiculous side, and there were a few smiles at first, but these faded as the legs on which they stood began to tire. About the time when bearing all their weight upon the muscle of one leg was beginning to become actively painful, Cletus ordered them to switch legs and kept them standing with all their weight on their left legs until the muscles of calf and thigh began to tremble under their full body weight. Then he switched them back to the right leg, and then again to the left, shortening the intervals each time as the leg muscles became exhausted more quickly. Very shortly they stood before him on legs as uncertain as those of men who had been bedridden for a period of weeks.

"All right, now," Cletus said then, cheerfully, "I want you all up in a handstand, the palms of your hands on the ground, your arms fully extended. You can balance yourselves this time by letting your legs rest against the bar."

They obeyed. Once they were all up, Cletus gave them a further order.

"Now," he said, "one hand off the ground. Do your handstand on one arm only."

When they were upside down, he went through the same process he had when they had been right side up. Only it took their arms a fraction of the time it had taken their legs to tire. Very shortly he released them from their exercise, and they all tumbled to the ground, virtually incapacitated in all their limbs.

"On your backs," ordered Cletus. Legs straight out, arms at your sides—but you don't have to lie at attention. Just straighten out on your back comfortably. Eyes on the sky."

They obeyed.

"Now," said Cletus, pacing slowly up and down before them, "I want you just to lie there and relax while I talk to you. Watch the sky . . ." It was one of those high, bright blue skies with a few clouds drifting lazily across it. "Concentrate on the feeling in your arms and legs, now that they've been relieved from the load of supporting your bodies against the force of gravity. Be conscious of the fact that now it's the ground supporting you—and them—and be grateful for it. Feel how heavy and limp your arms and legs are, now that they've given up the work of bearing weight, and are themselves being borne by the surface of the ground. Tell yourself—not out loud —in your own words how limp and heavy they are. Keep telling yourself that and watching the sky. Feel how heavy and relaxed your body is, with its weight being supported by the ground beneath your back. Feel the relaxation in your neck, in the muscles of your jaw, in your face, even in your scalp. Tell yourself how relaxed and heavy all these parts of you are and keep watching the sky. I'll be going on talking, but pay no attention to me. Just give all your attention to what you're telling yourself and what you're feeling and how the sky looks . . ."

He continued to pace up and down talking. After a while, the arm- and leg-weary men, soothed by their relaxed position and the slow movement of the clouds, lulled by the steady, pleasant, monotonous sound of his voice, ceased in fact to pay any attention to the sense of his words. He was merely talking. To Arvid, at one end of the line, Cletus' voice seemed to have gone off and

156

become as remote as everything else about him. Lying on his back, Arvid saw nothing but sky. It was as if the planet beneath him did not exist, except as a soft grassy pressure at his back, bearing him up. The clouds moved slowly in the endless blue, and he seemed to drift along with them.

A nudge at his feet brought him suddenly and sharply back to consciousness. Cletus was smiling down at him.

"All right," Cletus said, in the same steady low tone, "on your feet and step over there."

Arvid obeyed, getting heavily upright once more, and moving off, as Cletus had indicated, about a dozen feet. The rest were still on the ground, with Cletus talking to them. Then he saw Cletus, who was still pacing, pause at the feet of David Ap Morgan and nudge the sole of David's right foot with his toe.

"All right, David," Cletus said, without breaking the pace or tone of his talking, "up you get and join Arvid over there."

David's eyes, which had been closed, jerked open. He got to his feet and went over to stand by Arvid. As the two of them watched, one by one other members of the class went to sleep and were quietly wakened and weeded out until no one but Eachan still lay on the grass, his eyes wide open.

Cletus abruptly ended his talking with a chuckle. "All right, Eachan," he said. "There's no point in my trying to put you to sleep. You get up and join the others."

Eachan rose. On their feet and all together once more, the class looked at Cletus.

"The idea," said Cletus, with a smile, "is *not* to fall asleep. But we won't worry about that for a while yet. How many of you remember feeling any kind of a floating sensation before you did drop off?"

Arvid and three others raised their hands. Eachan was one of them.

"Well, that's it for today," Cletus said. "Tomorrow we'll try it without the muscle-tiring exercises first. But I want you all to go back to your quarters and try doing this again, by yourself, at least three times before tomorrow morning. If you like, you can try putting yourself to sleep tonight with it. We'll gather together here again tomorrow, at this same place at the same time."

In the next few sessions Cletus worked with the class until all of them could achieve the floating sensation without drifting off into sleep. With this accomplished, he led them by easy stages into autocontrol of pain and

157

deep bodily sensations. When they had become fairly adept at this, he began to move them gradually from a relaxed and motionless position into movement—first getting them to achieve the floating sensation while standing upright, then when walking slowly and rhythmically forward, and finally under any kind of activity up to the most violent. This achieved, there remained for them only the ability to make use of the trance state in various types of autocontrol under all conditions of activity, and he turned them loose to become teachers, in their turn to the other officers in training—who would, again, pass on the training to the enlisted men under their command.

By this time nearly three months had gone by, and the officers in training had advanced to the point where they could begin to pass on at least the physical end of their training to the troops that would be under their orders. Recruitment was started for Dorsais to fill the enlisted ranks—and for some few extra Dorsai officers to replace those who had dropped out of the training program.

Just at this time Cletus received a thick envelope of clippings sent him by a news-clipping service on Earth he had contacted before leaving Bakhalla. He opened the envelope, alone in Eachan's study, and spread the clippings out in order of their dates to examine them.

The story they told was simple enough. The Coalition, sparked by a few key speeches by Dow deCastries himself, was attempting to raise a storm of protest against mercenary troops on the new worlds in general, and the Dorsais in particular.

Cletus replaced the clippings in their envelope and filed them in the cabinet holding his own correspondence. He went out on the terrace to find Melissa there reading.

It was high summer in these Dorsai mountains, and the sun was in late afternoon position above the farther peaks. He paused for a moment, watching her as she sat unsuspecting that he watched. In the clear sunlight, her face was untroubled, and somehow more mature-looking than he remembered it back at Bakhalla.

He went out onto the terrace and she looked up from her reading spool at the sound of his feet. He caught her gaze with his own, and her eyes widened a little at the seriousness with which he stood looking down at her. After a minute he spoke.

"Will you marry me, then, Melissa?" he said.

The blueness of her eyes was as deep as the universe itself. Once again, as it had in the hospital in Bakhalla, her gaze seemed to evaporate the barrier of protective loneliness that his experience with life and people had led him to build about him. She looked up at him for a long moment before answering.

"If you really want me, Cletus," she said.

"I do," he replied.

And he did not lie. But, as the protective barrier flowed once more into position about his inner self, even as he continued to match her gaze with his, a cold interior part of his mind reminded him of the necessity that there would be now to lie, hereafter.

19

The wedding was set for a day two weeks away. Meanwhile, Cletus, seeing the formation of the force he had begun to raise on the Dorsai now beginning to operate under its own momentum, took time out for a trip back to Kultis and Bakhalla for a conversation with Mondar, and a farther trip to Newton seeking employment for the newly trained Dorsais of his command.

On Bakhalla, he and Mondar had an excellent dinner at Mondar's residence. Over the dinner table Cletus brought the Exotic up to date. Mondar listened with interest, which increased visibly when Cletus got into the matter of the special training in autocontrol he had initiated for the officers and men who would be under his command. After the dinner was over, they strolled out onto one of the many terraces of Mondar's home to continue their talk under the night sky.

"And there," said Cletus, as they stood in the warm night breeze, looking upward. He pointed at a yellowish star low on the horizon. "That'll be your sister world, Mara. I understand you Exotics have quite a colony there, too."

"Oh, yes," answered Mondar thoughtfully, gazing at the star.

"A pity," said Cletus, turning to him, "that they aren't as free there from Alliance and Coalition influence as you've been here on Kultis since the Neulanders were taken care of."

Mondar withdrew his eyes from the star, turned himself to face Cletus and smiled. "You're suggesting we Exotics hire your new battle unit to drive out the Alliance and Coalition forces?" he said, humor in his voice. "Cletus, we've strained our financial resources for you already. Besides, it's counter to our general philosophy to contemplate deliberate conquest of other peoples or territories. You shouldn't suggest it to us."

"I don't," said Cletus. "I only suggest you contemplate the building of a core-tap power station at the Maran North Pole."

Mondar gazed through the darkness at Cletus for a moment without speaking. "A core-tap power station?" he echoed at last, slowly. "Cletus, what new subtlety are you working at now?"

"Hardly a subtlety," replied Cletus. "It's more a matter of taking a square look at the facts on Mara, economic and otherwise. The Alliance and the Coalition are both still stretched to their economic limits to maintain their influence with various colonies on all the new worlds. They may have lost ground here. But they're both strong on Mara, on Freiland and New Earth under Sirius, on Newton and Cassida, and even to a certain extent on the younger old worlds of the solar system—Mars and Venus. In fact, you might say they're both overextended. Sooner or later they're bound to crack—and the one that's liable to crack first, because it's invested more of its wealth and manpower in influencing new world colonies than the Coalition has, is the Alliance. Now, if either the Alliance or the Coalition goes under, the one that's left is going to take over all the influence that the other formerly had. Instead of two large octopi, with their tentacles into everything on the new worlds, there'll be one extra-large octopus. You don't want that."

"No," murmured Mondar.

"Then it's plainly to your interests to see that, on some place like Mara, neither the Alliance nor the Coalition gets the upper hand," said Cletus. "After we took care of Neuland, and you invited the Alliance forces out, the personnel the Alliance had here were taken away and spread out generally—plugged in any place the Alliance seemed in danger of springing a leak in confrontation with the Coalition. The Coalition, on the other hand, took its people in Neuland—of which, granted, there weren't as many as there were of Alliance people, but it was a fair

160

number—and simply shifted them over to Mara. The result is that the Coalition is headed toward getting the upper hand over the Alliance on Mara."

"So you're suggesting we hire some of these newly trained Dorsais of yours to do on Mara what you did here?" Mondar smiled at him, a little quizzically. "Didn't I just say that philosophically we Exotics consider it inadvisable to improve our position by conquest—or any violent means, for that matter. Empires built by force of arms are built on sand, Cletus."

"In that case," said Cletus, "the sand under the Roman Empire must have been most solidly packed. However, I'm not suggesting any such thing. I'm merely suggesting that you build the power plant. Your Exotic colony of Mara occupies the subtropical belt across the one large continent there. With a core-tap power station at the North Pole, you not only extend your influence into the essentially unclaimed sub-arctic regions there, you'll be able to sell power to all the small, independent, temperate-zoned colonies lying between Mara and the station. Your conquest on that planet, if any, will be by purely peaceful and economic means."

"Those small colonies you refer to," said Mondar, his head a little on one side, watching Cletus out of the corners of his blue eyes, "are all under Coalition influence."

"All the better," said Cletus. "The Coalition can't afford very well to drill them a competing core-tap power plant."

"And how are we going to afford it?" Mondar asked. He shook his head. "Cletus, Cletus, I think you must believe that our Exotic peoples are made of money."

"Not at all," Cletus said. "There's no need for you to put yourself to any more immediate expense than that for the basic labor force required to set up the plant. It ought to be possible for you to set up an agreement for a lease-purchase on the equipment itself, and the specially trained people required to set up the plant."

"Where?" asked Mondar. "With the Alliance? Or the Coalition?"

"Neither," said Cletus, promptly. "You seem to forget there's one other colonial group out here on the new worlds that's proved itself prosperous."

"You mean the scientific colonies on Newton?" said Mondar. "They're at the extreme end of the philosophical spectrum from us. They favor a tight society having as little contact with outsiders as possible. We prize individualism above anything else, and our whole purpose of existence is the concern with the total human race. I'm afraid there's a natural antipathy between the Newtonians and us." Mondar sighed slightly. "I agree we should find a way around such emotional barriers between us and other human beings. Nonetheless, the barrier's there—and in any case, the Newtonians aren't any better off financially than we are. Why should they extend us credit, equipment and the services of highly trained people—as if they were the Alliance itself?"

"Because eventually such a power station can pay back their investment with an excellent profit—by the time the lease expires and you purchase their interest in it back from them," said Cletus.

"No doubt," said Mondar. "But the investment's still too large and too long-ranged for people in their position. A man of modest income doesn't suddenly speculate on distant and risky ventures. He leaves that to richer men, who can afford the possible loss—unless he's a fool. And those Newtonians, whatever else they are, aren't fools. They wouldn't even listen."

"They might," said Cletus, "if the proposition was put to them in the proper manner. I was thinking I might say a word to them myself about it—if you want to authorize me to do that, that is. I'm on my way there now, to see if they might not want to hire some of our newly trained Dorsai troops."

Mondar gazed at him for a second; the Exotic's eyes narrowed. "I'm utterly convinced, myself," he said, "that there's no chance in the universe of your persuading them to anything like this. However, we'd stand to gain a great deal by it, and I don't see how we could possibly lose anything by your trying. If you like, I'll speak to my fellow Exotics—both about the project and about your approaching the Newtonians for equipment and experts to put it in."

"Fine. Do that," said Cletus. He turned back toward the house. "I imagine I should start folding up, then. I want to inspect the Dorsai troops in the regiment you've got here now, and set up some kind of rotation system so that we can move them back by segments to the Dorsai for the new training. I want to be on my way to Newton by the end of the week."

"I should have our answer for you by that time," said Mondar, following him in. He glanced curiously at Cletus as they moved into the house side by side. "I must say I don't see what you stand to gain by it, however."

"I don't, directly," Cletus answered. "Nor do the Dorsais—we Dorsais, I have to get used to saying. But didn't you say something to me once about how anything that moved mankind as a whole onward and upward also moved you and your people toward their long-term goal?"

"You're interested in our long-term goal now?" Mondar asked.

"No. In my own," said Cletus. "But in this case it amounts to the same thing, here and there."

He spent the next five days in Bakhalla briefing the Dorsai officers on his training program back on the Dorsai. He invited those who wished to return and take it, along with those of their enlisted men who wished the same thing, and he left them with a sample plan for rotation of troops to that end—a plan in which his own trained men on the Dorsai would fill in for those of the Bakhallan troops that wished to take the training, collecting the pay of those they replaced for the training period.

The response from the Dorsais in Bakhalla was enthusiastic. Most of the men there had known Cletus at the time of the victory over Neuland. Therefore, Cletus was able to extend the value of the loan he had made from the Exotics, since he did not have to find jobs immediately for those Dorsais he had already trained, but could use them several times over as replacements for other men wishing to take the training. Meanwhile, he was continually building up the number of Dorsais who had been trained to his own purposes.

At the end of the week, he took ship for Newton, bearing credentials from the Exotics to discuss the matter of a core-tap power station on Mara with the Newtonian Governing Board as an ancillary topic to his own search for employment for his Dorsais.

Correspondence with the board had obtained for him an appointment with the chairman of the board within a day of his arrival in Baille, largest city and de facto capital of the Advanced Associated Communities—as the combined colonies of technical and scientific emigrants to Newton had chosen to call themselves. The chairman was a slim, nearly bald, youthful-faced man in his fifties by the name of Artur Walco. He met with Cletus in a large, clean, if somewhat sterile, office in a tall building as modern as any on Earth.

"I'm not sure what we have to talk about, Colonel," Walco said when they were both seated on opposite sides of a completely clean desk showing nothing but a panel of controls in its center. "The AAC is enjoying good relationships currently with all the more backward colonies of this world."

It was a conversational opening gambit as standard as king's pawn to king's pawn four in chess. Cletus smiled.

"My information was wrong, then?" he said, pushing his chair back from the desk and beginning to stand up. "Forgive me. I—"

"No, no. Sit down. Please sit down!" said Walco, hastily. "After you've come all the way here, the least I can do is listen to what you wanted to tell me."

"But if there's no need your hearing . . ." Cletus was insisting, when Walco once more cut him short with a wave of his hand.

"I insist. Sit down, Colonel. Tell me about it," he said. "As I say, there's no need for your mercenaries here at the moment. But any open-minded man knows that nothing's impossible in the long run. Besides, your correspondence intrigued us. You claim you've made your mercenaries more efficient. To tell you the truth, I don't understand how individual efficiency can make much difference in a military unit under modern conditions of warfare. What if your single soldier *is* more efficient? He's still just so much cannon fodder, isn't he?"

"Not always," said Cletus. "Sometimes he's a man behind the cannon. To mercenaries, particularly, that difference is critical, and therefore an increase in efficiency becomes critical too."

"Oh? How so?" Walco raised his still-black, narrow eyebrows.

"Because mercenaries aren't in business to get themselves killed," said Cletus. "They're in business to win military objectives *without* getting themselves killed. The fewer casualties, the greater profit—both to the mercenary soldier and to his employer."

"How, to his employer?" Walco's eyes were sharp.

"An employer of mercenaries," Cletus answered, "is in the position of any businessman faced with a job that needs to be done. If the cost of hiring it done equals or exceeds the possible profit to be made from it, the businessman is better off leaving the job undone. On the other hand, if the cost of having it done is less than the benefit or profit to be gained, then hiring the work accomplished is a practical decision. The point I'm making is that, with more efficient mercenary troops, military actions which were not profitable to those wishing them accomplished now become practical. Suppose, for exam-

164

ple, there was a disputed piece of territory with some such valuable natural resource as stibnite mines—"

"Like the Broza Colony stibnite mines the Brozans stole from us," shot out Walco.

Cletus nodded. "It's the sort of situation I was about to mention," he said. "Here we have a case of some very valuable mines out in the middle of swamp and forest stretching for hundreds of miles in every direction without a decent city to be found, worked and held onto by a backward colony of hunters, trappers and farmers. A colony, though, that is in possession of the mines by military forces supplied by the Coalition—that same Coalition, which takes its cut of the high prices you pay the Brozans for the antimony extracted from the stibnite."

Cletus stopped speaking and looked meaningfully at Walco. Walco's face had darkened.

"Those mines were discovered by us and developed by us on land we'd bought from Broza Colony," he said. "The Coalition didn't even bother to hide the fact that they'd instigated the Brozan's expropriation of them. It was piracy, literal piracy." Walco's jaw muscles tightened. His eyes met Cletus' across the desk top. "You picked an interesting example," he said. "As a matter of theoretical interest, suppose we do go into the matter of expense, and the savings to be gained by the efficiency of your Dorsais in this one instance."

A week later, Cletus was on his way back to the Dorsai with a contract for the three months' hire of two thousand men and officers. He stopped at Bakhalla on Kultis on the way back to inform the Exotics that their loan was already promising to pay off.

"Congratulations," said Mondar. "Walco has a reputation of being one of the hardest men on any world to deal with. Did you have much trouble persuading him?"

"There was no persuading involved," answered Cletus. "I studied the situation on Newton for a point of grievance before I first wrote him. The stibnite mines, which are essentially Newton's only native source of antimony, seemed ideal. So, in my correspondence after that I dwelt upon all those aspects and advantages of our troops under this new training, which would apply to just such a situation—but without ever mentioning the Brozan stibnite mines by name. Of course, he could hardly help apply the information I gave him to that situation. I think he was determined to hire us to recover the mines even

165

before he met me. If I hadn't brought up the subject, he would have."

Mondar shook his head with a slow smile of admiration. "Did you take advantage of his good humor to ask him to consider the Maran core-tap plan?"

"Yes," said Cletus. "You'll have to send a representative to sign the actual papers, but I think you'll find he'll be falling over himself in his eagerness to sign the agreement."

The smile vanished from Mondar's face. "You mean he's seriously interested?" Mondar demanded. "He's interested in a situation in which they'd put up that kind of equipment and professional services simply in return for a long-term financial gain?"

"He's not merely interested," said Cletus. "You'll find he's pretty well determined not to let the chance get away, no matter what. You should be able to write your own terms."

"I can't believe it!" Mondar stared at him. "How in the name of eternity did you get him into such a favorable mood?"

"There wasn't any real problem," said Cletus. "As you say, the man's a hard bargainer—but only when he's bargaining from a position of strength. I began, after our talk about the Dorsais was done, by just dropping the hint that I was on my way to Earth, where I had family connections who'd help me in getting Alliance funds to help you set up the Maran core-tap. He was interested, of course—I think, at first, more in the prospect in getting some such sort of Alliance aid for Newton. But then I happened to dwell on some of the financial benefits the Alliance would receive in the long run in return for their help, and that seemed to start him thinking."

"Yes," murmured Mondar, "the Newtonian appetite for credit is real enough."

"Exactly," Cletus said. "Once he showed that appetite, I knew I had him hooked. I kept drawing him on until he, himself, suggested his Advanced Associated Communities might possibly be interested in putting up a small share themselves—perhaps supply 20 per cent of the equipment, or an equivalent amount of the trained personnel, in return for no more than a five-year mortgage on property here on Bakhalla."

"He did?" Mondar's face became thoughtful. "It's a steep price, of course, but considering our chances of actually getting Alliance money are practically nonexistent—"

"Just what I told him," interrupted Cletus. "The price was so steep as to be ridiculous. In fact, I laughed in his face."

"You did?" Mondar's gaze sharpened. "Cletus, that wasn't wise. An offer like that from a chairman of the board on Newton—"

"Is hardly realistic, as I frankly told him," said Cletus. "I wasn't likely to put myself in the position of carrying an offer from them to you that was penurious to the point of insult. After all, as I told him, I had an obligation to my Dorsais to maintain good relationships with the governments of *all* independent new worlds colonies—and on second thought, I'd even begun to feel a little doubtful that I ought to have mentioned the matter to him in any case. After all, I'd only been given authority to speak to my relatives and contacts back on Earth."

"And he stood for that?" Mondar stared at Cletus.

"He not only stood for it," said Cletus, "he didn't waste any time in apologizing and amending his offer to a more realistic level. However, as I told him, by this time I was beginning to feel a little bit unsure about the whole business where he was concerned. But he kept on raising his offer until he was willing to supply the entire amount of necessary equipment, plus as many trained people as necessary to drill the core-tap and get it into operation as a power source. I finally agreed—reluctantly—to bring that offer back to you before going on to Earth."

"Cletus!" Mondar's eyes were alight. "You did it!"

"Not really," said Cletus. "There was still that matter of the Newtonians requiring Bakhallan property as security in addition to a mortgage on the core-tap itself. I was due to leave the next day, so early that morning, before I left, I sent him a message saying I'd thought it over during the night and, since there was absolutely no doubt that the Alliance would be happy to finance the project with a mortgage merely on the basis of the core-tap mortgage alone, I'd decided to disregard his offer after all and go directly on to Earth."

Mondar breathed out slowly. "With that much of an offer from him already in your hands," he said—and from anyone but an Exotic the tone of the words would have been bitter—"you had to gamble on a bluff like that!"

"There wasn't any gamble involved," said Cletus. "By this time the man had talked himself into buying a piece of the project at any cost. I believe I could even have gotten more from him if I hadn't already implied the

167

limits of what the Alliance would do. So, it's just a matter of your sending someone to sign the papers."

"You can count on that. We won't waste time," answered Mondar. He shook his head. "We'll owe you a favor for this, Cletus. I suppose you know that."

"The thought would be a strange one to overlook," said Cletus, soberly. "But I'm hoping Exotics and Dorsais have stronger grounds for mutual assistance in the long run than just a pattern of reciprocal favors."

He returned to the Dorsai, eight days later, ship's-time, to find the three thousand men, about whom he had messaged from Newton, already mobilized and ready to embark. Of these, only some five hundred were new-trained Dorsais. The other twenty-five hundred were good solid mercenary troops from the planet, but as yet lacking in Cletus' specialized training. However, that fact did not matter; since the untrained twenty-five hundred would be essentially, according to Cletus' plans, along only for the ride.

Meanwhile, before he left with them for Newton in three days' time, there was his marriage to Melissa to accomplish. The negotiations at Bakhalla and on Newton had delayed him. As a result, he arrived—having messaged ahead that he would be there in time for the ceremony if he had to hijack an atmosphere ship to make it—less than forty-five minutes short of the appointed hour—all this, only to find the first news to greet him was that perhaps all his hurry had been needless.

"She says she's changed her mind, that's all," Eachan Khan said to Cletus, low-voiced, in the privacy of the shadowed dining room. Over Eachan's stiff shoulders Cletus could see, some thirty feet away, the chaplain of his regiment of new-trained Dorsais, along with the other guests, eating and drinking in light-hearted ignorance of the sudden, drastic change in plans. The gathering was made up of old, fast friends of Eachan's and new, but equally fast, friends and officers of Cletus'. Among the mercenaries, loyalties were apt to be hard-won, but once won, unshakable. Those who were friends of Cletus' outnumbered those of Eachan's by more than two to one. Cletus had set up the invitation list that way.

"She says there's something wrong," said Eachan, helplessly, "and she has to see you. I don't understand her. I used to understand her, before deCastries—" He broke off. His shoulders sagged under the jacket of his dress uniform. "But not any more."

"Where is she?" asked Cletus.

"In the garden. The end of the garden, down beyond the bushes in the summer house," said Eachan.

Cletus turned and went out one of the French doors of the dining room toward the garden. Once he was out of sight of Eachan, he circled around to the parking area and the rented car he had flown out here from Foralie.

Opening the car, he got out his luggage case and opened it. Inside were his weapon belt and sidearm. He strapped the belt around his waist, discarding the weather flap that normally protected the polished butt of the sidearm. Then he turned back toward the garden.

He found her where Eachan had said. She was standing in the summer house with her back to him, her hands on the white railing before her, looking through a screen of bushes at the far ridge of the surrounding mountains. At the sound of his boots on the wooden floor of the summer house, she turned to face him.

"Cletus!" she said. Her face was quite normal in color and expression, although her lips were somewhat firm. "Dad told you?"

"Yes," he answered, stopping in front of her. "You should be inside getting ready. As it is we're going to have to go ahead just the way we are."

Her eyes widened slightly. A look of uncertainty crept into them. "Go ahead?" she echoed. "Cletus, haven't you been up to the house? I thought you said you'd already talked to Dad."

"I have," he said.

"Then . . ." She stared at him. "Cletus, didn't you understand what he said? I told him—it's wrong. It's just wrong. I don't know what's wrong about it, but something is. I'm not going to marry you!"

Cletus looked at her. And, as she gazed back at him, Melissa's face changed. There crept into her face that expression that Cletus had seen her wear only once before. It was the look he had seen on her face after he had emerged alive from the ditch in which he had played dead in order to destroy with the dally gun the Neulander guerrillas who had attacked their armored car on its way into Bakhalla.

"You don't . . . you can't think," she began, barely above a whisper. But then her voice firmed. "You can *force* me to marry you?"

"We'll hold the ceremony," he said.

She shook her head, disbelievingly. "No Dorsai chaplain would marry me against my will!"

"My regimental chaplain will—if I order it," Cletus said.

"Marry the daughter of Eachan Khan?" she blazed, suddenly. "And I suppose my father's simply going to stand still and watch this happen?"

"I hope so—sincerely," answered Cletus, with such a slow and meaningful emphasis on the words that color leaped into her face for a second and then drained away to leave her as pale as a woman in shock.

"You . . ." Her voice faltered and stopped. Child of a mercenary officer, she could not have failed to notice that, among those present for the wedding, those bound to Cletus by emotional or other ties outnumbered those bound to her father by two to one. But her eyes on him were still incredulous. They searched his face for some indication that what she saw there was somehow not the true Cletus.

"But you're not like that. You wouldn't . . ." Her voice failed again. "Dad's your friend!"

"And you're going to be my wife," Cletus answered.

Her eyes fell for the first time to the sidearm in the uncapped holster at his waist.

"Oh, God!" She put a slim hand to each side of her face. "And I thought Dow was cruel—I won't answer. When the chaplain asks me if I'll take you for my husband, I'll say no!"

"For Eachan's sake," said Cletus, "I hope not."

Her hands fell from her face. She stood like a sleepwalker, with her arms at her sides.

Cletus stepped up to her, took her arm and led her, unresisting, out of the summer house up through the garden, through a hedge and back in through the French doors to the dining room. Eachan was still there, and he turned to face them quickly as they came in, putting down the glass he held and stepping quickly forward to meet them.

"Here you are!" he said. His gaze sharpened suddenly on his daughter. "Melly! What's the matter?"

"Nothing," Cletus answered. "There's no problem, after all. We're going to get married."

Eachan's gaze switched sharply to Cletus. "You are?" His eyes locked with Cletus' for a second, then went back to Melissa. "Is this right, Melly? Is everything all right?"

"Everything's fine," said Cletus. "You'd better tell the chaplain we're ready now."

Eachan did not move. His eyes raked downward and

170

stared deliberately at the weapon in its holster on Cletus' hip. He looked back up at Cletus, and then at Melissa.

"I'm waiting to hear from you, Melly," Eachan said slowly. His eyes were as gray as weathered granite. "You haven't told me yet that everything's all right."

"It's all right," she said between stiff, colorless lips. "It was your idea I marry Cletus in the first place, wasn't it, Dad?"

"Yes," said Eachan. There was no noticeable change in his expression, but all at once a change seemed to pass over him, sweeping away all emotion and leaving him quiet, settled and purposeful. He took a step forward, so that he stood now almost between them, looking directly up into Cletus' face from a few inches away. "But perhaps I was making a mistake."

His right hand dropped, seemingly in a casual way, to cover Cletus' hand where it held Melissa's wrist. His fingers curled lightly about Cletus' thumb in a grip that could be used to break the thumb if Cletus did not release his hold.

Cletus dropped his other hand lightly upon the belt of the weapon at his side.

"Let go," he said softly to Eachan.

The same deadly quietness held them both. For a second there was no movement in the room, and then Melissa gasped.

"No!" She forced herself between them, facing her father, her back toward Cletus, his hand still holding her wrist, now behind her back. "Dad! What's the matter with you? I'd think you'd be happy we've decided to get married after all!"

Behind her, Cletus let go of her wrist and she brought the formerly imprisoned arm around before her. Her shoulders lifted sharply with the depth of her breathing. For a moment Eachan stared at her blankly, and then a little touch of puzzlement and dismay crept into his eyes.

"Melly, I thought . . ." His voice stumbled and fell silent.

"Thought?" cried Melissa, sharply. "What, Dad?"

He stared at her, distractedly. "I don't know!" he exploded, all at once. "I don't understand you, girl! I don't understand you at all."

He turned away and stamped back to the table where he had put his drink down. He picked it up and swallowed heavily from it.

Melissa went to him and for a second put her arm around his shoulders, laying her head against the side of his head. Then she turned back to Cletus and placed a cold hand on his wrist. She looked at him with eyes that were strangely deep and free of anger or resentment.

"Come along, then, Cletus," she said, quietly. "We'd better be getting started."

It was some hours later before they were able to be alone together. The wedding guests had seen them to the door of the master bedroom in newly built Grahame House, and it was only when the door was shut in their faces that they finally left the building, the echo of their laughter and cheerful voices fading behind them.

Wearily, Melissa dropped into a sitting position on the edge of the large bed. She looked up at Cletus, who was still standing.

"Now, will you tell me what's wrong?" she asked.

He looked at her. The moment he had foreseen when he had asked her to marry him was upon him now. He summoned up courage to face it.

"It'll be a marriage in name only," he said. "In a couple of years you can get an annulment."

"Then why marry me at all?" she said, her voice still empty of blame or rancor.

"DeCastries will be back out among the new worlds within another twelve months," he said. "Before he came, he'd be asking you to come to Earth. With your marriage to me, you lost your Earth citizenship. You're a Dorsai, now. You can't go—until you've had the marriage annulled and reapplied for Earth citizenship. And you can't annul the marriage right away without letting Eachan know I forced you to marry me—with the results you know, the same results you agreed to marry me to avoid, right now."

"I would never let you two kill each other," she said. Her voice was strange.

"No," he said. "So you'll wait two years. After that, you'll be free."

"But why?" she said. "Why did you do it?"

"Eachan would have followed you to Earth," said Cletus. "That's what Dow counted on. That's what I couldn't allow. I need Eachan Khan for what I've got to do."

He had been looking at her as he talked, but now his eyes had moved away from her. He was looking out the high, curtained window at one end of the bedroom, at the mountain peaks, now just beginning to be clouded with the afternoon rains that would in a few months turn to the first of autumn snows.

She did not speak for a long time. "Then," she said, at last, "you never did love me?"

He opened his mouth to answer, for the moment was upon him. But at the last minute, in spite of his determination, the words changed on his lips.

"Did I ever say I did?" he answered, and, turning, went out of the room before she could say more.

Behind him, as he closed the door, there was only silence.

20

The next morning Cletus got busy readying the expeditionary contingent of new-trained and not yet new-trained Dorsais he would be taking with him to Newton. Several days later, as he sat in his private office at the Foralie training grounds, Arvid stepped in to say that there was a new emigrant to the Dorsai, an officer-recruit, who wanted to speak to him.

"You remember him, I think, sir," said Arvid, looking at Cletus a little grimly. "Lieutenant William Athyer—formerly of the Alliance Expeditionary Force on Bakhalla."

"Athyer?" said Cletus. He pushed aside the papers on the float desk in front of him. "Send him in, Arv."

Arvid stepped back out of the office. A few seconds later, Bill Athyer, whom Cletus had last seen drunkenly barring his way in the in-town spaceship terminal of Bakhalla, hesitantly appeared in the doorway. He was dressed in the brown uniform of a Dorsai recruit, with a probationary officer's insignia where his first lieutenant's silver bars had been worn.

"Come in," said Cletus, "and shut the door behind you."

Athyer obeyed and advanced into the room. "It's good of you to see me, sir," he said, slowly. "I don't suppose you ever expected me to show up like this . . ."

"Not at all," said Cletus. "I've been expecting you. Sit down."

He indicated the chair in front of his desk. Athyer took

173

it almost gingerly. "I don't know how to apologize . . ." he began.

"Then don't," said Cletus. "I take it life has changed for you?"

"Changed!" Athyer's face lit up. "Sir, you remember at the Bakhalla Terminal . . . ? I went back from there with my mind made up. I was going to go through everything you'd ever written—everything—with a fine-toothed comb, until I found something wrong, something false, I could use against you. You said not to apologize, but . . ."

"And I meant it," said Cletus. "Go on with whatever else you were going to tell me."

"Well, I . . . suddenly began to understand it, that's all," said Athyer. "Suddenly it began to make sense to me, and I couldn't believe it! I left your books and started digging into everything else I could find in that Exotic library in Bakhalla on military art. And it was just what I'd always read, no more, no less. It was *your* writing that was different. . . . Sir, you don't know the difference!"

Cletus smiled.

"Of course, of course you do!" Athyer interrupted himself. "I don't mean that. What I mean is, for example, I always had trouble with math. I wasn't an Alliance Academy man, you know. I came in on one of the reserve officer programs and I could sort of slide through on math. And that's what I did until one day when I ran into solid geometry. All at once the figures and the shapes came together—it was beautiful. Well, that was how it was with your writing, sir. All of a sudden, the art and the mechanics of military strategy came together. All the dreams I'd had as a kid of doing great things—and all at once I was reading how they could be done. Not just military things—all sorts and kinds of things."

"You saw that in what I'd written, did you?" asked Cletus.

"Saw it!" Athyer reached up a hand and closed its fingers slowly on empty air. "I saw it as if it were *there,* three-dimensional, laid out in front of me. Sir, nobody knows what you've done in those volumes you've written. Nobody appreciates—and it's not only what your work offers now, it's what it offers in the future!"

"Good," said Cletus. "Glad to hear you think so. And now what can I do for you?"

"I think you know, sir, don't you?" Athyer said. "It's because of what you've written that I came here, to the Dorsai. But I don't want to be just one of your command. I want to be close, where I can go on learning from you. Oh, I know you won't have any room for me on your personal staff right away, but if you could keep me in mind . . ."

"I think room can be made for you," said Cletus. "As I say, I've been more or less expecting you. Go see Commandant Arvid Johnson and tell him I said to take you on as his assistant. We'll waive the full training requirement and you can go along with the group we're taking to employment on Newton."

"Sir . . ." Words failed Athyer.

"That's all, then," said Cletus, raking back in front of him the papers he had pushed aside earlier. "You'll find Arvid in the office outside."

He returned to his work. Two weeks later the Dorsai contingent for Newton landed there, ready for employment—and newly commissioned Force Leader Bill Athyer was among them.

"I hope," said Artur Walco several days after that, as he stood with Cletus watching the contingent at evening parade, "your confidence in yourself hasn't been exaggerated, Marshal."

There was almost the hint of a sneer in his voice, as the chairman of the board of the Advanced Associated Communities on Newton used the title Cletus had adopted for himself as part of his general overhaul of unit and officer names among the new-trained Dorsai. They were standing together at the edge of the parade ground, with the red sun in the gray sky of Newton sinking to the horizon behind the flagstaff, its flag already half-lowered, as Major Swahili brought the regiment to the point of dismissal. Cletus turned to look at the thin, balding Newtonian.

"Exaggeration of confidence," he said, "is a fault in people who don't know their business."

"And you do?" snapped Walco.

"Yes," answered Cletus.

Walco laughed sourly, hunching his thin shoulders in their black jacket against the northern wind coming off the edge of the forest that grew right to the limits of the Newtonian town of Debroy, the same forest that rolled northward, unbroken for more than two hundred miles, to the stibnite mines and the Brozan town of Watershed.

"Two thousand men may be enough to take those mines," he said, "but your contract with us calls for you to hold the mines for three days or until we get Newtonian forces in to relieve you. And within twenty-four hours after you move into Watershed, the Brozans can

175

have ten thousand regular troops on top of you. How you're going to handle odds of five to one, I don't know "

"Of course not," said Cletus. The flag was all the way down now and Major Swahili had turned the parade over to his adjutant to dismiss the men. "It's not your business to know. It's only your business to write a contract with me providing that we get our pay only after control of the mines has been delivered to your troops. And that you've done. Our failure won't cause your Advanced Associated Communities any financial loss."

"Perhaps not," said Walco, viciously, "but my reputation's at stake."

"So's mine," replied Cletus cheerfully.

Walco snorted and went off. Cletus watched him go for a second, then turned and made his way to the Headquarters building of the temporary camp that had been set up for the Dorsais here on the edge of Debroy under the shadow of the forest. There, in the map room, he found Swahili and Arvid waiting for him.

"Look at this," he said, beckoning them both over to the main map table, which showed in relief the broad band of forest, with Debroy at one end of the table and the stibnite mines around Watershed at the other. The other two men joined him at the Debroy end of the table. "Walco and his people expect us to fiddle around for a week or two, getting set here before we do anything. Whatever Brozan spies are keeping tab on the situation will accordingly pick up the same idea. But we aren't going to waste time. Major . . ."

He looked at Swahili, whose scarred, black face was bent with interest above the table top. Swahili lifted his eyes to meet Cletus'.

"We'll start climatization training of the troops inside the edge of the forest here, tomorrow at first light," Cletus said. "The training will take place no more than five miles deep in the forest, well below the Newtonian–Brozan frontier"—he pointed to a red line running through the forested area some twenty miles above Debroy. "The men will train by forces and groups, and they aren't going to do well. They aren't going to do well at all. It'll be necessary to keep them out overnight and keep them at it until your officers are satisfied. Then they can be released, group by group, as their officers think they're ready, and allowed to return to the camp here. I don't want the last group out of the forest until two and a half days from tomorrow morning. You leave the necessary orders with your officers to see to that."

"I won't be there?" asked Swahili.

"You'll be with me," answered Cletus. He glanced at the tall young captain to his right. "So will Arvid and two hundred of our best men. We'll have split off from the rest the minute we're in the woods, dispersed into two- and three-man teams and headed north to rendezvous five miles south of Watershed, four days from now."

"Four days?" echoed Swahili. "That's better than fifty miles a day on foot through unfamiliar territory."

"Exactly!" said Cletus. "That's why no one—Newtonians or Brozans—will suspect we'd try to do anything like that. But you and I know, don't we, Major, that our best men can make it?"

His eyes met the eyes in Swahili's dark, unchanging face.

"Yes," said Swahili.

"Good," said Cletus, stepping back from the table. "We'll eat now, and work out the details this evening. I want you, Major, to travel along with Arv, here. I'll take Force Leader Athyer along with me and travel with him."

"Athyer?" queried Swahili.

"That's right," replied Cletus, dryly. "Wasn't it you who told me he was coming along?"

"Yes," answered Swahili. It was true, oddly enough. Swahili seemed to have taken an interest in the newly recruited, untrained Athyer. It was an interest apparently more of curiosity than sentiment—for if ever two men were at opposite poles, it was the major and the force leader. Swahili was far and away the superior of all the new-trained Dorsais, men and officers alike, having surpassed everyone in the training, with the exception of Cletus in the matter of autocontrol. Clearly, however, Swahili was not one to let interest affect judgment. He looked with a touch of grim amusement at Cletus.

"And, of course, since he'll be with you, sir . . ." he said.

"All the way," said Cletus, levelly. "I take it you've no objection to having Arv with you?"

"No, sir." Swahili's eyes glanced at the tall young commandant with something very close—as close as he ever came—to approval.

"Good," said Cletus. "You can take off, then. I'll meet you both here in an hour after we've eaten."

"Yes."

Swahili went out. Cletus turned toward the door, and found Arvid still there, standing almost in his way. Cletus stopped.

"Something the matter, Arv?" Cletus asked.

"Sir . . ." began Arvid, and he did not seem to be able to continue.

Cletus made no attempt to assist the conversation. He merely stood, waiting.

"Sir," said Arvid again, "I'm still your aide, aren't I?"

"You are," said Cletus.

"Then"—Arvid's face was stiff and a little pale—"can I ask why Athyer should be with you in an action like this, instead of me?"

Cletus looked at him coldly. Arvid held himself stiffly, and his right shoulder was still a little hunched under his uniform coat, drawn forward by the tightening of the scar tissue of the burn he had taken back at the BOQ in Bakhalla, protecting Cletus from the Neuland gunmen.

"No, Commandant," said Cletus, slowly. "You can't ask me why I decide what I do—now or ever."

They stood facing each other.

"Is that clear?" Cletus said, after a moment.

Arvid stood even more stiffly. His eyes seemed to have lost Cletus, and his gaze traveled past him now to some spot on the farther wall.

"Yes, sir," he said.

"Then you'd probably better be getting to the evening meal, hadn't you?" said Cletus.

"Yes, sir."

Arvid turned and went out. After a second, Cletus sighed and also left for his own quarters and a solitary meal served there by his orderly.

At nine the following morning, he was standing with Force Leader Athyer five miles inside the forest fringe, when Swahili came up to him and handed him the match-box-sized metal case of a peep-map. Cletus tucked it into a jacket pocket of his gray-green field uniform.

"It's oriented?" he asked Swahili. The major nodded.

"With the camp as base point," Swahili answered. "The rest of the men tagged for the expedition have already left—in two- and three-man teams, just as you said. The captain and I are ready to go."

"Good," said Cletus. "We'll get started, too, Bill and I. See you at the rendezvous point, five miles below Watershed, in approximately ninety-one hours."

"We'll be there, sir." With a single, slightly humorous glance at Athyer, Swahili turned and left.

Cletus turned the peep-map over in the palm of his hand, exposing the needle of the orientation compass under its transparent cover. He pressed the button in the side of the case and the needle swung clockwise some forty degrees until it pointed almost due north into the forest. Cletus lined himself up with a tree trunk as far off as he could see through the dimness of the forest in that direction. Then he put the peephole at one end of the instrument to his eye and gazed through it. Within he saw the image of what appeared to be a ten- by twelve-foot relief map of the territory between his present position and Watershed. A red line marked the route that had been programed into the map. Reaching for another button on the case, he cranked the view in close to study the detail of the first half-dozen miles. It was all straight forest, with no bog land to be crossed or avoided.

"Come on," he said over his shoulder to Athyer. Putting the peep-map into his pocket, he started off at a jog trot.

Athyer followed him. For the first couple of hours they trotted along side by side without speaking, enclosed in the dimness and silence of the northern Newtonian forest. There were no flying creatures, neither birds nor insects, in this forest, only the amphibious and fish-like life of its lakes, swamps and bogs. Under the thick cover of the needle-like leaves that grew only on the topmost branches of the trees, the ground was bare except for the leafless tree trunks and lower branches but covered with a thick coat of blackened, dead needles fallen from the trees in past seasons. Only here and there, startling and expectedly, there would be a thick clump of large, flesh-colored leaves as much as four feet in length, sprouting directly from the needle bed to signal the presence of a spring or some other damp area of the jungle floor beneath.

After the first two hours, they fell into an alternate rhythm of five minutes at a jog trot, followed by five minutes at a rapid walk. Once each hour they stopped for five minutes to rest, dropping at full length upon the soft, thick, needle carpet without bothering even to remove the light survival packs they wore strapped to their shoulders.

For the first half hour or so, the going had been effortful. But after that they warmed to the physical movement, their heartbeats slowed, their breathing calmed—and it seemed almost as if they could go on forever like this. Cletus ran or walked, with the larger share of his mind abstract, far away in concentration on other problems. Even the matter of periodically checking their progress with the directional compass on the peep-map was an almost automatic action for him, performed by reflex.

He was roused from this at last by the fading of the already dim light of the forest about them. Newton's sun, hidden between its double screen of the treetops' foliage and the high, almost constant cloud layer that gave the sky its usual gray, metallic look, was beginning to set.

"Time for a meal break," said Cletus. He headed for a flat spot at the base of a large tree trunk and dropped into a sitting position, cross-legged with his back to the trunk, stripping off his shoulder pack as he did so. Athyer joined him on the ground. "How're you doing?"

"Fine, sir," grunted Athyer.

In fact, the other man was looking as good as he claimed to feel, and this Cletus was glad to see. There was only a faint sheen of perspiration on Athyer's face, and his breathing was deep and unhurried.

They broke out a thermo meal pack apiece and punctured the seal to start warming the food inside. By the time it was hot enough to eat, the darkness around them had closed in absolutely. It was as black as the inside of some sealed underground room.

"Half an hour until the moons start to rise," Cletus said into the darkness in the direction in which he had last looked to see the seated Athyer. "Try and get some sleep, if you can."

Cletus lay back on the needles, and made his limbs and body go limp. In a few seconds, he felt the familiar drifting sensation. Then it seemed that there were perhaps thirty seconds of inattention, and he opened his eyes to find a new, pale light filtering down through the leaf cover of the forest.

It was still only a fraction as bright as the filtered daylight had been, but already it was bright enough so that they could see to travel, and that brightness would perhaps double, since at least four of Newton's five moons should be in the night sky.

"Let's move," said Cletus. A couple of minutes later, he and Athyer, packs on back, were once more jog trotting upon their route.

The peep-map, when Cletus consulted it by its own inter-illumination, now showed a black line paralleling the red line of their indicated route for a distance of a little over thirty-one miles from their starting point. In the next nine hours of nighttime traveling, interrupted only by hourly rests and a short meal break around midnight, they accomplished another twenty-six miles before the setting of most of the moons dimmed the light once more below the level of illumination at which it was safe to travel. They ate a final, light meal and dropped off into five hours of deep slumber on the thick needle bed of the forest floor.

When Cletus' wrist alarm woke them, the chronometer showed that over two hours of daylight had already elapsed. They arose, ate and moved on as soon as possible.

For the first four hours they made good progress—if anything, they were traveling even a little faster than they had the day before. But around noon they entered into an area of bog and swamp thick with plants of the big, flesh-colored leaf, and something new called parasite vines, great ropes of vegetation hanging from the low limbs of the trees or stretching out across the ground for miles and sometimes as thick as an oil drum.

They were slowed and forced to detour. By the time night fell, they had made only an additional twenty miles. They were barely one-third of the distance to the rendezvous point below Watershed, nearly one-third of their time had gone, and from now on fatigue would slow them progressively. Cletus had hoped to cover nearly half the distance by this time.

However, the peep-map informed him that another twenty miles would bring them out of this boggy area and into more open country again. They had their brief supper during the half hour of darkness, and then pushed on during the night. They reached the edge of the bog area just before the moonlight failed them; they fell, like dead men, on the needle carpet underfoot and into slumber.

The next day the going was easier, but exhaustion was beginning to slow their pace. Cletus traveled like a man in a dream, or in a high fever, hardly conscious of the efforts and wearinesses of his body except as things perceived dimly, at a distance. But Athyer was running close to the end of his strength. His face was gray and gaunt, so that the harsh beak of his nose now seemed to dominate all the other features in it, like the battering-ram prow of some ancient wooden vessel. He managed to keep the pace as they trotted, but when they slowed to a walk, his foot would occasionally go down loosely and he would stumble. That night Cletus let them both sleep for six hours after the evening meal.

They made less than sixteen miles in the hours of moonlight that remained to them, before stopping to sleep again for another six hours.

They awoke with the illusion of being rested and restored to full strength. However, two hours of travel during the following daylight found them not much better than they had been twenty-four hours before, although they were traveling more slowly and more steadily now, portioning out their strength as a miser portions out the money for necessary expenses. Once again, Cletus was back in his state of detachment; his bodily suffering seemed remote and unimportant. The feeling clung to his mind that he could go on like this forever, if necessary, without even stopping for food or rest.

By now, in fact, food was one of the least of their wants. They paused for the midday meal break and forced themselves to swallow some of the rations they carried, but without appetite or sense of taste. The ingested food lay heavily in their stomachs, and when darkness came neither of them could eat. They dug down to the base of one of the flesh-colored leafed plants to uncover the spring that was bubbling there, and drank deeply before dropping off into what was now an almost automatic slumber. After a couple of hours of sleep, they arose and went on under the moonlight.

Dawn of the fourth day found them only half a dozen miles from the rendezvous point. But when they tried to get to their feet with their packs on, their knees buckled and gave under them like loose hinges. Cletus continued to struggle, however, and, after several tries, found himself at last on his feet and staying there. He looked around and saw Athyer, still on the ground, unmoving.

"No use," croaked Athyer. "You go on."

"No," said Cletus. He stood, legs stiff and braced, a little apart. He swayed slightly, looking down at Athyer.

"You've got to go on," said Athyer, after a moment. It was the way they had gotten in the habit of talking to each other during the last day or so—with long pauses between one man's words and the other's reply.

"Why did you come to the Dorsai?" asked Cletus, after one of these pauses.

Athyer stared at him. "You," said Athyer. "You did what I always wanted to do. You were what I always wanted to be. I knew I'd never make it the way you have. But I thought I could learn to come close."

"Then learn," said Cletus, swaying. "Walk."

"I can't," said Athyer.

"No such thing as can't—for you," said Cletus. "Walk."

Cletus continued to stand there. Athyer lay where he was for a few minutes. Then his legs began to twitch. He struggled up into a sitting position and tried to get his legs under him, but they would not go. He stopped, panting.

"You're what you've always wanted to be," said Cletus slowly, swaying above him. "Never mind your body. Get Athyer to his feet. The body will come along naturally."

He waited. Athyer stirred again. With a convulsive effort he got to his knees, wavered in a half-kneeling position, and then with a sudden surge lifted to his feet, stumbled forward for three steps and caught hold of a tree trunk to keep from going down again. He looked over his shoulder at Cletus, panting but triumphant.

"When you're ready to go," said Cletus.

Five minutes later, though Athyer still stumbled like a drunken man, they were moving forward. Four hours later they made it to the rendezvous point, to find Swahili and Arvid, together with perhaps a fifth of the rest of the men due to arrive at this point, already there. Cletus and Athyer collapsed without even bothering to take off their back packs, and they were asleep before they touched the needle-carpeted ground.

21

Cletus awoke about midafternoon. He felt stiff and a little lightheaded, but rested and extremely hungry. Athyer was still sleeping heavily, like a man under deep anesthesia.

Cletus ate and joined Swahili and Arvid.

"How many of the men are in?" he asked Swahili.

"There're twenty-six who haven't shown up yet," answered Swahili. "We got most of the rest in during the next hour after you got here."

Cletus nodded. "Good," he said. "Then they should be slept up enough to operate by twilight. We'll get busy right now with the ones that are already rested. The first thing we need is a vehicle."

So it happened that a Brozan truck driver sliding on his airjets down the single fused-earth highway leading into the small mining town of Watershed unexpectedly found his way barred by half a dozen armed men in gray-blue uniforms, each with a small blue and white flag of the Advanced Associated Communities stapled over the left breast pocket. One of these, a tall officer wearing a

183

circle of stars on each shoulder tab, stepped up on the foot-rest entrance to his cab and opened the door.

"Out," said Cletus, "we need this truck of yours."

Two hours later, just before sunset, that same truck drove into Watershed from a highway that had been strangely unproductive of traffic during the last 120 minutes. There were two men in the cab without caps on and they drove the truck directly to the headquarters of the small police detachment that had the duty of keeping law and order in the mining town.

The truck pulled into the parking compound behind the police headquarters, and a few moments later there was the sound of some disturbance within the headquarters itself. This, however, quietened, and a few moments later the fire siren above the police headquarters burst to life with a whooping like that of some mad, gigantic creature. It continued to whoop as the townspeople poured out of their houses and other buildings to find the town surrounded and the streets patrolled by armed soldiers with blue and white flags stapled over the left breast pockets of their uniform jackets. By the time the sun was down, Watershed had awakened to the fact that it was a captured community.

"You must be crazy! You'll never get away with it!" stormed the manager of the stibnite mines when, with the mayor of the town and the head of the local police contingent, he was brought into Cletus' presence at police headquarters. "The Brozan Army's headquartered at Broza City—and that's only two hours from here, even by road. They'll find out you're here in a few hours, and then—"

"They already know," Cletus interrupted him, dryly. "One of the first things I did was use your police communications here to announce the fact that we've taken over Watershed and the mines."

The mine manager stared at him. "You *must* be crazy!" he said at last. "Do you think your five hundred men can stand up to a couple of divisions?"

"We may not have to," said Cletus. "In any case, it's no concern of yours. All I want you and these other two gentlemen to do is to reassure the local people that they're in no danger as long as they keep off the streets and make no effort to leave the town."

There was a note in his voice that did not invite further argument. With a few additional half-hearted attempts at protest, the three officials of Watershed agreed to make a joint community call over the local phone system with the reassurance and warning he had asked them to deliver —following which, he had them placed under guard in the police headquarters.

It was in fact less than two hours before the first elements of the Brozan Army began to arrive. These were flying transports loaded with troops who quickly ringed the village at a distance of about two hundred yards inside the edge of the forest surrounding the town. Through the rest of the night, other troops, heavy weapons and armored vehicles could be heard arriving. By dawn, Swahili and Cletus concurred in an estimate that close to a division of Brozan soldiery, bristling with everything from belt knives to energy weapons, enclosed Watershed and its two hundred occupying Dorsai troops.

Swahili was in good humor as he handed the field glasses back to Cletus, after making his own survey of the surrounding forest area. They were standing together on top of the communications tower, which was the tallest structure in the town.

"They won't want to use those heavy weapons indiscriminately, with all these local people on hand," said Swahili. "That means they're going to have to come in on foot—probably all around the perimeter at once. I'd guess they'll attack inside the hour."

"I don't think so," answered Cletus. "I think they'll send someone in to talk, first."

He turned out to be correct. The surrounding Brozan troops did nothing for the first three hours of the morning. Then, toward noon, as the cloud-veiled sun over Newton was heating the northern landscape, a command car flying a white flag slowly emerged from the shadows of the forest and entered the town from the highway. It was met at the perimeter of Watershed by soldiers instructed in preparation for this meeting, and it was escorted by them to the police headquarters. There, a small, spare general in his early sixties, flanked by a round man perhaps ten years younger and wearing a colonel's insignia, dismounted and entered the headquarters building. Cletus received them in the office of the commander of the police detachment.

"I'm here to offer you surrender terms—" The general broke off, staring at Cletus' shoulder tabs. "I don't recognize your rank?"

"Marshal," Cletus answered. "We've shaken up our table of organization and our titles on the Dorsai, recently. Marshal Cletus Grahame."

"Oh? General James Van Dassel. And this is Colonel
185

Morton Offer. As I was saying, we're here to offer you terms of surrender—"

"If it was a matter of sending surrender terms, you'd hardly have needed to come yourself, would you, General?" Cletus broke in. "I think you know very well that there's no question of our surrendering."

"No?" Van Dassel's eyebrows rose politely. "Maybe I should tell you we've got more than a full division, with a full complement of heavy weapons, surrounding you right now."

"I'm aware of that fact," said Cletus. "Just as you're completely aware of the fact that we have something over five thousand civilians here inside our lines."

"Yes, and we're holding you strictly accountable for them," said Van Dassel. "I have to warn you that, if any harm comes to them, the liberal surrender terms we're about to offer you—"

"Don't try my patience, General," interrupted Cletus. "We hold those civilians as hostages against any inimical action by your forces. So let's not waste any more time on this nonsense about our surrendering. I've been expecting you here so that I could inform you of the immediate steps to be taken by the Advanced Associated Communities with regard to Watershed and the mines. As you undoubtedly know, these mines were developed on land purchased from Broza by the Advanced Associated Communities, and Broza's expropriation has since been ruled illegal by the international court here on Newton—although Broza has seen fit until now to refuse to obey that court's order returning the mines to the Advanced Associated Communities. Our expeditionary force has already notified the Advanced Associated Communities that the mines are once more under their proper ownership, and I've been informed that the first contingents of regular AAC troops will begin to arrive here by 1800 hours, to relieve my command and begin to function as a permanent occupying force. . . ." Cletus paused.

"I'm certainly not going to permit any such occupying forces to move in here," said Van Dassel, almost mildly.

"Then I'd suggest you check with your political authorities before you make any move to prevent them," said Cletus. "I repeat, we hold the townspeople here hostage for the good behavior of your troops."

"Nor am I willing to be blackmailed," said Van Dassel. "I'll expect notification of your willingness to surrender before the next two hours are up."

"And I, as I say," answered Cletus, "will hold you re-

186

sponsible for any hostile action by your command during our relief by the regular troops from the Advanced Associated Communities."

On that mutual statement, they parted politely. Van Dassel and his colonel returned to the Brozan troops encircling the village. Cletus called in Swahili and Arvid to have lunch with him.

"But what if he decides to hit us before the relieving troops get here?" asked Swahili.

"He won't," said Cletus. "His situation's bad enough as it is. The Brozan politicians are going to be asking him how he allowed us to take over Watershed and the mines here in the first place. He might survive that question, as far as his career is concerned—but only if there're no Brozan lives lost. He knows I understand that as well as he does, so Van Dassel won't take chances."

In fact, Van Dassel did not make any move. His division surrounding Watershed sat quietly while his deadline for surrender passed, and the relieving forces from the Advanced Associated Communities began to be airlifted in. During the following night, he quietly withdrew his forces. By the following sunrise, as the newly landed, AAC soldiery began to clear an area of the forest outside the town and construct a semipermanent camp for themselves, there was not a Brozan soldier to be found within two hundred miles.

"Very well done indeed!" said Walco, enthusiastically, when he arrived at Watershed with the last of his own troops and was ushered in to the office Cletus had taken over in the police headquarters building. "You and your Dorsais have done a marvelous job. You can move out any time now."

"As soon as we're paid," said Cletus.

Walco smiled, thinly. "I thought you might be eager to get your pay," he said. "So I brought it along with me."

He lifted a narrow briefcase onto the desk between them, took out a release form, which he passed to Cletus, and then began to remove gold certificates, which he stacked on the desk in front of Cletus.

Cletus ignored the form and watched coolly as the pile of certificates grew. When Walco stopped at last, and looked up at him with another broad smile, Cletus did not smile back. He shook his head.

"That's less than half of what our agreement called for," Cletus said.

Walco preserved his smile. "True," Walco said. "But in the original agreement we envisioned hiring you for a

187

three-month term. As it happens, you've been lucky enough to achieve your objective in less than a week and with only a quarter of your expeditionary force. We figured full combat pay for the whole week, however, for the five hundred men you used, and in addition we're paying you garrison scale not only for the rest of your men for that week but for your whole force for the rest of this month as well—as a sort of bonus."

Cletus looked at him. Walco's smile faded.

"I'm sure you remember as well as I do," said Cletus, coldly, "that the agreement was for two thousand men for three months, full combat pay for everybody during that period—and no pay at all if we weren't able to deliver the stibnite mines to you. How many men I used to make that recovery, and how long I took, was my concern. I expect full combat pay for three months for my entire command, immediately."

"That's out of the question, of course," said Walco, a little shortly.

"I don't think so," said Cletus. "Maybe I should remind you that I told General Van Dassel, the Brozan commander who had us encircled here, that I was holding the civilian population of Watershed hostage for his good behavior. Perhaps I should remind you that I and the men I brought here with me are still holding these people hostage—this time for *your* good behavior."

Walco's face became strangely set. "You wouldn't harm civilians!" he said, after a moment.

"General Van Dassel believes I would," replied Cletus. "Now I, personally, give you my word as a Dorsai—and that's a word that's going to become something better than a signed contract, in time—that no single civilian will be hurt. But have you got the courage to believe me? If I'm lying, and your takeover of the mines includes a blood bath of the resident townspeople, your chances of coming to some eventual agreement with Broza about these mines will go up in smoke. Instead of being able to negotiate on the basis of having a bird in the hand, you'll have to face a colony interested only in vengeance—vengeance for an action for which all civilized communities will indict you."

Walco stood, staring at him. "I don't have any more certificates with me," he said at last, hoarsely.

"We'll wait," answered Cletus. "You should be able to fly back and get them and return here by noon at the latest."

Shoulders slumped, Walco went. As he mounted the

steps of the aircraft that had brought him to Watershed, however, he stopped and turned for a parting shot at Cletus.

"You think you're going to cut a swath through the new worlds," he said, viciously, "and maybe you will for a while. But one of these days everything you've built is going to come tumbling down around your ears."

"We'll see," said Cletus.

He watched the door shut behind Walco and the aircraft lift away into the sky of Newton. Then he turned to Arvid, who was standing beside him.

"By the way, Arv," he said, "Bill Athyer wants to have the chance to study my methods of tactics and strategy at close hand, so he'll be taking over as my aide as soon as we're back on the Dorsai. We'll find a command for you, out in the field somewhere. It's about time you were brushing up on your combat experience anyway."

Without waiting for Arvid's response, he turned his back on the younger man and walked off, his mind already on other problems.

22

"Your prices," said James Arm-of-the-Lord, Eldest of the First Militant Church, on both the neighboring worlds of Harmony and Association—those two worlds called the Friendlies, "are outrageous."

James Arm-of-the-Lord was a small, frail, middle-aged man with sparse gray hair—looking even smaller and more frail than he might otherwise in the tight black jumper and trousers that were the common dress of those belonging to the fanatical sects that had colonized, and later divided and multiplied, on the surfaces of Harmony and Association. At first sight, he seemed a harmless little man, but a glance from his dark eyes or even a few words spoken aloud by him were enough to destroy that illusion. Plainly he was one of those rare people who burn with an inner fire—but the inner fire that never failed in James Arm-of-the-Lord was a brand of woe and a torch of terror to the Unrighteous. Nor was it lessened by the fact

189

that the ranks of the Unrighteous, in James' estimation, included all those whose opinions in any way differed from his own. He sat now in his office at Government Center on Harmony, gazing across the desk's bare, unpolished surface at Cletus, who sat opposite.

"I know we're priced beyond your means," said Cletus. "I didn't come by to suggest that you hire some of our Dorsais. I was going to suggest that possibly we might want to hire some of your young men."

"Hire out our church members to spend their blood and lives in the sinful wars of the Churchless and the Unbelievers?" said James. "Unthinkable!"

"None of your colonies on Harmony or Association have anything to speak of in the way of technology," said Cletus. "Your Militant Church may contain the largest population of any of the churches on these two worlds, but you're still starving for real credit—of the kind you can use in interworld trading to set up the production machinery your people need. You could earn that credit from us, as I say, by hiring out some of your young men to us."

James' eyes glittered like the eyes of a coiled snake in reflective light. "How much?" he snapped.

"The standard wages for conventional mercenary soldiers," replied Cletus.

"Why, that's barely a third of what you asked for each of your Dorsais!" James' voice rose. "You'd sell to us at one price, and buy from us at another?"

"It's a matter of selling and buying two different products," answered Cletus, unmoved. "The Dorsais are worth what I ask for them because of their training and because by now they've established a reputation for earning their money. Your men have no such training, and no reputation. They're worth only what I'm willing to pay for them. On the other hand, not a great deal would be demanded of them. They'd be used mainly as diversionary forces like our jump troops in our recent capture of Margaretha, on Freiland."

The taking over of Margaretha on Freiland had been the latest of a series of successful engagements fought by the new-trained Dorsai mercenaries under Cletus' command. Over a year had gone by since the capture of the stibnite mines on Newton, and in that time they had conducted campaigns leading to clear-cut and almost bloodless victories on the worlds of Newton's sister planet of Cassida, St. Marie, a smaller world under the Procyon sun with Mara and Kultis, and most recently on Freiland, which, with New Earth, were the inhabited planets under the star of Sirius.

Margaretha was a large, ocean-girt island some three hundred miles off the northeastern shore of the main continental mass of Freiland. It had been invaded and captured by the nearest colony adjoining it on the mainland mass. The island's government in exile had raised the funds to hire the Dorsais to recapture their homeland from the invaders.

Cletus had feinted with an apparent jump-belt troop drop of untrained Dorsais over Margaretha's main city. But meanwhile he had sent several thousand trained troops into the island by having them swim ashore at night at innumerable points around the coastline of the island. These infiltrators had taken charge of and coordinated the hundreds of spontaneous uprisings that had been triggered off among the island's population by word of the jump-troop drop.

Faced with uprisings from within and evident attack from without, the mainland troops that had seized the island chose discretion as the better part of valor and abandoned the island for their home colony. They reached home only to discover how few had been the troops that had actually driven them out, and turned swiftly about to return to Margaretha.

When they reached the island this second time, however, they found watch fires burning on all the beaches, and the population aroused, armed and this time ready to die between the tide marks rather than let a single mainlander invader ashore.

As with Cletus' other military successes, it had been a victory achieved through a careful blending of imagination and psychology with what was now beginning to be regarded, on the other colony worlds, as the almost superhuman abilities of the trained Dorsai soldiers. Clearly, for all his apparent unwillingness to listen to Cletus' offer, James was not unaware of the hard facts and advantages of the proposition. It was typical of elders such as James that they were either pro or con, but never admitted to indecision.

Cletus took his leave, accordingly, having planted the seed of an idea in a Friendly mind, and being content to bide his time and let it grow.

He took a spaceship to New Earth, that sister planet of Freiland, where his command of Dorsais and a new military campaign were waiting for him. Marcus Dodds, Eachan's old second-in-command, met him at the Dorsai camp just outside of Adonyer, the main city of Breatha Colony, their employers on New Earth. In spite of the two new stars on each of his shoulder tabs, marking him as a field commander with a full division of mercenaries under him, Marcus' face was solemn with concern.

"Spainville's formed an alliance with four of the five other city-states of the interior plains," he told Cletus, as soon as they were alone in Marcus' office. "They call it the Central Combine, and they've mustered a combined army of better than twenty thousand regular troops. Not only that, they're ready and waiting for us. We aren't going to be able to use surprise the way we have in other campaigns, and this short division you've given me here has less than five thousand men."

"True enough," said Cletus, thoughtfully. "What do you suggest I do about it?"

"Break the contract with Breatha," said Marcus, strongly. "We can't possibly go up against this Central Combine now without more men. And how many other new-trained Dorsais are there? Certainly not more than a couple of hundred. We've got no choice but to break the contract. You can cite the fact that the situation has changed since we were hired. Breatha may squawk, but responsible people in other colonies wanting to hire us will understand. If we don't have the troops, we don't have the troops— that's all there is to it."

"No," said Cletus. He got up from his seat beside Marcus' desk and walked across the room to a map showing the flat plains area of the continental interior, which Breatha shared with its rivals, five other colonies, each of which was essentially farming communities centered around one large city—hence their common name of city-states. "I don't want to start breaking contracts, no matter how well justified we are."

He studied the map for a minute. Breatha, with a narrow corridor running to the coast, was surrounded by the city-states of the interior on four of its five sides. Originally it had been the manufacturing center that supplied the city-states with most of their factory-made equipment and brought farm produce from the city-states in return. But then Spainville, the largest of the five city-states, had ventured into manufacturing on its own, sparking off a similar action in the other city-states—one of which, called Armoy, had chosen to construct a deep-space spaceport in competition with the one existing in Breatha Colony.

Now, with economic ambition burning bright in the

former agricultural colonies of the central plain, Spainville, which bordered on Breatha's corridor to the sea, had chosen to lay claim upon that corridor and threaten to take it over by armed force if Breatha did not yield it peacefully. Hence, the presence of the Dorsais on the Breatha payroll.

"On the other hand," said Cletus, turning back to Marcus, "if they believed we'd been reinforced, that might be almost as good as our actually getting the necessary extra troops in here."

"How're you going to make them think that?" demanded Marcus.

"It may take some thought." Cletus smiled. "At any rate, I'll make a quick trip back to the Dorsai now, as though I was going after extra men, and see if I can't work out a plan on the way."

Having announced his intentions, Cletus wasted no time. By late that evening, after a wild trip halfway around the circumference of New Earth in an atmosphere ship, he was on board a deep-space vessel that had the Dorsai as its next port of call. Three days later he was back in Foralie. Melissa met him at the doorway of Grahame House with a warmth that was surprising. Since the marriage, she had slowly been softening toward him, and since the birth of their son, three months ago, that process had accelerated even while it seemed that all those others who had once been close to Cletus were becoming more and more estranged to him.

Typical of these was Eachan, whose greeting to Cletus was almost as detached and wary as that which might be accorded a stranger. At the first opportunity, he got Cletus away from Melissa and the child to speak bluntly to his son-in-law.

"Have you seen these?" he asked, spreading an assortment of news clippings out on the desk before Cletus. They were standing in Cletus' office-study, in the west wing of Grahame House. "They're all from Earth news services—Alliance and Coalition alike."

Cletus glanced over the clippings. Unanimously, they were concerned with the Dorsais and himself. Not only that, but their vituperative tone was so alike that they could have been the product of a single voice.

"You see?" Eachan challenged, as Cletus finally looked up from the clippings. "It was the Coalition news service that started calling you a pirate after the Bakhalla business. But now the Alliance has taken it up too. These citystates you're hired to go against on New Earth are backed by Alliance as well as Coalition aid and investment. If you don't look out you'll have the Alliance as well as the Coalition laying for you. Look"—his brown right forefinger stabbed at one of the clippings—"read what Dow deCastries said in a speech in Delhi—*'If nothing else, the peoples of the Coalition and the Alliance both can join in condemning the brutal and bloody activities of the ex-Alliance renegade Grahame....'* "

Cletus laughed.

"You think this is funny?" said Eachan, grimly.

"Only in its predictability," answered Cletus, "and in the obviousness of Dow's intentions."

"You mean you've been expecting this—expecting deCastries to make speeches like that?" demanded Eachan.

"Yes," answered Cletus. He dismissed the subject. "Never mind that. I'm back here to go through the motions of transporting an imaginary extra division of troops to Breatha Colony. I'll need at least two deep-space transports. Maybe we can arrange to lease some empty cargo spaceships for a diversionary trip—"

"You'd better listen to something else first," Eachan interrupted him. "Did you know you're losing Swahili?"

Cletus raised his eyebrows. "No," he murmured. "But it's not surprising."

Eachan opened a drawer of Cletus' library desk and took out a resignation form, which he dropped on the table on top of the news clippings. Cletus looked down at it. Sure enough, it was made out and signed by Swahili, now a one-star general field commander. Promotions had come thick and fast among those men who had been with Cletus from the beginning. Only Arvid, now in the field, was still a commandant—the equivalent of his old grade of captain—and Eachan, who had refused the one promotion offered him. By contrast, the once ineffective Bill Athyer was now a rank above Arvid as commandant senior grade, less than two ranks away from field commander, with command of a regiment.

"I suppose I'd better talk to him," said Cletus.

"Not that it'll do you any good," replied Eachan.

Cletus invited Swahili up from his post at the main new-training center, now on the far side of Foralie. The next day they met briefly in that same office-study where Eachan had confronted Cletus with the news clippings shortly after his arrival home.

"Of course, I'm sorry to lose you," said Cletus, as the two faced each other. Swahili, a single star gleaming gold on each of his shoulder tabs, bulked larger than ever in

194

his blue dress uniform. "But I imagine you've completely made up your mind."

"Yes," said Swahili. "You understand, don't you?"

"I think so," said Cletus.

"I think you do," echoed Swahili softly, "even if it is just the opposite of the way you like to do things. You've taken all the life out of war—you know that, don't you?"

"It's the way I like it," said Cletus.

Swahili's eyes flashed a little in the soft light of the peaceful library-office. "It's not the way I like it," he said. "What I like is what nearly everyone else hates—hates or is scared sick of. And it's that you've taken out of the business for everybody who serves under you."

"You mean the combat, itself," said Cletus.

"That's right," said Swahili, softly. "I don't like being hurt and all those weeks in the hospital any more than the next man. I don't want to die. But I put up with all the rest of it—all the training, all the hurry-up-and-waiting, all the marking time between engagements—I put up with all that, just for the few hours when everything turns real."

"You're a killer. Or don't you admit that to yourself?" asked Cletus.

"No," said Swahili. "I'm a special fighter, that's all. I like to fight. Just the killing itself wouldn't do anything for me. I told you I didn't want to get hurt, or killed, any more than the next man. I feel just as hollow inside when the energy weapons start burning the air over my head. At the same time, I wouldn't miss it for anything. It's a dirty, damn universe, and every once in a while I get a chance to hit back at it. That's all. If I knew in the morning when I started out that I was going to be killed that day, I'd still go—because I couldn't die happier than to go down hitting back."

He stopped talking, abruptly. For a moment he simply looked at Cletus in the silence of the room.

"And it's that you've taken out of mercenary work," he said. "So I'm going someplace else where they still have it."

Cletus held out his hand. "Good luck," he said.

They shook hands.

"Luck to you," said Swahili. "You'll need it. In the end the man with gloves on always loses to the bare-knuckle fighter."

"You'll have your chance to test that belief, at least," said Cletus.

23

A week later Cletus returned to New Earth with two leased cargo vessels, the crew and officers of which had agreed to being held in a locked room during the embarking and disembarking of the troops they were supposed to carry. They could testify afterward only to hearing the sounds of boots entering the ship for two and a half hours, on the Dorsai, and to some four hours of similar sounds as they hung in orbit above New Earth, while landing craft shuttled from their ships to some unannounced spot on the planet below. Agents for the Central Combine of city-states, however, observed these landing craft making their sit-downs in a wooded area just inside Breatha Colony's border with Spainville. On attempting to investigate further, the agents found themselves stopped and warned back by a cordon of armed Dorsais, but their estimate of the troops landed, taken from the number of trips from the spaceships in orbit, was of at least five thousand men.

General Lu May, commander of the city-states combined forces, grunted when this information was brought to him.

"That's the sort of thing this Grahame likes to pull," said Lu May. The general was in his mid-seventies, and had been retired from active soldiering until the new ambitions and war-like fervor of the city-states had summoned him back to take over-all command of their new army. "He'd like to shake us up with the idea that we've got to watch two separate invading commands. But I'll lay you odds he pulls them together at the first opportunity, as soon as he thinks he's got us out in the open where he can pull all sorts of fancy maneuvers. But we aren't going to fall for it. We'll stay dug in here in Spainville, and make him come to us."

He chuckled. He was fat as well as old, and the thought of being able to frustrate this unorthodox young upstart while remaining comfortably seated in his own home in Stanleyville tickled him. He ordered heavy energy weapons dug in all around the perimeter of the city and all approaches heavily mined. It would take more than the light-weaponed and light-armored Dorsai mercenaries to break through defenses such as these, even if they were equal in number to the men he had under arms inside the city.

Meanwhile, Cletus' forces were already in motion. A motley horde of civilian trucks and other heavy-duty, air-cushioned sliders had earlier converged on the area where the shuttleboats had landed from the spaceships. These now moved out like a transport and supply convoy, with an armed Dorsai driving each of them. This force crossed the border into Armoy, and swung inland toward Armoy City and its new spaceport, thereby raising flutters of alarm within the community's citizens.

"Sit tight!" grunted Lu May to the frantic messages that reached him from Armoy City for an expeditionary force to defend them against the oncoming Dorsais. He did not send the force, but instead followed his own advice, sitting tight and watching Cletus' other command, which was also in movement now, across the Spainville border, heading apparently through Spainville toward one of the other adjoining city-states. Still Lu May made no move, and sure enough, once it had passed the city of Spainville, Cletus' first command of Dorsais swung about and came up on the city's rear. At the same time, the command that had been threatening Armoy City swung away and cut in to come up before the city of Spainville, so that within a few days the city was ringed by the Dorsai troops.

Lu May chortled and slapped his fat knees. Curiously enough, in Cletus' headquarters outside the city, there was hardly less satisfaction to be found in the person of Chancellor Ad Reyes, representative of the government of Breatha Colony, who was accompanying Cletus, ostensibly as an "observer."

"Excellent, Marshal. Excellent!" Reyes, who was a thin, eager, scholarly-looking man with a high forehead, dressed in the long, black, official gown of his chancellorhood, rubbed his thin hands with pleasure. "You've managed to trap their army here. And there're no other forces who can come to their rescue. Excellently done!"

"You should thank General Lu May for that, instead of me," Cletus answered, dryly. "He has a good deal less to fear from us, sitting back behind his mine fields and his perimeter defenses, than he does in the open field, where the Dorsais are a great deal more mobile than his troops. He has more men and he's in an entrenched position."

"But you don't have to try to take the place by assault!" protested Reyes. "You can live off the country or supply yourself from Breatha as you want. Lu May's cut off from outside supplies. It's just a matter of starving him out!"

"That may not be easy," said Cletus, "unless he's been strangely forgetful, while preparing for everything else, to stock enough provisions for the city and his troops so that they can hold out longer than we can afford to sit here besieging them."

Reyes frowned. Plainly, it seemed to him that this Dorsai marshal was taking an entirely too gloomy a view of the situation.

"Do you object to besieging the city?" Reyes demanded. "If so, I should probably mention that the Breatha government considered this the optimum—indeed the only— course you could pursue, if you were lucky enough to trap Lu May in a fixed position."

"I don't object—for now," Cletus answered, quietly. "But that's because there're military reasons for it, far removed from the opinions of your government. I might remind you, Chancellor, that one of my stipulations in accepting employment with Breatha Colony, as it is with every government with whom I sign a contract, is that I, alone, be in charge of the conduct of the campaign."

He turned and sat down behind the desk in the office of the field structure in which they had been talking. "And now, if you'll excuse me, I've got work to do."

Reyes hesitated, then turned on his heel and walked out.

Cletus continued the siege for three weeks, throwing up breastworks and digging his own trenches behind them to encircle the city, as if he had every intention of staying indefinitely. Meanwhile, outside of an occasional exchange of small-arms fire, there was little open conflict between the city defenders and its Dorsai attackers.

Meanwhile, overhead, a similar unspoken truce existed. Dorsai aircraft patrolled the atmosphere above and about the city to prevent city-state vessels from entering or leaving it. But beyond this, there was no aerial conflict. As in most inter-colony armed conflicts on the new worlds, air warfare was being avoided by the sort of tacit agreement that had interdicted the use of poison gas during World War II in the twentieth century on Earth. The object of armed struggle between opposed technology-poor communities, such as the young colonies, was not so much to destroy the enemy's productive capacity as to take it away from him. One did not obliterate by bombing that which one had started a war to obtain. And if the factories and other hardware of civilization were valuable, the men who had the skills to operate them were almost as valuable.

Therefore, bombing and even the indiscriminate use of heavy weapons in the vicinity of built-up areas was avoided, and—atmosphere craft being almost as expensive as spacecraft—any other use of the skies other than for reconnaissance or the transporting of troops was likewise avoided.

At the end of three weeks, however, Cletus apparently lost patience with this stalemate and issued orders, orders that brought Chancellor Ad Reyes literally running to Cletus' headquarters office, the black gown tucked up to allow free movement to the chancellor's legs.

"You're pulling out half your forces and sending them to take Armoy City and its spaceport!" Reyes accused him, bursting into Cletus' office.

Cletus looked up from the desk at which he was working. "You've heard of that, have you?" Cletus asked.

"Heard of it!" Reyes strode up to the edge of the desk and leaned over it almost as though he would have liked to have thrust his face nose-to-nose with Cletus'. "I've *seen* them! All those civilian trucks you requisitioned to transport your secondary command are headed off toward Armoy! Don't tell me that isn't where they're headed!"

"That's where they're headed," said Cletus, agreeably. "The rest of us will be following them in twenty-four hours. There's plainly no point in continuing this siege any longer. I'm going to raise it, move on Armoy City and take that spaceport of theirs."

"Raise the siege? . . . What kind of trick is this? If you'd been paid by the city-states to betray us, you couldn't have picked a better—" He broke off abruptly, shrinking a little at the sudden sound of his own words in his ears. Cletus was on his feet behind the desk.

"I hope I don't hear you correctly, Chancellor." Cletus' voice and eyes had changed. "Are you accusing Dorsais of dishonoring a contract with your government?"

"No . . . that is, I didn't mean . . ." Reyes stammered.

"I'd advise you to be careful of what you do mean," said Cletus. "The Dorsais don't break contracts, and we don't tolerate talk that we do. And now, for the last time, let me remind you that I—I, alone—am in command of this campaign. Perhaps you should get back to your own quarters, now."

"Yes, I . . ." Reyes fled.

Just before dawn the following morning, the rest of the Dorsais besieging Spainville mounted their military vehicles and pulled out with all armor and weapons. Only their aircraft remained above Spainville to discourage pursuit by air reconnaissance.

Dawn rose on the empty trenches and breastworks that the mercenaries had thrown up, but it was nearly noon before their silence and appearance of abandonment could tempt patrols out from Spainville to investigate. When, however, the former Dorsai positions had been investigated and found to be abandoned, the patrols took note of the direction of the signs of departure visible in the pasture earth and summer grass south of the city, and passed the word hastily to General Lu May.

Lu May, roused with this news from his slumbers after a late evening, swore in a way that had gone out of fashion forty years ago.

"We've got him!" the old man exploded, rolling out of bed and beginning hastily to struggle into his clothes. "He couldn't stand the waiting—now he's cut his own throat!"

"Sir?" protested the colonel who had brought him the news. "Cut his own throat? I don't understand—"

"That's because you kids know nothing about war the way it's really fought!" trumpeted Lu May, getting into his trousers. "Grahame's headed for Armoy City, idiot!"

"Yes, sir," said the colonel. "But I still don't see—"

"He's faced the fact that there was no hope of his taking the city here!" snapped Lu May. "So he's pulled out and decided to take Armoy City, instead. That way he can claim that he did the best he could, and at least got Breatha Colony the spaceport that was giving them competition! With the spaceport, he'll tell them, they can make a deal to protect their corridor to the sea! Don't you see? Grahame's finally faced the fact that it was a bad contract he signed. He wants to get out of it on any terms—but he can't get out unless he has at least something to offer Breatha. Armoy City and that spaceport will be it!"

"Yes, sir," said the colonel, earnestly. "I see all that. But what I don't understand is why you say he cut his own throat. After all, if he's able to give Breatha Colony the spaceport and Armoy City to bargain with—"

"Idiot! Double idiot!" roared Lu May. "He has to take Armoy City first, doesn't he, fool?"

"Yes, sir—"

"Then he's going to have to occupy Armoy City with his forces, isn't he?"

Dressed at last, Lu May waddled hastily toward the door. Over his shoulder, he continued, "If we move fast after him, we'll catch him inside Armoy City, and we can surround him! He's got no supplies to last in a city like that very long—and if we need to, we even have the men and weapons to take the city by storm! Either way we can wrap his Dorsais up and have him as a prisoner to do what we want with!"

Lu May wasted no time in getting his army in pursuit of Cletus and the Dorsais. But for all his hurry, he did not fail to move out in good marching order, or without the heavy energy weapons he had dug in around the perimeter of the city, and which he now took with him, even though having them with him would necessarily slow his movement. Ponderous, but deadly, he slid along over the plain track Cletus' two departing commands had left behind through the standing grass and grain.

The direction of the track aimed directly at Armoy City, perhaps three days' travel away for Cletus' lightly equipped Dorsais. Lu May would be lucky to do it in four with his command, but the extra day should bring the Spainville general on the scene at Armoy City, as he calculated, just in good time to take advantage of that moment in which Cletus' troops were letting down, after having made their conquest of Armoy City and the spaceport an accomplished fact.

All the same, it was wise—thought Lu May—to give himself a little time margin if at all possible. If he should find himself ahead of schedule, he could always dawdle a bit in coming up to the city at the far end of his pursuit. Therefore, he issued orders after the evening meal for his command to continue after dark, under the moonless but star-bright New Earth sky. He pushed them on through the darkness until men began falling asleep at the controls of their vehicles, or on their feet. Finally, reluctantly, he called a halt for the night about three hours after midnight.

His army had just managed to get deeply into exhausted slumber, when a series of sharp, blasting explosions jerked them back to wakefulness, and they sat up to see the heavy energy weapons they had been hauling burning with sparkling red-white flames as their energy storage units melted under their own fierce heat like butter in a furnace. In the same moment, dark-clad Dorsais were suddenly among Lu May's troops stripping them of their body weapons and heading them into groups under the watchful eyes and guns of other mercenaries standing guard.

General Lu May, himself, started out of deep slumber, and sat up in his field bed to find Cletus standing over him, an uncapped holster showing the sidearm at Cletus' side. Lu May stared in befuddlement.

"But you're . . . up ahead of me . . ." he stammered, after a moment.

"I've got a detachment of empty civilian trucks up ahead of you," answered Cletus. "Trucks that never had any men in them except the drivers. What men I had are here with me now—and your command is taken prisoner, General. You'll make things simpler by giving me your surrender, right now."

Lu May fumbled out of bed. Suddenly he was very old, and chilly, and helpless, standing there in his pajamas. Almost humbly, he went through the motions of surrender.

Cletus went back to the field unit that had already been set up as his temporary headquarters. Waiting inside for him was Chancellor Ad Reyes.

"You can inform your government that the effective military forces of the combined city-states are now our prisoner, Chancellor . . ." he began, and broke off as Arvid entered, bearing a yellow message slip.

"Signal from Colonel Khan on the Dorsai," said Arvid, "forwarded on by our base camp at Adonyer, back in Breatha Colony."

Cletus took the message sheet and unfolded it. He read:

> Attack made through Etter's Pass from Neuland into Bakhalla territory beaten off. Alliance and Coalition forces combined in a joint "Peace Force" for the new worlds. Dow deCastries has supreme command of this force.

Cletus folded the message and put it in a pocket of his battle tunic. He turned to Reyes.

"You've got twenty-four hours," he said, "to get Breatha troops here to take charge of these prisoners we've just captured. I and my troops must return immediately to the Dorsai."

Reyes stared at him in combined awe and amazement. "But we'd planned a triumphal parade in case of victory . . ." he began, uncertainly.

"Twenty-four hours," said Cletus, brusquely. He turned on his heel and left the chancellor standing.

24

Landing back on the Dorsai, Cletus phoned ahead to order Major Arvid Johnson, now acting field commander, to meet him at Grahame House. Then with Bill Athyer like a smaller, beak-nosed shadow at his side, he took a hired atmosphere craft to Foralie and Grahame House, still wearing his battle uniform.

Melissa, with Arvid and Eachan, met him just inside the front door. Athyer, diffident still in spite of his present rank, stood at the far end of the entrance hall as Cletus greeted Melissa and Eachan briefly before striding on toward the door to his office-study and beckoning Eachan and Arvid to follow him.

"You too, Bill," he said to Athyer.

He closed the door of the office behind them. "What's the latest word?" Cletus demanded of his father-in-law, as he walked around to stand behind the pile of message blanks on his desk and stare down at them.

"It seems deCastries was appointed to this position as Commander-in-Chief of the joint Alliance–Coalition troops on the new worlds several months ago," answered Eachan. "The Coalition and the Alliance just kept it secret while the two high commands built up a news campaign to get the common citizens of Earth on both sides ready for the idea. Also, Artur Walco's here to see you. Seems like deCastries is already making trouble for him at those stibnite mines on Newton."

"Yes, there'll be brush wars breaking out all over the new worlds now. . . . I'll see Walco tomorrow morning," said Cletus. He turned to Arvid.

"Well, Arv," he said. "If the Dorsai had medals to give I'd be handing you a fistful of them right now. I hope someday you can forgive me for this. I had to have you thinking I'd shoved you aside into the field for good."

"You didn't, sir?" asked Arvid, quietly.

"No," said Cletus. "I wanted a development in you. And I've got it."

In fact, it was a different man who stood before them to answer to the name of Arvid Johnson. Not the least of the change was that he looked at least five years older. His white-blond hair had darkened as though with age, and his skin was more deeply suntanned than it had been. He looked as though he had lost weight, and yet he appeared larger than ever, a man of gaunt bone and whip-cord muscle, towering over all of them.

At the same time, something was gone from him for good. A youthfulness, a friendly softness that had been a basic part of him before was vanished now. In its place was something grim and isolated, as though he had at last become coldly conscious of the strength and skill in him that set him apart from other men. A quality like the sheer, physical deadliness of Swahili had entered into him.

He stood without moving. When he had moved earlier, it had been almost without a sound. He seemed to carry about him now a carefulness born of the consciousness that all others were smaller and weaker than he, so that he must remember not to damage them without intent. Like someone more warrior than man, prototype of some line of invincible giants to come, he stood by Cletus' desk.

"That's good to hear," he said softly, to Cletus, now. "What do you want me to do?"

"Fight a campaign—if necessary," said Cletus. "I'm going to give you a world to defend. And I'm promoting you two grades to a new rank—vice-marshal. You'll be working in team with another officer also holding an entirely new rank—the rank of battle operator."

He turned slightly to look at Bill Athyer. "That'll be Bill, here," he said. "As battle op, Bill will rank just below you and above any other officer in the field with you, except myself."

Arvid and Bill looked at each other.

"Battle operator?" said Eachan.

"That's right," Cletus answered him. "Don't look so surprised, Eachan. This is something we've been headed toward from the start, with the reorganization and re-training of the men."

He looked back at Arvid and Bill. "The marshal, or vice-marshal, and the battle operator," Cletus said, "will form a general commander's team. The battle op is the theoretical strategist of that team and the vice-marshal is the field tactician. The two will bear roughly the same relationship to each other as an architect and a general contractor in the construction of a building. The battle op will first consider the strategical situation and problem and lay out a campaign plan. And in this process he will have complete authority and freedom."

Cletus had been watching Bill in particular as he spoke. Now, he paused. "You understand, Bill?" he said.

"Yes, sir," he replied.

"Then, however"—Cletus' eyes swung to Arvid—"the battle op will hand his strategical plan to the vice-marshal, and from that point on, it'll be the vice-marshal who has complete authority. His job will be to take the plan given him, make any and all alterations in it he thinks it needs for practical purposes and then execute it as he sees fit. *You* understand, Arv?"

"Yes, sir," said Arvid, softly.

"Good," said Cletus. "Then you and Bill are released from your present duties as of now and you'll begin immediately on your new jobs. The world I'm giving you to start with is the Dorsai here, and the first force you'll be working with will be made up of the women and children, the sick, the injured, and the average men."

He smiled a little at them. "Then get at it, both of you," he said. "None of us has any time to waste nowadays."

As the door to the office closed behind the two of them, a wave of the fatigue he had been holding at bay for a number of days and hours now suddenly washed over him. He swayed where he stood and felt Eachan catch him by the elbow.

"No—it's all right," he said. His vision cleared and he looked into Eachan's concerned face. "I'm just tired, that's all. I'll take a nap and then we'll hit things after dinner."

With Eachan walking guardedly beside him, he walked out of the office-study, feeling as though he were stepping on pillows, and went up to his bedroom. The bed was before him; he dropped onto its yielding surface without bothering even to take off his boots. . . . And that was the last he remembered.

He awoke just before sunset, ate a light meal and spent half an hour getting reacquainted with his son. Then he closeted himself in his office with Eachan to attack the pile of paper work. They sorted the correspondence into two piles, one which Cletus had to answer himself and one

205

which Eachan could answer with a few words per letter of direction from him. Both men dictated until nearly dawn before the desk was cleared and the necessary orders for the Dorsai and off-world troops were issued.

The interview in the study next day with the Newtonian chairman, Walco, was brief and bitter. The bitterness might have gone into acrimony and the interview prolonged unduly if Cletus had not cut short Walco's scarcely veiled accusations.

"The contract I signed with you," said Cletus, "promised to capture Watershed and the stibnite mines, and turn them over to your own troops. We made no guarantee that you'd stay in control of the mines. Holding onto them was up to you, and to whatever agreement you could make with the Brozans."

"We made our agreement!" said Walco. "But now that they've suddenly been reinforced by fifteen thousand Alliance and Coalition troops, courtesy of this fellow deCastries, they're refusing to honor it. They claim they made it under duress!"

"Didn't they?" Cletus said.

"That's not the point! The point is, we need you and enough troops from the Dorsai, right away, to match those fifteen thousand soldiers from Earth that the Brozans're holding over us like a club."

Cletus shook his head. "I'm sorry," he said. "I'm facing unusual demands on my available mercenaries right now. Also, I'm not free to come to Newton, myself."

Walco's face went lumpy and hard. "You help get us into a spot," he said, "and then when trouble comes, you leave us to face it alone. Is that what you call justice?"

"Was justice mentioned when you signed us to the original contract?" replied Cletus, grimly. "I don't remember it. If justice had been a topic, I'd have been forced to point out to you that, while it was your funds and experts who developed the stibnite mine, that was only because you were in a position to take advantage of the Brozan poverty that was then keeping them from developing the mines themselves. You may have a financial interest in the mines, but the Brozans have a moral claim to them—they're a Brozan natural resource. If you'd faced that fact, you'd hardly have been able to avoid seeing their moral claim, which would have to be recognized by you, eventually—" He broke off.

"Forgive me," he said, dryly. "I'm a little overworked these days. I gave up long ago doing other people's thinking for them. I've told you that neither I, nor an expeditionary force of the size you ask for, is available to you right at the moment."

"Then what will you do for us?" muttered Walco.

"I can send you some men to officer and command your own forces, provided you contract to let them make all the military decisions, themselves."

"What?" Walco cried out the word. "That's worse than nothing!"

"I'll be perfectly happy to let you have nothing, then, if that's what you prefer," said Cletus. "If so, let me know now. My time's limited at the moment."

There was a second's pause. Gradually the lumpiness of Walco's features smoothed out into an expression almost of despair.

"We'll take your officers," he said, on a long exhalation of breath.

"Good. Colonel Khan will have the contract ready for you in two days. You can discuss the terms with him then," said Cletus. "And now, if you'll excuse me . . ."

Walco left. Cletus called in David Ap Morgan, one of Eachan's old officers, now a senior field commander, and gave him the job of heading up the officers to be sent to command the troops of the Associated Advanced Communities on Newton.

"You can turn the job down, of course," Cletus wound up.

"You know I won't," said David Ap Morgan. "What do you want me to do?"

"Thanks," said Cletus. "All right. I'm going to give you about twelve hundred and fifty men, each one bumped up at least one rank from what he's holding now. You'll have ex-noncoms to be your force leaders. Use them to replace all the local commissioned officers—I mean *all*. And the contract's being written to give you sole command in military matters. Be sure you keep that command. Don't take any advice from Walco and his government, under any circumstances. Tell them if they don't leave you alone, you'll pull out and come back here."

David nodded. "Yes, sir," he said. "Any plan for the campaign?"

"Just make sure you don't fight any stand-up battles," said Cletus. "I probably don't need to tell you that. Your AAC troops wouldn't be any good in a stand-up battle anyway. But even if they would be, I still wouldn't want you to fight. Tease the Alliance–Coalition forces into chasing you—and then keep them chasing. Lead them all over the map. Hit them just enough to keep them hot after you and break up into guerrilla groups if they get too close. Do anything needed to keep them worried and your own casualties down as much as possible."

David nodded again.

"I think"—Cletus looked at him seriously—"you'll find you'll lose 70 or 80 per cent of your AAC troops through desertion in the first four to six weeks. The ones that hang on will be the ones who're starting to have faith in you. You may be able to start training them as they go to turn into fairly effective soldiers."

"I'll do that," said David. "Anything else?"

"No. Just make it as expensive for the enemy as possible," answered Cletus. "Don't hit their troops when you can avoid it. Make their casualties light, but make it expensive for them in material. The more active duty soldiers they have, the more there'll be around to miss the food, equipment and other supplies I'm counting on you to destroy, every chance you get."

"Got it," said David, and went off, whistling, to his nearby home of Fal Morgan, to pack his gear for the campaign. Like all his family, he had a fine singing voice and he also whistled sweetly and intricately. Unexpectedly, hearing that tune fade away down his entrance hall and out the front door of Grahame House, Cletus was reminded of a song Melissa had played and sung for him once. It was a small, sad, beautiful tune made by a young member of the Ap Morgan family who had died in some campaign when Melissa had been even younger, long before Cletus had come to the Dorsai.

He could not remember it all, but it dealt with the young soldier's strong memories of the house where he had grown up, remembered while he was waiting for an engagement to begin on some other world.

. . . Fal Morgan, Fal Morgan, when morning is gray,
Your wall stones and rooftree stand near me, today . . .

Cletus shook the emotional tag end of recollection from his mind. He turned to the task of picking out the men he would promote and send with David.

During the weeks that followed, the demand upon the Dorsai professional soldiers continued. Everywhere that Cletus had won a campaign, the combined Alliance–Coalition forces were in action, trying to reverse whatever situation his successful actions had created.

The efforts of the forces from Earth were ponderous and awesome. Together, the Alliance and the Coalition had better than half a million military people scattered out upon the new worlds. If the full half million could have been made effective in the campaigns Dow deCastries was trying to conduct, any opposition by the Dorsais or the attacked colonies could not have lasted more than a few days in each case.

As it was, however, nearly half the half million were engaged in military occupations other than those of a fighting soldier or officer. And of the more than two hundred and fifty thousand men that this left technically available for active duty in the field, more than a hundred and fifty thousand at any one time were rendered—or managed to render themselves—ineffective through a variety of means and for a variety of causes.

Among these were deep suspicions and old rivalries between former Alliance officers and their new Coalition partners; also, there was laziness and inefficiency among those of all ranks and political backgrounds, and the sheer blundering that inevitably resulted from the disorganization in such a large, hastily formed partnership of military units.

In spite of this, with all these subtractions, there remained a hard core of perhaps eighty thousand well-trained and superbly equipped troops from Earth to face a couple of hundred thousand almost useless and practically nonequipped local Colonial troops, plus a relative handful of Dorsais. Cletus could hardly have put twenty thousand Dorsai men in the field, even if he had scraped together every male from that small world, including walking cripples, between the ages of twelve and eighty.

Sending small contingents of Dorsais to officer Colonial troops was one solution; but only where the Colonial troops had at least a shred of training and effectiveness. Where this was not the case—as on Cassida—or where there simply were no native Colonial troops to officer—as on St. Marie—actual contingents of Dorsais had to be sent.

"But why don't we just stop?" demanded Melissa, anguished one day after she had come back from visiting a neighboring household that had lost yet another of the family's men. "Why can't we just stop sending men out?"

"For the same reason the Coalition and the Alliance have combined to send men to reverse everything we've accomplished," Cletus answered her. "If they beat us at every point, they'll destroy our value as soldiers for hire to the other colonies. That's what Dow's really after. Then they'll come on to the Dorsai and destroy us."

"You can't be sure of that—that they're out to destroy us!"

"I can't be other than sure. Nor can anyone who's thought the matter through," said Cletus. "We were winning every campaign and proving ourselves superior to their own troops. A little more of that, and troops from the Alliance and the Coalition wouldn't be needed any more on the new worlds. And with the need gone for any military support from Earth, there'd go Earth's influence among the colonies. This way, if they win, they protect their hold on the new worlds. While if we win—"

"Win!" snorted Eachan, who was in the room at the time.

"If we win," repeated Cletus, looking steadily at the older man, "we break that hold for good. It's a battle for survival between us now—when it's over, either Earth or the Dorsai are going to be counted out on the new worlds."

She stared at him, her eyes unnaturally wide, for a long moment of silence. "I can't believe that!" she said at last. She turned to her father. "Dad—"

"Oh, it's true enough," said Eachan flatly, from across the room. "We *were* too successful—with Cletus' early campaigns on Newton and worlds like that. We scared the Alliance and the Coalition, both. Now they're out to make themselves safe. And they're very big, and we're very small. . . . And we've already sent out the last men we've got to send."

"They haven't any left in reserve either," said Cletus. Eachan said nothing. Melissa turned back to Cletus.

"No," said Cletus, although she had not spoken, "I don't intend to lose."

Eachan still said nothing. In the silence, distantly, the front door annunciator chimed. A second later, an aide opened the door.

"Rebon, Exotic Outbond to the Dorsai, sir," he said.

"Bring him in," said Cletus. The aide stood aside and a slight man in blue robes entered the room.

His face held the eternal Exotic calm, but his expression was serious nonetheless. He came up to Cletus as both Cletus and Eachan got to their feet.

"I've got some bad news I'm afraid, Cletus," he said. "A military force of the Alliance–Coalition Peace Force has seized the Maran core-tap site and all the equipment and technicians there."

"On what basis?" snapped Eachan.

"The Coalition has filed claims against the Associated

Advanced Communities of Newton," said Rebon, turning slightly to face Eachan. "They've seized the core-tap site as an AAC asset pending settlement of their claim. Mondar"—he turned back to Cletus—"asks your help."

"When did this happen?" asked Cletus.

"Eight hours ago," said Rebon.

"Eight hours!" exploded Eachan. The fastest spaceship —and there was no known swifter way of transmitting messages across interstellar space—required at least three days to cover the light-years between Mara and the Dorsai. Rebon's eyes veiled themselves slightly.

"I assure you it's true," he murmured.

"And where'd the troops come from?" demanded Eachan. He threw a glance at Cletus. "They weren't supposed to have any more available!"

"From the Friendlies, undoubtedly," replied Cletus.

Rebon lifted his gaze back to Cletus, slowly. "That's true," he said, on a note of surprise. "You expected this?"

"I expected deCastries to hire help from Harmony or Association eventually," said Cletus, brusquely. "I'll leave right away."

"For the core-tap site on Mara?" Relief sounded in Rebon's voice. "You *can* raise men to help us, then?"

"No. Alone. For Kultis," said Cletus, already striding out of the room, "to talk to Mondar."

Boarding the spaceship that would take him to Kultis, he encountered at the foot of the boarding ladder Vice-Marshal Arvid Johnson and Battle Operator William Athyer, who had been ordered to meet him here. Cletus stopped for a moment to speak to them.

"Well," said Cletus, "do you still have any notion I gave you a nothing job when I put you in charge of defending the Dorsai?"

"No, sir." Arvid looked calmly at him.

"Good. It's up to you then," said Cletus. "You know the principles behind whatever action you'll need to take. Good luck."

"Thank you," said Bill. "Good luck to you, too, sir."

"I make it a point not to know the lady," said Cletus "I can't afford to count on her."

He went up the boarding ladder and the entry port of the ship closed behind him.

Five minutes later it leaped skyward in thunder and was lost into space.

25

Mondar had changed in some indefinable way, since Cletus had seen him last, when they met again in Mondar's garden-enclosed residence in Bakhalla. There were no new lines in the calm face, no touch of gray in the Exotic's hair, but the blue eyes, like Melissa's, were becoming strangely deeper in color, as though the time that had passed had dredged new levels of understanding in the mind behind them.

"You can't help us on Mara, then, Cletus?" were the words with which he greeted Cletus on the latter's arrival.

"I don't have any more troops to send," said Cletus. "And if I had, I'd strongly suggest we not send them."

They passed through the halls of Mondar's house, walking side by side, and emerged into an enclosure half-room, half-arbor, where Mondar waved Cletus to a wide, basket-weave chair, and then took one like it himself. All this time Mondar had not spoken; but now he did.

"We stand to lose more than we can afford, if we lose our present investment in the core-tap," said Mondar. "We've still got a contingent of your Dorsais here in Bakhalla. Can't we use some of them to retake the core-tap site?"

"Not unless you want the additional Alliance–Coalition troops that have been put into Neuland to come boiling over the border into your colony, here," said Cletus. "You don't want that, do you?"

"No," said Mondar. "We don't want that. But what's to be done about the Friendly mercenaries occupying the core-tap site?"

"Leave them there," said Cletus.

Mondar gazed at him. "Cletus," he said softly after a second, "you aren't just trying to justify this situation you've created?"

"Do you trust my judgment?" countered Cletus.

"I've got a high regard for it," Mondar answered slowly, "personally. But I'm afraid that most of the other

Outbonds here and in the Maran colonies of our people don't share that high regard at the moment."

"But they still trust you to make the decisions about me, don't they?" asked Cletus.

Mondar gazed at him, curiously. "What makes you so sure of that?" he asked.

"The fact that I've gotten everything I've ever asked the Exotics for, through you—up until now," answered Cletus. "You're the man who has to recommend me as a bad bet or a good one, still, aren't you?"

"Yes," said Mondar, with something of a sigh. "And that's why I'm afraid you won't find me as personally partial to you now as I might be, Cletus. I've got a responsibility to my fellow Exotics now that makes me take a harder view of the situation than I might take by myself. Also, I've got a responsibility to come to some kind of a decision between you and the Alliance–Coalition combination."

"What's the procedure if you decide for them—and against us?" asked Cletus.

"I'm afraid we'd have to come to the best possible terms with them that we could," Mondar answered. "Undoubtedly they'd want us to do more than dismiss the troops we've now got in hire from you, and call in your loan. They'd want us to actively throw our support on their side, hire their troops and help them against you on the Dorsai."

Cletus nodded. "Yes, that's what they'd want," he said. "All right, what do you need to decide to stick with the Dorsai?"

"Some indication that the Dorsai stands a chance of surviving the present situation," said Mondar. "To begin with, I've told you we face a severe loss in the case of the Maran core-tap, and you said just now, even if you had the troops to spare, you'd suggest doing nothing about the Alliance–Coalition occupation of the site. You must have some reasoning to back that suggestion?"

"Certainly," said Cletus. "If you stop and think for a moment, you'll realize the core-tap project itself is perfectly safe. It's a structure with both potential and actual value—to the Alliance and Coalition, as well as to anyone else. Maybe they've occupied the site, but you can be sure they aren't going to damage the work done so far by the men or machines that can finish it."

"But what good's that do us, if it stays in their hands?"

"It won't stay long," said Cletus. "The occupying troops are Friendlies and their religious, cultural discipline makes them excellent occupying troops—but that's all. They look down their noses at the very people who hire them, and the minute their pay stops coming they'll pack up and go home. So wait a week. At the end of that time either Dow will have won, or I will. If he's won, you can still make terms with him. If I've won, your Friendlies will pack up and leave at a word from me."

Mondar looked at him narrowly. "Why do you say a week?" he asked.

"Because it won't be longer than that," Cletus answered. "Dow's hiring of Friendly troops gives away the fact that he's ready for a showdown."

"It does?" Mondar's eyes were still closely watching him. Cletus met them squarely with his own gaze.

"That's right," he said. "We know the number of the available field troops in the Alliance–Coalition force that Dow's put together. It can be estimated from what we already knew of the number of troops the Alliance and the Coalition had out on the new worlds, separately. Dow had to use all of them to start enough brush wars to tie up all my Dorsais. He hadn't any spare fighting men. But, by replacing his fighting troops with Friendlies, he can temporarily withdraw a force great enough, in theory, to destroy me. Therefore the appearance of Friendly troops under Dow's command can only mean he's forming such a showdown force."

"You can't be sure his hiring of Friendlies as mercenaries means just that, and not something else."

"Of course I can," said Cletus. "After all, I was the one who suggested the use of the Friendly troops in that way."

"*You* suggested?" Mondar stared.

"In effect," said Cletus. "I stopped off at Harmony myself some time back, to talk to James Arm-of-the-Lord and suggest he hire out members of his Militant Church as raw material to fill uniforms and swell the official numbers of my Dorsais. I offered him a low price for the men. It hardly took any imagination to foresee that once the idea'd been suggested to him, he'd turn around as soon as I'd left and try to get a higher price from Dow for the same men, used the same way."

"And Dow, of course, with Alliance and Coalition money, could pay a higher price," said Mondar, thoughtfully. "But if that's true, why didn't Dow hire them earlier?"

"Because exposing them to conflicts with my Dorsais would have quickly given away the fact that the Friendlies

214

hadn't any real military skills," replied Cletus. "Dow's best use of them could come only from putting them into uniform briefly, to replace the elite Alliance–Association troops he wanted to withdraw secretly, for a final battle to settle all matters."

"You seem," said Mondar slowly, "very sure of all this, Cletus."

"That's natural enough," said Cletus. "It's what I've been pointing toward ever since I sat down at the table with Dow and the rest of you on board the spaceship to Kultis."

Mondar raised his eyebrows. "That much planning and executing?" he said. "Still, it doesn't mean you can be absolutely sure Dow will do what you think he'll do."

"Nothing's absolutely sure, of course," said Cletus. "But for practical purposes I'm sure enough. Can you get your fellow Exotics to hold off action on the occupation of the Maran core-tap site for seven days?"

Mondar hesitated. "I think so," he said. "For seven days, anyway. Meanwhile, what are you going to do?"

"Wait," said Cletus.

"Here?" said Mondar. "With Dow, according to your estimate, gathering his best troops to strike? I'm surprised you left the Dorsai to come here in the first place."

"No need to be surprised," said Cletus. "You know I know that the Exotics somehow seem to get information of events on other worlds faster than the fastest spaceship can bring it. It merely seemed to me that information might reach me as fast here as it would any place. Would you say I was wrong?"

Mondar smiled slightly. "No," he answered. "I'd have to say you weren't wrong. Be my guest, then, while you wait."

"Thank you," said Cletus.

Mondar's guest, then, he remained—for three days during which he inspected the Dorsai troops in Bakhalla, browsed in the local library that had been the scene of Bill Athyer's discovery of a new occupation life and renewed his old acquaintance with Wefer Linet.

On the morning of the fourth day, as he and Mondar were having breakfast together, a young Exotic in a green robe brought in a paper, which he handed to Mondar without a word. Mondar glanced at it and passed it over to Cletus.

"Dow and fifteen shiploads of Coalition elite troops," Mondar said, "landed on the Dorsai two days ago. They've occupied the planet."

Cletus got to his feet.

"What now?" Mondar looked up at him from the table. "There's nothing you can do now. Without the Dorsai, what have you got?"

"What did I have before I had the Dorsai?" retorted Cletus. "It's not the Dorsai Dow wants, Mondar, it's me. And as long as I'm able to operate, he hasn't won. I'll be leaving for the Dorsai immediately."

Mondar got to his feet. "I'll go with you," he said.

26

The shuttleboat, with the Exotic sunburst emblem inlaid on its metal side, was allowed to land without protest on the Dorsai at the Foralie shuttleboat pad. But on emerging with Mondar, Cletus was immediately disarmed of his sidearm by competent-looking and obviously veteran troops in Coalition uniforms, with the white band of the Alliance–Coalition Joint Force fastened about their right sleeves. The same soldiers escorted the three men through a Foralie town where none of the local people were to be seen—only the occupying soldiers—to a military atmosphere craft that flew them up to Grahame House.

Word of their arrival had obviously been sent ahead. They were escorted to the door of the main lounge of the house, ushered inside and the door closed firmly behind them. Within, seated with drinks in which they obviously had little interest, were Melissa and Eachan, in their stiffness and unnaturalness, like set pieces arranged to show off Dow deCastries, slim in the gray-white Coalition uniform, standing beside the bar at the far end of the room with a drink also in his hand.

Across the room, Swahili, also in Coalition uniform, stood holding a heavy energy handgun.

"Hello, Cletus," Dow said. "I was expecting to find you here when I landed. I'm surprised you came on in when you saw my transports in orbit. Or didn't you think we'd have occupied all of the Dorsai yet?"

"I knew you had," said Cletus.

"But you came in anyway? I wouldn't have," said Dow.

He raised his drink and sipped from it. "Or did you come down to trade yourself if I'd turn the Dorsai loose? If you did, that was foolish. I'm going to turn it loose anyway. All you've done is save me the trouble of hunting you down on some other world. I've got to take you back to Earth, you know."

"To be sure," said Cletus. "So I can have a trial—which will end in a death sentence. Which you can commute to life imprisonment—after which I'll be imprisoned secretly somewhere, and eventually just disappear."

"Exactly right," said Dow.

Cletus looked at the watch on his wrist. "How long is it since your scanning screens picked up the approach of the spaceship I came in?" he asked.

"About six hours." Dow put his drink down and straightened up. "Don't tell me you came in here expecting to be rescued? Maybe the handful of officers you left here do have a screen that picked your ship up, and maybe they did know it was you aboard her. But Cletus, we've been chasing them twenty-four hours a day since I brought my troops in here. They're too busy running to worry about you, even if they had enough men and guns to do something."

He stared at Cletus for a second. "All the same," he said, turning to Swahili, "we won't take any chances. Go give the local commander my orders to set up a security cordon to the shuttleboat landing pad in Foralie. And order a shuttle down from one of the transports. We'll get Grahame aboard as soon as possible." He looked back at Cletus. "I'm not going to start underestimating you now."

Swahili went out, handing his weapon to Dow and closing the door carefully behind him.

"You've never stopped underestimating me," said Cletus. "That's what brought you here."

Dow smiled.

"No. What I'm saying is quite true," said Cletus. "I needed a lever to change history and I picked you. From the time I sat down at your table on the ship to Kultis, I was busy working you into this situation."

Dow leaned the elbow holding the heavy handgun on the bar beside him, keeping its muzzle pointed steadily at Cletus.

"Move a few feet away from him, Mondar," Dow said to the Exotic, who had been standing beside and a little behind Cletus all this time. "I can't imagine you sacrificing yourself to give him a chance to escape, but there's no point in risking it."

217

Mondar moved.

"Go on, Cletus," said Dow. "We've got a few moments to wait anyway. I don't believe what you're saying at all, but if there's even a slight chance you've been able to maneuver me, I want to know about it."

"There's not much to tell," said Cletus. "I started out first by attracting your attention to myself. Then I showed you I had military genius. Then I began to make a name for myself on all the new worlds, knowing this would suggest an idea to you—the idea you could use what I was doing as an excuse to get what you wanted for yourself."

"And what was that?" The gun in Dow's hand was steady.

"Personal control of both the Alliance and the Coalition—and through them the new worlds," answered Cletus. "You talked up my successes on the new worlds as a threat to both the Alliance and the Coalition, until they agreed to combine their outworld forces and put you in command of them. Once in command, you thought all you needed was to stretch the Dorsais out so thin you could defeat them. Then you'd capture me and use your popularity and military power to put military juntas in place of the political leaders at the head of both the Coalition and Alliance, back on Earth. Naturally, the generals you picked for the military juntas would be your men—and in time they'd be yielding up the government of all Earth to you."

Swahili came back into the room. Dow handed him the handgun and, carefully covering Cletus all the while, Swahili crossed once more to his position on the other side of the room.

"How long?" Dow asked him.

"Twenty minutes," Swahili answered. Dow looked thoughtfully back at Cletus.

"Maybe a trial would be too much of a risk after all—" He broke off.

There were shouts, and the sharp, chorused whistling of cone rifles outside the house, followed by the heavy sizzle of at least one energy weapon. Swahili ran toward the door of the room.

"No!" snapped Dow. Swahili checked and spun about. Dow pointed at Cletus. "Shoot him!"

Swahili brought the energy handgun up and there was a sound like the snapping of a small stick. Swahili checked abruptly, turning toward Eachan, who was still sitting in his chair, but now holding the same flat little handgun—minus the long sniper's barrel—that he had used long ago from under the overturned command car in which he, with Melissa, Mondar and Cletus, had been trapped on the road to Bakhalla.

Swahili went suddenly, heavily, to his knees on the carpet. The energy pistol dropped from his grasp. He fell over on his side and lay there. Dow moved sharply toward the fallen weapon.

"Don't!" said Eachan. Dow stopped abruptly. There were more sounds of voices shouting outside the house.

Eachan got to his feet and walked across to the fallen energy weapon, still holding his own pistol. He picked up the fallen gun and bent over Swahili, who was breathing raggedly.

"Sorry, Raoul," Eachan said, gently.

Swahili looked up at him and almost smiled. The almost-smile continued and did not change. Eachan reached down in an old-fashioned gesture and softly closed the lids over the unmoving eyes. He straightened up as the door burst open and Arvid, a cone rifle in one large hand, strode into the room closely followed by Bill Athyer.

"All right, here?" said Arvid, looking at Cletus.

"All right, Arv," Cletus answered. "How about outside?"

"We've got them all," Arvid answered.

"You'd better start running in a hurry, then," said Dow, dryly. "All these detachments of mine are in constant open-channel communication with each other. There'll be other detachments moving in here within minutes. And where are you going to run to?"

"We're not going to run at all." Arvid looked at him. "All your troops on the Dorsai are now captured."

Dow stared at him. Black eyes locked with pale blue.

"I don't believe it," Dow said, flatly. "There are nothing but women, children and old men left on this world."

"What of it?" Cletus asked. Dow turned to look at him. Cletus went on: "Don't you believe I could defeat a few thousand Coalition elite troops with a worldful of women, old men and children to help me?"

Dow regarded him for a few seconds without speaking. "Yes," he said at last. "You, Cletus—I'll believe you could do it. But you weren't here." He lifted his right hand and pointed his index finger at Cletus. "The thing you forget—"

There was a small, momentary, soundless puff of white vapor from the sleeve of his jacket. What felt like a sledgehammer smashed into Cletus' upper right chest. He

219

stumbled backward and the edge of a table stopped him from falling.

Arvid took one long, swift pace toward Dow, his nearer hand flinging up and starting to descend, edge-on.

"Don't kill him!" snapped Cletus, with what little breath was left in him.

Arvid's hand changed direction in midair. It came down to close on Dow's outstretched arm. He peeled back the sleeve, and they all saw a dead-man's tube, a reflex single-dart thrower, strapped to Dow's wrist. Arvid broke the strap fastening loose and tossed the tube into a corner of the room. He caught up Dow's other arm and peeled the sleeve back, but the wrist was bare.

"Don't move at all," Arvid said to Dow, and stepped back from him. Melissa was already at Cletus' side.

"You've got to lie down," she said.

"No." He shook his head, resisting the pull of her hands. He could not feel the extent of the damage from the shock-point of the dart, but his right upper body was numb and a weak dizziness was threatening to overwhelm him. He fought it back with all the strength of physiological discipline he had. "There's something I've got to tell him."

He leaned gratefully back against the supporting edge of the table top behind him.

"Listen to me, Dow," he said. "I'm going to send you back to Earth. We're not going to kill you."

Dow looked at him fearlessly and almost curiously.

"If that's so, I'm sorry I shot you," he said. "I thought I was on my way out and might as well take you with me. But why send me back to Earth? You know I'll just raise another army and come back. And next time I'll beat you."

"No." Cletus shook his head. "Earth's lost its influence on the new worlds. You'll tell them that, back there. From now on any colony can hire half the number of Dorsai troops that the Alliance or the Coalition supplies to their enemy—and defeat the Earth troops easily. The Dorsais will always win, and any colony can afford to hire them."

Dow frowned. "It's you that make Dorsais potent," he said. "And you won't last forever."

"But I will." Cletus had to pause to fight off the encroaching dizziness again. Barely, once more, he won the battle and went on. "Just as you said—I wasn't here when you landed. And a planetful of women, children and oldsters beat you. That's because I was as good as here.

You see these two?" He nodded weakly toward Arvid and Bill.

"There're the two parts of me," he said, almost whispering now. "The theoretician and the field general. The only orders I left them was to defend Dorsai. But they defended it just the way I would have—right down to being here, when I knew they would, to rescue me from you. There's no end to the Dorsais now. Earth won't ever have troops able to beat them." The dizziness surged in on him and he forced it back.

". . . why?" he heard Dow saying. He looked about for the man and saw the lean face under the black hair and graying temples floating as if on a field of mist.

"It's time for the new worlds to go free," Cletus said. "They had to break loose from the Alliance, the Coalition —from all Earth—and make themselves into what they're meant to be. It was time. I did it."

". . . because of the books you wanted to write, you said." Dow's voice faded out almost to nothingness and then roared like the sound of surf on his ears.

"That . . . too . . ." Cletus held hard to the table edge behind him with both hands, for the floor was threatening to dissolve under his feet. "The last sixteen volumes will be tactics only as Dorsais-to-come can use . . . no use to ordinary military, back on Earth. Only with a new sort of soldier . . . with restraint . . . obligation . . . mind and body . . ."

There was no more.

After what seemed many centuries of nothingness, he drifted back to fuzzy consciousness to find himself lying on a bed. A young commandant wearing medical insignia was just finishing a broad bandage across his upper chest, and behind the commandant stood Melissa and Mondar.

"I'm not dead . . . then?" he asked, hearing the words come out in a whisper so weak it was ridiculous.

"Dow used the wrong weapon on you, Cletus," said Mondar. "Darts that trigger a state of physical shock and collapse are all right for killing ordinary men, but not one like you, who's trained his physiological processes to obey his will automatically. You're going to live—isn't he, Doctor?"

"Absolutely." The medical commandant straightened up and stepped back from the bedside. "He should have died on his feet within the first minute and a half after he was hit. When he got past that point, there was no place for his system to go but toward recovery."

221

He handed a hypospray arm band to Melissa. "See that he does a lot of sleeping," he said. "Come on, Outbond."

The figures of the two men moved out from Cletus' field of vision. He heard a door close at a little distance. Melissa sat down in the chair the doctor had occupied and began to strap the hypospray around Cletus' sleeveless right arm.

"You don't have to do that," he whispered to her. "You can go now, to Earth or anywhere you want. It's all over."

"Don't talk," she said. "It's all nonsense, anyway. If I'd wanted to go, I'd have gone right after you made me marry you. I could have dreamed up some excuse—to explain it to Dad. You know he'd believe anything I told him."

He stared at her. "Then why didn't—"

"Because you told me you loved me," she said. "That was all I wanted to know."

He rolled his head a little, weakly and negatively, on the pillow. "I said—"

She finished strapping the hypospray on his wrist and bent down and kissed him, stopping the words on his lips.

"You idiot!" she said, fiercely and tenderly. "You magnificent, genius-idiot! Do you think I paid any attention to what you *said?*"